Standing on her toes, eyes heavy with desire: "Will I have to do penance if I ask for a real kiss?"

His mouth came down softly on her parted lips and lingered until she tightened her grip on his arm. Will seemed to read her silent expectations. His kiss became urgent and fiery. When he moved away, her entire body was hot and needy. She leaned against him and he traced her mouth with his tongue.

His lips devoured hers. His tongue explored the recesses of her mouth. He raised his mouth from her and silently gazed into her eyes before brushing his lips against her face. Breathing an intoxicated sigh, she loosened her grip and he took her face in his hands.

"You won't have to do penance, but I will unless we stop right now."

# *LOOK BOTH WAYS*

*JOAN EARLY*

Genesis Press, Inc.

# INDIGO

An imprint of Genesis Press, Inc.
Publishing Company

Genesis Press, Inc.
P.O. Box 101
Columbus, MS 39703

Copyright © 2009 by Joan Early

ISBN: 13 DIGIT : 978-158571-284-7
ISBN: 10 DIGIT : 1-58571-284-1
Manufactured in the United States of America

First Edition 2009

Visit us at www.genesis-press.com
or call at 1-888-Indigo-1

# *DEDICATION*

To Dale,
My love and my strength

# CHAPTER 1

Susan Cross, a devout believer in controlling that short wink between birth and infinite peace, picked a path over hot concrete that led from a parking garage to an angular glass building in the heart of Houston's financial district. Pride dueled with anxiety as she stepped into the lobby. She had declined the offer of a car and driver, or a personal escort, for her first day as executive vice president and head of lending for Sealand Prime Financial. She wanted to begin the day without fanfare.

She crossed the lobby and slipped into the ladies' room for a final inspection. Age had certainly altered the awkwardness, she thought while glancing in the mirror. Long legs that had caused her grief as an adolescent were now a source of pride. She always listed her height as five feet, nine inches, which was a quarter-inch exaggeration. Her figure had changed slightly since maturity, but she could still wear the size six dresses from her college years. She had inherited her mother's copper skin, her father's straight, auburn hair, and a smile that highlighted deep dimples.

She checked for remnants of a hurried breakfast on her teeth, and reflected on her journey to the present. What had begun as a part-time position for a newlywed college student had catapulted her to the big time. Being plucked from the security of her family in Ohio and dropped into the sprawling environs of Houston was not the most desirable route, but Susan always knew the road to the top would have a few sharp curves. She had always considered her career to be more important than remaining in her comfort zone. She had made the necessary compromises, and at twenty-seven, she was proud of her achievements; the only casualty was her four-year marriage to Stan.

She saw her name on the building directory facing the elevators. Susan Cross, suite 2600. The top floor. Impressive, she thought. Very impressive. Her parents had built the foundation for an amazing flight pattern for her and her brothers. Her life had taken shape with few bumps: no awkward growth spurts, no teen traumas, no adolescent angst—not even pimples. When those years of growth and discovery were over, she had followed the path her parents had carefully outlined without complaints or objections, and she had never strayed.

Her college years were a time of awakening and developing a higher level of consciousness. Away from the watchful eyes of her parents, she understood and accepted the responsibilities of newfound freedom. With her best friend from high school, Barbara Calloway, at her side, she made new friends, studied hard and stayed focused on her goals. She was popular but unreceptive to romantic overtures, not promiscuous, which meant most of her dates were friendly outings with someone she liked and trusted. And then she met Stanford Arceneaux.

Susan had been touched and intrigued when she learned the shy basketball jock had paid a friend to find out if she was available. She had accepted his dinner invitation and had been captivated by his easy smile. He talked of the things he wanted to accomplish and she listened attentively. He complimented her large brown eyes, dazzling smile, and the way she pronounced each syllable of her words. By evening's end, Susan had fallen in love.

She had felt him in life and in her heart, almost from the moment they had met. Both were ambitious, thrifty, and mature beyond their years, but Stan did not share her deeply held beliefs on pre-marital sex. Determined to stay true to the decision she had made in her early teens, Susan struggled with her own longing and Stan's urgent needs during months of mutual frustration. She suggested taking a break, and he suggested marriage.

"I won't lie about what I'm feeling right now. I'm having trouble concentrating on anything but having you in my arms," he proclaimed, his eyes dilated with lust. "And if that's all it was, I would find someone to ease the pain. I'm in love with you. I want to be married to you for the rest of my life. Will you please marry me, Susan?"

She remembered the dismay on her father's face when Stan asked for her hand in marriage. Of course, the elegant wedding her parents had arranged on short notice spawned the expected rumors, but her parents accepted and applauded her choices, and that was all that mattered. For their honeymoon, they went on a five-day trip to Hawaii, where she fell in love with Stan all over again. He had just enough experience to make her feel comfortable with her body and with his. The memory of that painfully delightful first time still made her hands shake. It had been well worth the wait.

They had moved to a small apartment off campus with Stan working at an electronics plant in the evenings and Susan working as a bookstore clerk. Believing that fortune sides with those who dare, Susan responded to an advertisement for a loan processor. The post required more experience than she had, but Susan had persuaded the branch manager at Sealand Prime Financial that she was a quick study. Armed with a load of manuals, she had rushed home to tell Stan.

"Instead of checking the employment ads, we can start looking for a house. My salary is almost twice what I've been making. We'll have a down payment in no time."

They celebrated with pizza and beer, but it soon became clear that Stan's reaction was less supportive than she had expected. It seemed that each upward step she took toward success brought the dissolution of their marriage closer.

After the divorce, she succumbed to a brief interlude of insanity, including a weeklong shopping trip to New York with Barbara. Realizing she was making a dent in her savings, Susan returned to her parents' home and her usual careful approach to the choices before her. Dating proved more disappointing than she had imagined. She soon gave up and threw herself into her work. Often the first to arrive, she worked well after other employees had gone. She volunteered for any project that would broaden her overall knowledge of lending rules and regulations.

Her hard work did not go unnoticed. Promotions were frequent, and so were the salary increases.

Her parents were happy to have her home, and suggested she stay there until she was ready to purchase a home of her own. Her days consisted of work and church volunteer projects, while nights and weekends were spent with friends and family.

The planes of reality shifted again when Waylon Deeds, president of Sealand, called her to the boardroom and made an unexpected offer. Having been promoted to branch manager only six months earlier, Susan had stared in disbelief. Deeds offered her the highest position in the company's mortgage-lending division. Disregarding the fact that she was black and found tokenism conceptually demeaning, Susan had chosen to believe her promotion had been prompted by hard work and dedication.

Now standing in the company's lobby, she was still floored by the huge thrust forward. When the elevator door opened, she took a deep breath and pressed number twenty-six. The summit. The top of the heap. She tried, but could not remember ever feeling so rattled.

"Miss Cross?"

A stumpy fireplug of a man with thinning hair and a cunning smile approached and extended his hand as she looked around the reception area on the twenty-sixth floor.

"I'm Price Bishop, mortgage loan production manager. Welcome to Houston."

She acknowledged his greeting and tried not to stare at the strawberry mole on the end of his oversized nose or to react to the tension she felt immediately.

"Mr. Deeds is in California, so I'm the welcoming committee this morning. I'll be happy to show you around. This way." He gestured to the door on his left. "Is this your first trip to our city?"

"No, I've been to Houston many times." She walked at his side. "I've attended four computer training classes here at Sealand."

"I must have missed those classes." He turned his head toward her, but his eyes landed on her chest. "I certainly would remember someone as lovely as you are."

She felt a rush of blood under her skin, but chose to ignore his comment. "Sealand is an innovator among lenders. I've occupied several positions during my time with the company, and I'm proud to be part of the team."

Allowing him to lead the way, Susan followed him down the hallway while taking in the opulent décor. Artwork decorated the cerulean blue walls, and each office they passed shared a back wall of glass and had just enough wood to add a touch of warmth.

"Have you found an apartment? There are tons of nice accommodations in this area, one or two within walking distance. They're pricey, but I'm sure you can afford the rent."

"Thanks, but I'm living in one of Sealand's executive suites for the time being. It's only a few blocks away."

"Yes." His transparently insincere smile faded. "I know exactly where they're located. What did they give you to drive?"

She decided not to mention the company car parked in her garage. "After experiencing Houston's high water during my last training class, I decided to drive my Jeep down from Ohio. I feel safer in a vehicle that rides high."

Studying his puckish expression, Susan noticed that he seldom made eye contact. She also speculated that the easily detectable acid in his voice meant he had expected to occupy the big office by the window. His next statement supported that assumption.

"*Your* office is over there," he said with increased sharpness, and pointed to the right of the reception area.

She flinched at the change in his tone and walked ahead of him. "How many offices are on this floor?" she asked.

"The entire floor is being remodeled for Sealand's executives, but for now the boardroom to your left divides the area. Appraisals, marketing and most of production are on the other side of the boardroom. Your office is this way, mine is on the other side of the reception area, and our support staff is here in between."

He introduced her to the receptionist and two executive assistants. The women welcomed her politely and with gleaming smiles, but did not interrupt their tasks.

"You're getting Mr. Deeds's old office, so everything you need should be right at your fingertips. If you have any questions, Laura is the one to ask." He nodded to a tall brunette with a pixie haircut. "She has the longest tenure and knows where all the bodies are buried. Your new business cards have been delivered. They're on your desk." He fumbled with the keys on a heavy key ring until he found the one to her door. He unlocked it and stood aside.

"Production meets every Monday morning, but I rescheduled the meeting for tomorrow and requested full attendance so you can meet the rest of the staff. Just production, of course."

"Why is that?" She walked in and swallowed a gasp. Her office was large and more lavishly furnished than the others they passed, from the plush carpeting to expensive wood furnishings that were polished to a high gloss. "Why not all of the managers?"

"Well, for one, I don't know if we could fit everyone into the boardroom." He seemed annoyed. "Besides, their interests and problems are completely different from ours. Accounting, marketing, and appraisals are considered part of production, but the others have their own meetings."

Susan wanted to say that she viewed the company as one large wheel working together for maximum efficiency and profitability, but decided against sharing her work philosophy at this time.

Price left and she was alone in the largest office she'd ever had. Leather and wood dominated the décor and defined the previous occupant as male. Drawings of the Houston skyline hung on the paneled walls, a mahogany table in one corner had seats for six, and the floor-to-ceiling windows behind the desk offered a spectacular view of Houston.

Feeling suddenly alone, she took a family photograph and a business card holder from her briefcase. She rearranged a set of lending manuals on the ebony credenza behind her desk and placed the photograph in the center. Instead of bringing solace, her mother's smile and her father's kind eyes heightened her sense of aloneness.

"Miss Cross."

A clean-cut man wearing a blue business suit was standing in her doorway.

"Hi, I'm Travis Polk, head of appraisals. I just stopped by to welcome you to the fold."

"Thank you, and please call me Susan." They had spoken on the phone, and she was delighted to see that Travis was black. A quick once-over also revealed that he was tall and handsome and had smooth skin free of razor tracks. His dark eyes were cloudy, as though he concealed a secret, but they were also dangerously appealing. Susan noted that the ridges in his forehead were at odds with his smile and wondered if she was also the source of his irritation.

"Come in and visit for a minute if you're not in a hurry." She flashed her corporate face to forestall any misinterpretation of her invitation. She was not looking for love or trouble. She simply wanted a friend.

He walked in and started to close the door.

"Just leave it open. I'm sure the bugs were already in place when I arrived."

Watching his frown deepen, she regretted her attempt at levity. "As the new kid on the block, I have a million questions. Yours is the friendliest face I've come across so far, so I hope you don't mind clarifying some of my concerns."

"Glad to help if I can." He eased into the chair, but did not return her smile.

"I remember speaking with you at least two years ago. How long have you been with the company?"

"This is my fifth year. I worked as an independent appraiser for two years after college. Worked out of my home and was doing well, but I really had to hustle. I took the rush jobs that no one else wanted. Worked weekends. Late hours. I met Price while I was doing work for FHA. He later hired me to head Sealand's appraisal department."

Quickly deciding that Travis was probably loyal to Price, she refrained from seeking the answers she needed and kept the conversation light. "Are you originally from this area?"

"Yeah, I'm a native Houstonian. One of the few. I joined the marines after high school and completed my education courtesy of my Uncle Sam." He returned to her reason for inviting him in. "Is there something specific you wanted to ask?"

"No, not really, just trying to get my bearings." She smiled and crossed her fingers in her lap. "But I am curious about the steady decrease in loan originations over the past three months." Having been told her promotion and transfer were necessitated by a steep increase in volume, she had noticed contrasting figures on the production chart that was left on her new desk.

"Decreasing interest rates is the only thing that comes to mind. You know how that goes. People see the rates dropping and hold out to see just low they'll go. Sealand has grown tremendously over the past few years. The volume of new loans generated from this office alone is staggering," he explained, finally looking directly into her eyes. "Price can answer your questions about trends in lending better than anyone. He can also provide statistical and historical data on fluctuations in new home construction."

"Yes, I'll certainly discuss this with Price." She caught sight of Price pacing the hallway.

"I know he planned to introduce everyone at the meeting, but I wanted to stop by and offer my congratulations on your promotion. Deeds informed us by memo that you were given the position. I'm glad you were transferred here."

His smile was warm. She wanted very much to feel that she had found a friend, but felt little trust between them. Worrisome notions kept popping into her head. Had she been chosen because she had earned the recognition and reward? Did Mr. Deeds have ulterior motives for sending her to Houston? She decided it best to keep her eyes open and trust no one.

"Thank you," she said as he left. Before she could gather her thoughts, Price poked his head into the door.

"Hi, again." He had removed his jacket, revealing a severe laxity in gym visits. "I thought you might like to look at the production breakdown for the past three months. I know the home prices here in Houston are vastly different from those in your hometown."

Susan considered the difficulty of working in an atmosphere of animosity and tried to sound especially cordial. "Oh, yeah. Big difference. There is certainly more new home construction here than in Canton. I'm also glad to see the resale market doing so well."

He offered an opinion on the housing trends in Houston, and she thanked him for his input.

"I'll take these home for evening reading." She smiled. "Travis stopped by earlier to extend a personal welcome. We spoke several times when I was in Ohio, and he was always helpful. It's good to finally place faces with names."

"We have a group of very capable employees in this office. I'm happy to welcome one more. I'm certainly glad to have additional help. Now my wife can quit nagging me to spend more time with her and the kids. I'm sure your marital status was a factor in your promotion. It's a lot easier to transfer a single person than one with a family."

He started for the door and looked over his shoulder. "By the way, Travis is also single."

She smiled but said nothing. She recalled reading the results of a study on the progression of single females in the corporate world. Price could be right. Of course, the cost of moving a family as opposed to a single employee would not have been a consideration if Price has been promoted; he already lived in Houston. Trying to unclutter her mind, Susan filled her head with pleasant thoughts.

Travis was a pleasant thought. He was handsome, and she had noticed that even when his voice quivered, his hands remained steady and strong. Her mother had always said the hands always betray the heart and that steady hands were a sign of strong character. What she did not see was confidence and potency. She also did not feel a physical attraction.

She thought of Stan and wondered if he was happy. She had not wanted to end her marriage, but it was the only thing that made sense. His needs for constant reassurance and ego boosts became draining. The more she gave, the more he required. She shook her head free of those thoughts, the tension and emptiness she was feeling. A man, a husband, was not paramount to her happiness. Nonetheless, emotional and physical merging of souls and bodies was part of her prescription for a totally satisfying life. She knew she would one day find the right combination.

After purchasing a sandwich from the first-floor deli, Susan returned to her office, closed the door, and started reviewing the reports Price had provided. Remembering the customary lull in home buying after school started, she planned to use the weeks of late August and early September to get acquainted with her new surroundings. She finished the sandwich and turned to reapply her lipstick.

"Miss Cross?" The receptionist tapped on her door and came inside.

"Sorry to disturb you, but there are some people here to see you."

Surprised, she asked, "Did they ask for me specifically?"

"No, they said they wanted to speak with . . . I believe the exact words were 'head honcho,' and Mr. Bishop said to have them see you. The leader of the group is Rev. Willard Cartwright. He didn't introduce the others."

Ignoring Ann's Cheshire cat grin, Susan checked her inter-office directory and dialed Price's extension.

"Who is Rev. Cartwright, and why is he here?"

"I'm not sure why he's here, but Rev. Cartwright is one of the city's leading ministers and community activists," Price said. "He does a lot of moralizing and makes a lot of waves. He said he's here about our lending practices, and since you're head of lending, I had Ann direct him to your office. Is that a problem?"

When she didn't answer, he made an openly patronizing offer.

"I'll be happy to sit in on the meeting if you don't feel you can handle it."

Resisting the urge to scream, she spoke calmly. "Just remain available until they leave, please." She hung up. "Show them in, Ann."

Susan took a deep breath and stood as the five people were ushered in. She stopped in mid-exhalation. The man in front was larger than life—not just in size, which was considerable, but also in sheer magnetism. Standing tall and proud, his broad shoulders were squared with military erectness. His eyes were large and dark, almost black, she thought. His features were in perfect symmetry: a wide, unlined forehead, prominent nose, and strong, square chin.

Susan thought of old Western movies in which tribal warriors stood on hilltops watching their people. This man reminded her of such a warrior. His expression and his stance spoke clearly; he was chief of his tribe. His companions faded into the background, overshadowed by his prominence and the most intriguing smile Susan had ever seen. Impeccably dressed in a gray suit, white shirt, and red print tie, his broad shoulders and smooth black skin were enough to make him stand out, but the thundering baritone of his "good afternoon" was as electrifying as an echo in a canyon.

She anchored her right hand on the edge of the desk and spoke above the pounding of her heart. "Good afternoon. I'm Susan Cross. How may I help you?"

"I'm Rev. Willard Cartwright, and I certainly hope you can help us, Miss Cross," he said, gesturing to his companions. "This is Mrs. Whitehead, Deacon Roosevelt Jones, and Mr. and Mrs. Jessie Carter."

Susan acknowledged each with a nod and a smile, ending with Deacon Jones, who was touring her body with his eyes. She refocused on Rev. Cartwright. His looks. His presence. His calm effervescence. His generous mouth remained in a crooked smile as if he sensed her uneasiness.

"Please have a seat," she said, pointing to the six chairs around the mahogany conference table.

Rev. Cartwright held a chair for Mrs. Whitehead and waited until everyone was seated before unbuttoning his jacket and taking the chair across from Susan, who sat facing the window. She watched his every move. Something new was happening to her heart.

"We came here to discuss a serious problem, but before we get into that, may I first ask why we were directed to you?"

His deep voice was insistent but had a hint of sweetness. Susan was insulted and angry, and she was sure it showed as she looked from one to the other. Ashamed of her intensely sexual response to a stranger, and a minister at that, she chose her words carefully.

"The receptionist said you asked to see the person in charge. In the absence of the company president, that would be me. If you'd like to speak to someone else, I'll be more than happy to redirect you, although I must advise you, we rarely see visitors without appointments."

She spoke with measured clarity, hoping her voice did not convey her inward irritation. "We do have a customer service department on the nineteenth floor, but since you described your problem as serious, I doubt customer service would be of much help."

The ire she had hoped to mask brought stern looks from his associates and a big smile from the reverend. She shivered, but her face was scalding hot.

"I apologize to you, Miss Cross." His smile widened and his dark eyes danced merrily. "Is it Miss or Mrs.?"

"Miss is just fine."

"Miss Cross, I apologize, first for barging in without an appointment and then for questioning your authority. I assure you, it was not intended as an insult." His eyebrows drew together inquisitively. "If you don't mind my asking, what is your position with Sealand?"

She turned and lifted one of her brand new business cards from the crystal holder, a gift from her parents, and held it out to him. "Executive vice president. My responsibilities include, but are not limited to, managing the company's mortgage-lending division. I report to the president of the company, which, in his absence, makes me the head honcho in charge of this division."

His penetrating gaze was weakening her resolve. "Now, how can I help you?"

She tilted her head to the right and tried not to come undone, but out of sight, her legs trembled and her heart pounded furiously.

"I didn't mean to get off on the wrong foot, Miss Cross. I'm here on behalf of six individuals, maybe more, who were turned down for loans with your company. The only common thread is that all six were attempting to purchase homes in the same neighborhood, Cedargrove Heights. Four of the six were easily approved elsewhere. Our concern, Miss Cross, is the reason they were denied credit with this company."

Deacon Jones grunted as Rev. Cartwright continued.

"Other lenders readily approved their applications. Since there were no problems with the applicants, it must have been the neighborhood. That's redlining, Miss Cross; a practice that's severely frowned upon by all bodies that govern the lending industry."

"I'm familiar with redlining, Rev. Cartwright, and it is a serious matter. Do you have proof of your suspicions?" she asked calmly, having regained some control over her runaway emotions.

"The proof is obvious, Miss Cross. Cedargrove Heights is a predominately black community. It's an old neighborhood with some blight, but its residents are mostly proud and conscientious homeowners. Quite a few professionals live in the older section. They've raised their families there. First-time homeowners, some newly-weds, and quite a few older couples are purchasing the less expensive homes in newly developed areas. The neighborhood is very special to me. I grew up there."

Awestruck by his charm and still angry at his intrusion, she tried to concentrate. There was a gleam in his eyes, a sparkle. She imagined his inviting lips on hers and felt at once ashamed, angry, and aroused.

"May I ask how all of this concerns you, Rev. Cartwright? If you're here in a legal capacity, you should speak with the honcho in—"

"No, no; I'm not an attorney, Miss Cross. My church, Cedargrove Baptist, is in the heart of this community. The six families in question attempted to purchase homes in this particular community, and those attempts were met with discrimination. I'm a concerned citizen, as is everyone here. We want to try and settle this matter amicably."

His smile had disappeared. Susan was happy to have riled him almost as much as he had rattled her.

"I'll certainly take your concerns under advisement, Rev. Cartwright. If this problem exists, I can assure you, Sealand will handle it in a responsible and equitable manner. Please provide the names and phone numbers of the applicants in question and I will forward my findings to them."

Deacon Jones stood and shook his head, saying, "No way, sugar pie. We ain't giving you nothing. You ought to have records of the people you turned down. We don't want you to get back to us. We want answers now. That's why we come down here." His fingers fumbled with the breast pocket of his jacket while his eyes strayed to the crystal ashtray on the table. "You don't mind if I smoke, do you?"

Susan watched his elastic jaws fold and elongate like an accordion. In this gnat of a man, she saw generations of crusaders whose tireless fight for equality had not ceased. That, and her profound respect for his age, prevented an equally nasty reply.

"I'm sorry," she said softly, "but this is a no-smoking building, Deacon Jones. You're correct; we do keep files for all loans. Unless what you say is true, there is no reason for our files of approved or rejected loans to be segregated by subdivision. So then, I could spend days, weeks, searching for information that you can readily provide."

Arms flailing and projectile drops of spittle skidding across the polished wood of the conference table, Deacon Jones took loud exception to the smoking ban. "Well, somebody in this building must smoke. Where do they go when they want a cigarette? You're supposed to facilitate everybody, handicapped and all. Why you got this big ashtray here if nobody smokes?"

Before she could respond to the deacon's rant, Mr. Carter rose from his chair and declared. "Your company turned us down, and I want to know why. There's nothing wrong with our credit. We moved here from Silsbee six years ago. We been renting since we got here. We worked hard to save enough money for a down payment, and now you say we don't qualify. I just want to know why."

"Mr. Carter, if you don't mind, please allow me to answer Deacon Jones," Susan responded, looking at the wrinkled black face with more admiration than anger. "Deacon, I have no knowledge of the smoking habits of the employees, and while I consider cigarette smoking a grave annoyance and definite health hazard, to the best of my knowledge, it's not a handicap. This building has proper facilities for the blind and those in wheelchairs, but smoking is not allowed. As for the ashtray, it was here when I arrived. Maybe someone smoked in here at one time, but I'm sure you're aware of recent laws prohibiting smoking in public buildings."

She turned to Mr. Carter, who had slumped back into the chair. "Mr. Carter, I'll be happy to pull your file, review your loan application, and provide further information on the outcome. I will reply in writing, in person, or over the telephone if you prefer, but I will not, cannot, give you an answer at this time."

No longer interested in presenting a calm posture, she stood, trembling and legless. Holding onto the table with both hands, she looked into Rev. Cartwright's enthralling eyes. "Why are you really here? Is this about lending practices, working conditions, or did you just drop by to insult me?"

"We've—"

She stopped Rev. Cartwright with a wave of her hand. "You didn't bother to make an appointment." She spread her hands and shrugged. "You've questioned my authority and my ability. You've made allegations of faulty lending practices. And, you want immediate and specific answers. It doesn't work that way."

She saw Price walking past her door for the third time.

"The proper sequence of events entails a written complaint or an appointment that will make your concerns known before your arrival. I have no knowledge of the community in question, and I will not disrupt the work schedule of every other employee to satisfy your concerns."

She stopped and took a deep breath. "If that is not to your liking, please feel free to file any complaint your facts will substantiate, or return when the *real* honcho is in. His name is Waylon Deeds. He is chairman of the board and CFO of Sealand." She tilted her head in Rev. Cartwright's direction.

"Miss Cross, please—"

She held up her hand. "I haven't finished, Rev. Cartwright. Do you know how many loans are originated within this company? I could possibly find Mr. and Mrs. Carter's file, review it quickly and give you a preliminary answer. But I certainly can't discuss files for the unnamed people you're supposed to represent. As for your concerns that everyone receive fair and equitable treatment, I doubt that any of you would have . . ."

Leaving the thought unfinished, she struggled for calmness and a way to stand firmly on rubber legs. Cartwright's obtrusive approach was annoying. She abhorred violence, but would have found great satisfaction in slapping his wonderfully arresting face. In the midst of her anger, his image conjured up thoughts that put her dreams to shame. The physical attraction was immediate and amazing.

Rev. Cartwright stood. "Let me apologize again, Miss Cross. You're correct. We should have made an appointment and allowed you time to research this matter. It was not our intent to blindside you, but I felt certain you would be familiar with Cedargrove Heights, if not this specific problem."

"I'm sorry to disappoint you, Rev. Cartwright, but I've been in this city for seven days, and this is my first day on the job. I'm not familiar with your neighborhood, or even the one in which I reside."

His eyes widened. "Oh, were you just hired by Sealand?" he asked, sitting.

"No, I've been with the company since my junior year in college. I just transferred here from Ohio."

He nodded. "Again, I wish to apologize for the intrusion. We'll wait for your response, and I would simply appreciate your reviewing any loan rejections for purchase of properties in Cedargrove for the last thirty days, if that's not too much trouble. We have substantial proof of our allegation or we never would have bothered you."

He paused to adjust his fetching smile. "And since you're new in Houston, let me extend a welcome to our worship service at Cedargrove Baptist Church. We have eight and eleven o'clock services each Sunday, with adult Sunday school classes in between. We also have a great singles' group, which I chair. We meet in the sanctuary on Wednesdays at six-thirty, and would love to have you join us. Here's my card if you're interested."

The back of his fingers brushed her hand and lingered. She felt a rush of warmth and a deep desire to hold on. In spite of his occupation and the anger he triggered, she could not ignore the obvious. He was as enticing as a snow cone on a blistering afternoon, and almost as cool. His expression changed with the conversation, but his deep voice remained perfectly modulated. He was a minister and a warrior.

"I appreciate the invitation, Rev. Cartwright. I'll review your concerns and let you know my findings as quickly as possible."

Mrs. Whitehead lingered behind the others. "I want to apologize if we upset you, Miss Cross. Just seeing you in this position makes me proud. God bless you."

"Thank you." As soon as they left, she began assembling pieces of a puzzle that made her blood boil. Looking up, she saw Price walking toward her, his face plastered with victorious smugness.

"I waited for your call." He leaned across her desk. His eyes again fell on her cleavage. "What did they want?"

"I've got it covered, Price. Thanks for standing by."

He left, and she stared at her name on the buff-colored cards.

*You know why they were here, you condescending little worm. You may even know why I'm here.*

# CHAPTER 2

Susan spent the remainder of the afternoon gathering data on loan applications for the past two months, and pulled everything connected to Cedargrove Heights. She compared the number of loans approved to those rejected and reviewed each denial. In the first two files, she found glaring reasons to preclude approval, but the reasons given to the applicants were not only vague, they were largely unsubstantiated.

Comprehension struck.

If this was a set-up, if Sealand planned to use her, and she found that a distinct possibility, she would not accept the blame for Price Bishop's bias. Like Rev. Cartwright and Deacon Jones, she had to walk on the side of fairness. She had to fight for her dignity and her career. If her promotion had been the company's saving grace for their faulty lending practices, she would have to prove her worthiness and seek retribution for the families who were wronged.

Taking the street names from one of the files, she reviewed the numbers on all active loans for the area, and those paid in full, foreclosed, or sold. After drafting a summary of her preliminary findings, and not knowing whom to trust, she typed it herself and made an appointment with the head of Sealand's legal department.

Susan had noticed that Angie Edwards, the collection manager who provided part of the information, was nowhere on the management flowchart. She returned from legal and called out to Price on his next stroll past her door.

"I need several more collection reports. What can you tell me about Angie Edwards?" Not of major concern, but certainly worth noting, was that Angie Edwards was black.

"She hasn't been here very long." He fiddled with the buttons on his shirtsleeve. "She replaced Bill Styles when he got a recording contract. He's a big star now. Ever hear of him?"

She had not, and said so.

"Why are you looking at delinquency reports?" he asked.

She evaded his questions just as he had dodged hers, and added Angie to the mystery she had catalogued in less than a day on the job.

Angie delivered the last of the reports just before five o'clock. Susan thanked her and she started to leave, but turned and stood in the door. With her lower lip firmly clasped between her teeth, she frowned and stared into the hallway.

"Is there a problem, Angie?"

"Yes and no." She faced Susan. "I was just trying to decide whether to tell you about Cedargrove, or just keep my mouth shut. Like any other company, the politics here can do you in, and I need my job."

Susan's interest was piqued. "Did someone ask you not to divulge information about Cedargrove?"

"I wouldn't put it that way. I just know a little about this situation, and I know a lot about Rev. Willard Cartwright. He's a powerful man in this community. His father, a minister and civil rights activist, was slowed by a stroke, but both father and son have the respect of city officials and the news media. You just got here, so I'm sure there are things you don't know."

"Angie, if you'd rather not talk about this, I'll understand. If you'd feel better talking away from the office, I'll arrange that as well."

After work, she met Angie in the parking garage and followed her to a little restaurant in the Third Ward, not an area where Sealand's hierarchy was likely to congregate. Taking a back table in the dimly lit room, Susan sat opposite Angie and studied her features.

A pleasant-looking woman with a hearty laugh and a doubtful eye, Angie was no more than thirty-five and under five feet tall. Her round face became animated when she spoke, and the movement of her eyebrows alone conveyed a forceful message. They ordered a cosmopolitan for Susan and a margarita on the rocks for Angie. Susan asked Angie if she wanted anything from the limited selection on the appetizer menu.

"No, thanks; I can't stay long. I have to pick up my girls." She sat erect, as if signaling Susan to begin.

"I appreciate your talking to me. I came into this position with a litany of concerns. If my first day is any indication of what's to come, I think my concerns are well founded. If there is something I should be aware of, please let me know."

"I just thought you should know the truth, and I knew you wouldn't get it from Price Bishop. He's mad because you got that position instead of him. Anyone loyal to him won't cooperate with you, but that may be fewer people than he thinks. Mr. Deeds is away most of the time, which puts a lot of decisions in Price's hands, and that makes him dangerous. He isn't the sharpest tool in the shed, but his ego could fill the Grand Canyon."

She moved to the edge of her chair and leaned forward.

"Deeds brought you here, so maybe he's more insightful than I thought. Truth is, Price is inefficient to a fault, but smart enough to hire people to cover his ignorance."

She stretched and sipped her drink. "The only loans I see are the delinquencies, and that's how I overheard Price's comment about Cedargrove. As you probably know, the delinquency ratio is the main concern in servicing. When Price didn't know I was listening, he cautioned the loan officers to stop making loans in Cedargrove or Sealand would own a ton of ghetto foreclosures and a sucker's reputation to boot."

She flexed her eyebrows. "Servicing is the company's stepchild. The production staff rarely talks to us, but a few days after Price mouthed off in that meeting, word came down the pike that Price had pulled three files from the underwriters. He told them to take their time getting back to the applicants. The properties on those files were all in Cedargrove. Knowing him the way I do, I'm certain he instructed them to deny as many loans as they could."

"Can you rely on the person who told you this?"

"Actually, she's the only person up there that I do trust. I talk to Travis Polk, but only when I need an appraisal for foreclosure. He's Price's puppet and was the highest ranking black in this office, maybe in the whole company, until you came along. I was glad when you showed up, and I wanted you to know the truth. That's the reason I'm here."

"What can you tell me about Rev. Cartwright?" Her interest was only partly related to business.

"Willie Cartwright is one of the few remaining soldiers, sort of in the vein of Martin Luther King Jr. He gives his time and lends his name to a large number of causes, and I don't mean just those benefiting blacks—if any of our problems can actually be segregated. He chairs a foundation to send financial help to children in Nicaragua, works with the Anti-Defamation League, and is on the board of many civic groups. He is also on the board of the Houston Grand Opera and heavily involved in promoting the arts here in the city. Anything consequential going on in Houston is bound to have his name on the list of sponsors and supporters."

Susan was already impressed.

"He's not one to cross, that's for sure. If there's something fishy going on in Cedargrove, he'll find it and make those responsible look like dirt. He has done it many times before, and to people with a lot more weight than Sealand's production staff."

"I'm grateful that you decided to talk to me. I've already sampled Price's venom, and I've notified legal of the Cedargrove situation."

"I'd hate to see you leave, and I'm not the only one. Just keep in mind that Willie Cartwright and those people from Cedargrove are not to be taken lightly. I've seen him destroy some pretty powerful people." She shook her head admiringly and smiled. "And he does it with such finesse."

That part was not hard for Susan to believe. She was still trying to recover from his crushing invasion. "How long have you been with Sealand?"

"Four years. The collection department is usually a stepping-stone to upper management, unless that's where they choose to stick you." She smiled. "I got stuck. I started as a collector, went on to collection supervisor, and then on to collection manager. That's it for me, but I don't mind. The salary is good and I'm getting great experience. I probably make more than any collection manager in the city. I also maintain a low delinquency ratio and have excellent rapport with every entity that does business with Sealand."

She sipped her margarita and then made an unexpected offer. "I don't often get involved in things like this, but I'm willing to make an exception. If you need my help to fight this, I'll be happy to pitch in."

Susan outlined her immediate plan, but Angie disagreed with it.

"Price is not going to incriminate himself by allowing his people to state the real reasons for those rejections."

"I'm not planning to rely on their information. I'll ask for their assistance, but I know they won't tell the truth. I'm going to re-underwrite the loans myself. Given the insistent nature of this problem, I don't know if I'll have time to finish before I have to provide answers to Cartwright and his people, but I'll do enough to prove my point."

"That will do for now, but sooner or later you'll have to account for every one of those loans. They only mentioned the recent ones, but this has been going on for a long time. If you fail to flag just one, that'll be the one they throw in your face. You have to review every file, and you will. I'll help."

"I wasn't aware that you—"

"That I could underwrite?" Angie interrupted. "I handle commercial as well as residential delinquencies. I have to determine if the debts were properly underwritten in the first place and went bad, or if they never should have been approved. I can underwrite better than most of those people upstairs, and I have a decided advantage." She twisted her mouth to the side. "Nobody knows I can underwrite."

They both laughed.

"Don't get me wrong," Angie added, "I'm not a disgruntled employee. I like what I do, and if my last salary increase is any indication, I must do it well. Mr. Deeds was impressed that I've reduced the ratio from the second highest in the region to the second lowest. It would be the lowest if we didn't have areas like Cedargrove, and believe me, that's not the only area with a high foreclosure rate. I'm good, and I'm industry respected. That's all that matters. Titles don't pay the rent."

They talked much longer than expected. Angie left after repeating her offer to help, and giving Susan directions back to her apartment. This time, Susan felt she really had made a friend.

The middle child and only daughter of Ralph and Tammy Cross collapsed on the mouse-gray sofa and idly drew patterns in the moisture on her martini glass. Then she felt a need to call home, dialed the phone, and waited. Her mother's voice had always been a soothing lullaby, and tonight was no exception.

"As first days go, Mom, this was a baptism by fire." She relayed her suspicions. "I understood the situations surrounding my previous promotions, but this one is different. I would be crazy not to stop and wonder. There were four people that I'm aware of, including the one here, all male and all white, with more tenure. I know I'm good and I'm dedicated, but it's quite possible that Sealand needed a black face to extinguish the flames over this Cedargrove mess, especially if they knew about Price Bishop's fishy role."

"So you think this group is going to continue making trouble for the company?" her mother asked.

"Yes, I do." Frustration singed her heart when she thought of Willard Cartwright's handsome face. She wanted to tell her parents about the fascinating minister and the way he had made her feel, but instead she focused on Deacon Jones's prickly disposition.

"I know how hard some people have worked for equal rights, but you should have heard the way this man came at me. He's very old. His little face was shriveled like a peach pit, and I really felt his pain, but I'm not the enemy. I wanted to tell them that I've worked hard, made sacrifices, and refused to settle for mediocrity. I may not have gotten this position simply on merit, but I am qualified to handle it."

Her father joined in. "You earned this position, honey. Don't let anyone make you feel differently. You've always been far ahead of the crowd. You made good grades in school, but you read and studied out of school. While your friends were still wading through Judy Blume, you were devouring Tolstoy. You asked for books, not toys, when we went to the shopping center."

"And I have you to thank for that, Daddy." The man with the iron fist also had the voice of an angel. She began to feel better.

"And this beautiful woman standing next to me gave you strength and courage. You've always been self-assured, sensible, and confident. If this is a setup, I know you'll handle the situation with your usual proficiency."

"Your father is right," Tammy declared. "Remember, honey, for hundreds of years, skin color has barred us from the corporate boardrooms of this country. If that is what got you into this one, you should use it to your advantage. Don't let anyone make you feel out of place."

Not wanting to give her parents further cause to worry, she changed both the subject and her tone. "You guys should see this apartment. The name Executive Quarters says it all. The living room is spacious enough to throw a party. The kitchen is small but functional. There's a breakfast bar with four stools, a dining room, and a half bath with a laundry room in back, all on the first floor. My bedroom, bath, and a small sitting room are on the second floor. And there's a really nice balcony."

Keeping it light, she described the ostrich and leather boots she had purchased in a whimsical salute to Texas. And then she told them about the furry little companion lying next to her.

"I went to the Galleria to shop for lightweight suits and this beautiful Himalayan just jumped out of that pet store window and into my heart. I named him Dino and spent a small fortune on gourmet pet food and cat toys."

After promising she would thread carefully through the confusion at Sealand, she stretched out on the sofa and let her mind drift back to Stanford and the marriage she had thought would last forever. She missed having his arms around her and touching him during the night. She needed the assurance and comfort he brought to her life before their marriage soured.

She shook off the ghosts of regret, checked the time and called Barbara. "I've got a question for you. Do you believe in love at first sight?"

She told Barbara about Willie Cartwright. Her friend's advice was to take it slow.

"You're in unfamiliar surroundings and maybe you're just a little lonely. He sounds divine, but don't move too quickly."

"I'm not about to jump into anything with this man. It's just that I've never felt this way before, especially for someone I don't know. It's a little frightening."

After her call to Barbara, she polished off the container of leftover Chinese food, snuggled up next to Dino, and fell asleep.

*SP*

"I'm sure I'm right," Willard Cartwright Jr. insisted. "We sent people over there last month just to see what would happen, and the only one approved was the one who applied for a government-insured loan. The other two, one being Dr. Carroll, were denied. Miss Cross is new to this office and may not have been aware of it, but she is now."

He pulled his chair next to where his father sat on the sofa. He hesitated long enough to remember her toast-brown skin and chestnut brown hair that curved along high cheekbones and feathered around her shoulders. Speaking softly, he continued: "The other thing is . . . she's the most beautiful woman I've ever seen."

"So you think she's a decoy?" his father asked.

"Could be. She was just transferred to this office, so they may be using her to front their defense, or as a scapegoat. For her sake, I hope that's not the case."

"It wouldn't be the first time some poor unsuspecting woman was sent to squelch these situations. If that is the case, they'll probably keep her around until things cool off and then she's history. Make sure you keep in touch with her, because if that happens something should be done. Did she seem knowledgeable?"

"Her capability was very obvious. A great body filled with passionate spirit." His voice drifted and his eyes were almost closed. His heart had leaped when he saw her standing there. By the time the discussion ended, her anger and his frustration had only increased his attraction to her. He imagined his fingers skimming her face and felt rippling heat through his body. Still daydreaming, he imagined her almond-shaped eyes locking on his with the same intensity they had when he had first walked into her office. Her strong female essence came back with staggering clarity. Will knew that if he never saw Susan Cross again, the face that was seductive even in anger would always be with him.

"She's very beautiful. And mean as a wet cat."

"Doesn't exactly fit the profile. Is this woman someone you might like to date?"

"Why do you ask that?"

Rev. Cartwright Sr. leaned on his son's shoulder and moved to the wheelchair. "I love my children equally, but I know you best of all. The look on your face when you talk about this woman is one I haven't seen in a very long time."

When Will did not answer, Rev. Cartwright reached over and patted his knee. "You've made me proud, son. I didn't expect you to follow in my footsteps, but I'm happy you did. I know your personal life has been filled with turmoil, and I pray that will change. Losing Trey was devastating. Losing Trey's mother was a blessing in disguise, but I'm sure it hurt."

"I'm okay with it, Dad. I'll always love my son." He smiled. "And I want another one more than anything. When the right woman comes along, I know that will happen."

"Then you'd better get cracking, Willie Joe. Your mother and I married before construction began on the original Cedargrove Baptist building. The congregation was small and the responsibilities were few, but it was still a handful. You made your accounting firm profitable before you were thirty, and then you inherited a monster of a congregation when I suffered this stroke. The congregation wanted you. My heart swells each time I see you in the pulpit, but you have to think of your personal life. You could have any number of beautiful women, but a goodly number of them would have dollar signs in their eyes. Culling out the worthy ones takes time. If you think this woman at Sealand is so special, don't you dare let her get away."

Will helped his father prepare for bed, and assured him that he was coping with the trials of the ministry and with his private life. He drove two blocks to the house that had been home to his wife and son. He called out to the big yellow lab that came bounding around to meet him. Each time he opened the door and walked into the hallway, the terror rushed out to greet him. Time had only slightly diminished the horror of finding his son's tiny body tangled, lifeless, in the sheet, and finding Tracey, still dressed in party clothes and smelling of booze, snoring on the couch.

Passing the blame had been her defense. He had agreed to stay home with the baby while she attended a bridal shower for her younger sister. When the call came that a member of Cedargrove's choir had been involved in a fatal accident, he mumbled his regrets and rushed to the hospital. The venom in her voice when he called two hours later was harsher than ever before. She screamed accusations of disinterest and neglect before informing him that she would attend the shower even if she had to take the baby with her. He promised to come home as quickly as possible, but knew there was no way to swiftly console a grieving family. She screamed that his family always came last and she would not wait for his arrival.

In the heartache and grief that followed, he repeatedly told himself that hate was not an emotion he could consider, but animosity grew rapidly. Tracey was an enticing woman and knew how to use her body to bring him to his knees, but soon even that seemed sordid. When she asked for a divorce, he agreed immediately. The dates he had after their divorce only reminded him of how difficult relationships can be, and coming home alone reminded him how desperately he needed a woman.

He thought of Susan and became painfully aroused. The way her nose crinkled in anger. Her perfect body and charming wit. Even her height, which, judging from his own six-foot, three-inch frame, he estimated at close to six feet in heels, was a perfect match. Was she a decoy? Was romance all a game where women said what they thought men wanted to hear and vice versa? Could he trust his heart to another woman?

"I'll have to, because I don't know how much longer I can survive this way."

The next day, Susan drafted her response to Rev. Cartwright's allegations. She reviewed the files again, and noted the reasons Price's staff had given for denying the loans, as well as the reasons she would have denied them. With each word she wrote, Willard Cartwright's face was there, staring, smiling. The thought of facing him filled her with excitement and terror.

As she dialed his number, her heart skipped several beats. She felt sixteen again and twitched with the same excitement as when Bobby Reynolds had escorted her to the school dance. The rush was invigorating, but the thought of succumbing to Rev. Cartwright's undeniable charm produced fear.

"Miss Cross. It's nice of you to respond so quickly."

The sparkle in his voice evoked an appealing image. She took a deep breath and held her hand over her heart as if she were trying to keep it in place or protect it from feelings she could not control.

"It's my job, Rev. Cartwright. When would you like to meet to discuss my findings? Also, please let me know if you plan to bring your entourage so I can round up a posse of my own. I'll have a hard time matching Deacon Jones, but I'll do my best."

"Tomorrow is fine. I'll be alone, and I apologize for Deacon Jones. He's an old war-horse who has logged many hours defending the rights of others. His eyesight is poor and his mobility limited, but he refuses to pass the torch. He meant no disrespect. Is two o'clock good for you?"

Susan said it was and spent the rest of the day and most of the night rehearsing what she would say and trying to still her frazzled nerves. She dressed with him in mind the following morning. Ignoring her mother's advice to dress to impress, not entice, she chose a stylish suit that highlighted her curves. It was red with a neckline just a little lower than she normally wore to the office. The jacket was long and sleek and showed just a hint of the lacy camisole underneath. She added pearls and a dragonfly pin to the lapels. She dusted her cheeks and eyelids with sienna and smoothed a lightly frosted glaze over her lipstick. Instead of the usual straight hairdo, she added curls and combed her auburn tresses to one side.

"I heard you, Mom." She reached for the red bottle of Samsara and spritzed her neck and wrists. "But today I need to impress . . . and entice."

The workday was wasted. Susan was simply unable to concentrate. She was anxious to see him again, but terrified of what would happen when she did. She willed herself to remain calm; this was no ordinary day, and Willard Cartwright was no ordinary man. Going to the restroom mirror, she practiced putting on several faces—indifference, intolerance, and anger—before concluding that control was all she could reasonably hope to attain.

Her planning was in vain. When the big man walked through the door, her knees weakened. Her efforts to remain calm failed, and the walls seemed to close in around her. Everything about him intrigued her. Her hands trembled, and a woozy sensation caused her to hold onto the arms of her chair.

"Hello, Miss Cross." His thundering voice was filled with pleasantness. "Thank you for your prompt response."

He wore a deep-blue suit, periwinkle shirt, and no tie. His black alligator loafers were spit-shined to perfection. She imagined standing next to him, lying next to him, having his mouth on her body.

"No need to thank me. As I told you yesterday, I'm just doing my job. The charges leveled by your group are serious, and I'm as anxious to get to the bottom of this as you are." She sensed a speck of displeasure in his eyes when she did not return his smile.

"Rev. Cartwright, I went back two months into Sealand's records. In that time, eleven applications were taken for loans in your community. Five were approved and six were rejected. For my own peace of mind, I underwrote each one, using industry-approved guidelines. Even with a friendly and liberal approach, I could not, in keeping with my duty to this company, approve any of the loans."

He frowned and she held up her hand. "At least, not without further information."

As she had expected, her voice faltered. Her words failed her. Anguish grew in her heart. She could not tell the complete truth, which made everything she said sound like a lie in her mind, and she was sure in his as well. She was angry with him, with Price, and with herself for not having better control over the situation.

"In some cases only minor documentation was missing, but from my perspective, none of the files were green lights. I'm sending letters to each applicant with a complete explanation. I'm offering my services to help them through the paperwork, and I'm offering to waive origination fees once their loans are approved."

Her offer was sincere, but she knew her tone was a bit too forceful. She wanted to prove her point and humble Rev. Cartwright, and it showed.

"Did they get to you already?"

She leaned forward, wanting to meet his gaze. "You're out of line, Rev. Cartwright. Way out of line. I don't own or run this company, but I can guarantee you, I call the shots as I see them. The loan application packages in question were incomplete. If you doubt my word, I'll gladly review each file with the applicant in the presence of an attorney of your choice. I'll—"

He held up both hands. "I'm sorry. And you're right. I am out of line."

His frown faded, but doubt and mistrust still lurked in his eyes.

"Miss Cross, before we go any further, do you think it would be possible to declare some sort of armistice? I misspoke. I didn't mean to accuse you personally. I'm sure you had no knowledge of what transpired here, especially since you weren't here when it happened, but the facts are still there. You said five loans were approved. Did you notice anything that distinguished these loans from the ones that were rejected?"

She knew exactly where he was heading. "The approvals were government-backed loans, and the rejected loans were conventional. I'm sure you knew that because two of the applicants who were approved never returned to complete the deal."

He looked away and she intensified her rebuttal.

"They were obviously sent here by you or someone else, just to see if they could get approval. I don't know how familiar you are with lending criteria, but I can assure you, government loans have fewer and less stringent policies than conventional loans because they're less of a risk for the lender."

"So you're offering a little bonus, no origination fee, if they reapply and qualify?" Even though he had asked for a truce, his tone was gritty and critical.

"I've activated the files so that reapplication isn't necessary. Each letter will explain what is needed for approval. In two cases, unless there's been a drastic change in their financial situation, I doubt that we can approve the loans, and certainly not for the requested amount, but the rest can qualify."

His eyes narrowed. He was clearly weighing what she had said.

"Let me see if I understand. You're admitting that most of the loans could be approved, so you're offering a little something for their inconvenience? We don't want handouts, Miss Cross, just the truth."

She placed her hands in her lap, laced her fingers, and still felt she might throw something at him. She had told the truth. Each loan application package lacked at least one vital document. What she could not say was that the letters to the applicants simply stated they did not qualify without advising them that they probably could.

"Waving origination fees is not to be considered a handout." She searched for a way to fully disclose her feelings without admitting what she suspected Price had done. "I'm waiving origination fees because each applicant should have been clearly advised of the documentation needed for approval, and I don't see that this was done, certainly not to my satisfaction."

She thought back to her reason for applying for a job at Sealand. She and Stan had rented a small studio apartment when they married, and had plans to purchase a home as soon as possible. When Sealand offered her a part-time position that paid twice the salary of her bookstore clerk job, she'd placed most of the money in savings for their dream of home ownership. Those individuals whose loans had been denied, she felt, had the same dream. She would have handled each one differently. She would have handled them fairly.

"I'm sure it's very disappointing to learn you can't purchase the home you dreamed of owning. I'm not sure these prospective borrowers were told they could qualify by providing additional information. Copies of pay stubs, gift letters for money being used as a down payment, proof of clear title to an automobile—all minor issues, but critical to prove their ability to repay the debt."

Trying not to wilt under his stare, she began speaking more slowly, watching him watching her.

"You must also know that this institution is in the middle of the conservative spectrum. While trying to be the best, not necessarily the biggest, we follow established guidelines, and it's that practiced caution that has kept Sealand afloat and profitable while many others have gone under. Like selling cars or anything else, our production employees are rewarded by the number of loans they approve, not the ones they turn away."

He said nothing, but his wary expression sent Susan's temperature soaring. He wasn't buying her story, and her confidence was slipping. Her heart had been weakened by his intense appeal. Her emotions kept getting in the way of rational thinking. Feeling frustrated and overwhelmed, she coiled into strike position and lashed out.

"You must be a busy man, Rev. Cartwright. How do you find time for these little confrontations? You say it wasn't your intention to initiate a combative relationship, but that's exactly what you did from the moment you first walked through that door. I understand and admire your need to serve your community, but this is strictly business. It's not about race or boundaries."

He finally blinked. "I came here, not so much for answers, but to end the discrimination Sealand imposed on my neighborhood. I could have gone to the press and, if nothing else, created a lot of bad publicity. I've apologized for our earlier meeting. We fired the first shot and you retaliated, but this is not a personal attack. Can you abandon your defensive anger and just concentrate on the facts?"

"I will if you will, Rev. Cartwright," she said impassively.

"I'll just state the facts as I see them, no conjecture, no editorializing. Our records clearly show that some loan applications for properties in your neighborhood were denied. Others were approved. I've reviewed the rejects and I agree that the loans, as they stand, should have been denied. I remain doubtful regarding Sealand's communication efforts to the applicants, so I am offering to meet with them individually, waive fees, and make a concerted effort to rectify the situation. Any loans that can be approved, which are probably all but two, will be expediently reviewed. That's the best I can do."

"Now, Miss Cross, you know as well as I do that Sealand had to approve those government applications. The others were rejected because Sealand didn't want to make any loans in Cedargrove Heights unless it had to do so. Redlining is prohibited. If this practice were known to exist, the government agencies involved would void any commitments formerly issued to this company. I want those loans approved, Miss Cross, without further delay. As head of production, were you not given the authority to set this right?"

"Questioning my weight again, are you?" Her tone was still controlled and even, but the fire in her eyes raged brightly. "I have full authority to carry out the duties of this position, Rev. Cartwright. Let me reiterate that I cannot approve any of the loans unless issues related to the applicant's credit, employment, or past payment history are resolved. I can only discuss the particulars with the applicants."

He shook his head and looked into her eyes. Her thoughts zigzagged. She was losing control. Gripping the arms of the chair with trembling hands, she wondered if she was not convincing because she could not convince herself, or because the man before her had everything that was missing in her life. She searched for concluding words that would pack the punch she needed to win the round. Smiling slightly, she continued.

"As I stated, most of the situations are easily rectified."

"Well, if it's so simple, you should be able to approve them now. I'm sure you know the courts will uphold what I'm saying."

"Rev. Cartwright, court dockets are packed with claims that are not only frivolous and unfounded, but just plain stupid. Unfortunately, a lot of these nuisance claims are settled simply to defray the cost of a defense, but I will not put aside this company's underwriting guidelines just to rid myself of a nuisance."

His body jerked as if he had been struck, and she immediately regretted her choice of words and her inflammatory delivery. His smile became rigid.

"I see. I'm very sorry to have been a nuisance, and I'm sorry you and I couldn't have met under different circumstances. I will trouble you no further, Miss Cross. Good day." He nodded and left.

Her heart sank. No matter how well prepared she had been, looking into those eyes and watching the movements of his powerful body had turned her to putty. She started to run after him, but by the time she was able to command her feet to move, Price had charged into her office at a full trot and was bombarding her with questions.

"That man is determined to create a lot of public speculation about this company, and that's not good for our image. What did he want this time?"

"Just a continuation of our earlier discussion."

She blurted out a question that had been in the back of her mind since the Cedargrove matter had been dropped on her shoulder. "In case of an emergency, how do we contact Mr. Deeds?"

"From what I heard he's out of the country."

He turned to leave, but suddenly realizing the weight of her question, he turned and gleefully asked, "Is it that bad? Don't you think you should tell me what's going on? Are those people suing Sealand?"

"I plan to inform everyone at the same time. I have a few other assessments to make, which, hopefully, I can conclude this weekend. We'll discuss the matter in detail at the next management meeting."

# CHAPTER 3

Rev. Cartwright left the emotionally charged meeting with Susan and joined an even more daunting one in the meeting hall at Cedargrove Baptist Church. As his father's assistant, he had felt the arrows of discontent from congregation members, but his father had been there to deflect the sting. He wondered if his father had been a stronger man. Feeling dejected and physically beat, he stopped in front of his parents' home and tried to calm his frayed nerves.

The wonderful aroma of his mother's cooking was comforting, even in his agitated state. "Hi, Mom," he said, kissing her forehead. "Something smells mighty good in here."

"Thanks, dear. It's pork roast and yams. I'll call when dinner is ready and you can help your father in to the table."

He stopped in the doorway and looked at his father. He knew a wide vein of pain and helplessness was hidden under the senior Cartwright's façade of indomitability.

"Hey, Pop," he said, briefly resting his hand on the old man's shoulder.

"What put that frown on your face? The meeting at Sealand or the one at the church?" Rev. Cartwright Sr. asked.

"Both."

"I don't know what transpired at Sealand, but I know why Clyde Otis is so fired up. He's a skunk, and simply put, he aims to turn the spotlight on himself by any means available to him. He's always been that way. He still wants my pulpit, and it's eating him up that you got it. If he had bat brains, he would recognize his own shortcomings. The church voted him down because they knew he couldn't stand up. He's a weasel."

Will listened to the sounds of home. His mother in the kitchen. His father watching the news and offering his usual support. It was the only part of his life that felt right.

"He as much as accused me of being the weasel because I advised against legal action. On top of that, I went down to Sealand and made matters worse. I can't seem to have a good exchange with Miss Cross, and I did try," he said, rubbing his chin. "I don't know what it was today. It was as if she was trying to say something without actually admitting wrongdoing. I antagonized her, and that's not what I wanted to do."

"You want to ask her out, so why don't you?"

"That's not even a thought right now. She can't stand the sight of me. I'll keep trying to make this right, but I'm afraid Otis will act out of his own selfishness and initiate legal action. I don't want that for the people involved, or for her."

He heard his mother setting the table. "Come on, Pop, I'll help you into the kitchen. Or do you prefer to use the walker?"

"Since you're standing with me, I'll try the walker." Using his son's arm, he pulled himself up from the chair and grasped the rubber-covered handles. "I feel like I dumped my problems on you when I had this stroke. Don't let Clyde or this situation get you down."

Will put an arm around his father's shoulder and guided him into the kitchen. Mrs. Cartwright brought filled glasses of lemonade to the table.

"What did crazy Clyde do now?" she asked.

"Same crazy stuff he's always done to get attention. I knew he'd make things hard for Willie."

"Don't worry about me, Pop. I can handle Clyde Otis."

"You shouldn't have to. He's a self-centered braggart." Rev. Cartwright Sr. elaborated, looking at his wife, "I've always known he was a crook, but your mother didn't. She even dated him back before we married. I suspect that's the reason he's been carrying a grudge all these years. He is angry because I married her and he didn't."

Mrs. Cartwright grunted her disagreement, saying, "I didn't date Clyde Otis. I went to the movies with a group of my friends and he happened to be in the group." She placed a comforting hand on her son's arm. "Can I get you a glass of wine?"

"I must look pretty bedraggled if you're offering me wine, Mom. I'm fine with the tea."

"Looks like you've had a hard day. You need to relax." She sat next to her husband and looked across the table at her son. "How did your meeting with the mortgage company go?"

"Awful," Will answered. He could not stop thinking of Susan Cross. He had sat in his car after their heated discussion and tried to collect his thoughts. His vivid memory of her body didn't help. He was ashamed and frustrated. "I'm trying to keep peace here, but I went down to that company and spoke out of mind, not my heart."

"You've got that backwards, son." His father spoke matter-of-factly. "Your heart did the talking. Your mouth just didn't say the right things."

The rest of Susan's week was filled with associating names with faces. She used her special mnemonic system to remember who did what, but the task proved to be more taxing than she had imagined. Her catalogue of who's who in the Canton office was miniscule compared to the staff roster for the Houston office. There appeared to be at least two people for each position. No one seemed particularly busy, but most of them needed her input before decisions were made. While fulfilling daily duties, she continued to gather information for her report. She also added possible overstaffing to her growing list of concerns.

"I was able to get copies of all rejected loan files for Cedargrove Heights since inception of the development," she told Angie over lunch. "I know Price's people are not on my side, but no one suspects my motives for requesting the files and no questions were asked."

"Just as I said, you have the upper hand when the people around you underestimate your abilities or your intentions. That has always been my insurance."

"I also decided that economic fluctuations dictate I review several loans that were approved at the time each Cedargrove loan was denied. That will give us a comparative basis."

"Good thinking," Angie said.

"I wish I had more time to devote to Cedargrove, but whenever I get a little free time another crisis develops. I'm beginning to wonder what they did before I arrived, and that maybe I was shortchanged on my new salary. When I take one of those files and start a review, I already know the outcome. So far, I have only seen two loan applications with denials that wouldn't hold up in court, and Sealand got lucky both times. One applicant had a job-related accident and decided to wait for an insurance settlement before purchasing a house. The other is a young couple now in the middle of a divorce."

She rubbed the back of her neck to ease the tension. "These files were sloppily underwritten, to say the least. I know some, if not all, of Price's employees are involved. I can't help wondering if Price is the highest link in the chain."

Friday was a day of pure torture. She regretted every recent decision she had made, including accepting her current position. She wanted to call Rev. Cartwright and apologize, but feared he would hear the hypocrisy in her regrets. Her other fear was of weakening at the sound of his voice.

She worked through lunch, as she did most days, but somehow found time to thank Tom Waverly, the source of her extensive knowledge of the lending industry. One of the founding partners at Sealand, he had become a figurehead when she was hired, and readily admitted he was just waiting "to be put out to pasture." With lots of time and a wealth of information to share, he seemed happy to have a willing listener. The knowledge he passed along to Susan was priceless, especially now.

Fondly and gratefully remembering an old man in English tweed with elbow patches, she called her favorite florist in Canton and had the largest plant they offered delivered to Mr. Tom Waverly with her heartfelt thanks.

Thankful the day had lurched to an end, Susan crammed her briefcase with loan files, picked up a stack of reports, and prepared to leave. After locking her office door, she turned and literally ran into Travis in the hallway.

"Here, let me help you with that," he offered.

Shifting the binders that teetered uncertainly against her chest brought her close enough to be reminded of the pleasure a man's arms could bring.

"Don't tell me you have nothing better to do on the weekend than ponder over this mess. Get out and explore the city. Houston has a great theater district, and a few clubs that actually cater to those of us who are over twenty-five."

"I'm sure it's a wonderful city, but its size and my poor sense of direction tend to dampen my adventurous spirit. I'm basically confined to the area between my apartment and here, except for shopping and eating. That leaves entertainment. Are there any good jazz clubs in town?"

"Well, if I may be so bold, I'd love to take you to this great little jazz club in Montrose tomorrow night. It's an area north of here." He pointed to her right. "The place is small, so we would have to arrive early to find a seat, but I know you'll like the band. Can you make it?"

"Sure, I'd love to. Thank you." His smile was not as sweet and inviting as Rev. Cartwright's, she thought, and she did not trust his professional loyalties, but she needed a night out. "I enjoy live music. I actually prefer the kind with lyrics I can sing without having to do penance. With the current crop of singers and musicians, that means listening to the oldies or jazz. "

"I agree. When I'm not listening to jazz, I put on the oldies. Motown. The Philly sound. It doesn't get better than that. Of course, your oldies are probably a lot newer than mine."

"I guess my oldies are a little more current, but I can listen to Al Green for days." She put her purse on the hood of her Jeep and reached in for a pen. "Let me give you my address . . . or I can meet you there if you prefer."

"I'm an old-fashioned guy. I'll pick you up."

She tore the address corner of a page from her new checkbook and jotted her cell phone number on the edge. "What time should I expect you?"

"Let's have dinner first, say seven? The restaurant is close by, so I'll pick you up around six-thirty. I'll introduce you to our Tex-Mex cuisine if your stomach can handle the challenge."

Feeling more carefree than she had since arriving in Houston, she shopped for groceries before going home.

As soon as she got home, she made a hearty salad and called her mother. Tammy sensed her mood change right away.

"You sound much more upbeat than you did on Monday. Have you discovered anything new?"

"Not really. I know the ship is full of rats, and I'm almost certain Price Bishop leads the pack. Guess I'll have to find out if Mr. Deeds was also involved before I can determine my intended role."

"Well, don't let it bother you," Tammy replied. "I was an oddity in the operating room when I began, but I learned to live with it, and the people around me learned to stay out of my way. It's called respect and, believe me, that is the key. I want to be liked by my coworkers, but I insist on respect, and I never let cynics or assholes get me down. "

"I'm not worried, just curious. I did meet a nice man at work, Travis Polk, head of the appraisal department. He asked me out for dinner and jazz tomorrow night."

"O-h-h-h! So that accounts for the lilt in your voice. I knew there was a man behind the change," Tammy bubbled, sounding relieved. "Your father and I hoped you'd find romance in your new city."

"Don't go there, Mother. He probably felt sorry for the lonely newcomer and invited me on a pity date. Besides, if my salary was a problem for Stanford, imagine how Travis will feel. I'm his boss's boss."

Her father joined in. "Don't worry, honey, you'll find the right man. Enjoy your evening out, but stay clear of office romances. They're usually more trouble than they're worth."

Not for the first time, her mother shared a few memories of her first year as a scrub nurse and Susan began to relax. She would enjoy her weekend and try not to worry about Sealand, Cedargrove, or the handsome Rev. Cartwright.

Sleeping late on Saturdays was a holdover from her college days, but this Saturday Susan awakened before daybreak and began her day with a cup of coffee and a toasted bagel. In short order, she fed Dino, did a load of laundry, and tackled household chores.

Sealand provided a housecleaning service on Fridays, but this was home for now and she wanted to add her personal touch. She arranged brightly colored placemats on the table and lit candles, igniting fond memories of her marriage. She knew Stan had loved her. His fingerprint on her life would be hard to remove, but the finality of their divorce precluded any hope of reunion. She was alone, but she was not afraid.

She put on a simple black dress, pulled her hair back in a loose twist, and waited for her date. Travis was on time, earning his first plus of the evening. Casually sharp in dark slacks, plaid jacket, and open-collar shirt, he looked much younger than he had the day before, and more relaxed. He wore his hair closely trimmed, and his mustache formed a heavy line across smooth brown skin.

"You look radiant," he said, beaming when she opened the door. "I hope you're hungry. The restaurant serves huge portions of fantastic food. It's also close to the club."

"As a matter of fact, I am hungry. I got carried away with household chores and forgot to eat."

After she locked the door, he then took her arm and escorted her to the elevator. "Tell me you're not one of those women who constantly counts calories. You have a perfect figure."

She quickly adjusted her bodice to cover the area of her chest on which his eyes were resting.

"The only problem with a perfect figure is keeping it that way. I don't gain weight easily, but with two brothers and a former college all-star father, I was very active back home. Since my 'teammates' are all in Ohio, I might have to join a gym."

"What sports did you and your family play?"

"You name it. Dad loves basketball, and so do my brothers. Even Mom likes to shoot hoops. Mom and Dad both play golf. I played occasionally."

"So what's your handicap?" he asked, escorting her to his car that was parked in front of her apartment building.

She laughed. "I was too bad to have a handicap. I would swing and pray I had hit the ball."

They continued talking sports while he toyed with the radio dial. Casual conversation turned more personal once they were inside the restaurant.

"I hope this doesn't offend you, but I always wonder about pretty women who are still single. You're not just pretty; you're accomplished, confident, and gracious. Even Mr. Van Dyke, the building maintenance superintendent, called you an angel, and he never seems to like anyone. Is being single a matter of choice or just not finding the right guy?"

"I'm not offended by your question. I married when I was still in college. My career took off, his didn't. The ensuing friction drove us apart over a year ago. Since then, I haven't met anyone to occupy that special place in my life, and I'm not really looking. If it happens, it happens. If not, I'll still make the best of my life. What about you?" she asked, brushing Stan's image from her mind. "Divorced? Never married?"

"I was married. We became engaged in high school. I joined the military, and she decided to find someone else. She was divorced with a child when I returned, but she and one of my sisters were friends and my mother adored her, so we saw each other often. We got back together and married. I adopted her son, Michael, and we had a daughter, Kayla."

She saw the light in his eyes when he mentioned the children. "If you'd rather not talk about it, I understand."

"Oh, no. I'm long over her. I just miss the kids. Mike was only two when we married, so he's as much mine as if I had fathered him. Her first husband was an irresponsible jerk, and the one she's married to now isn't much better," he said, ruefully. "I'll never understand how any man could ignore his child, especially one as lovable as Mike. My little girl is adorable. A real know-it-all. I miss them both."

She listened sympathetically, while choking her way through a jalapeno-laced dish.

"Alfreda wanted it all, and she wanted it immediately. I wanted security. I said the word portfolio and she began counting the pairs of shoes in her closet. My family was poor. Not uneducated or unskilled, just too many mouths to feed. I'm one of seven children, and we watched both parents work hard to make ends meet. There's no way I'm going to slave all of my life and end up with no more than I was born with, or so deep in debt I can't rest at night."

"So you basically divorced over money, too. What a shame."

"Yeah. She gave me an ultimatum: buy her a nicer home or she'd take the kids and leave. I didn't, she did." There was no bitterness in his voice.

"I hope you have a good relationship with your children. I hate seeing kids suffer during divorce. That's one reason I'm glad Stan and I didn't have children."

"I have a good, but distant, relationship with the kids. Freda married a lawyer, and they live from paycheck to paycheck in that nice house she wanted. I suppose that compensates for having a husband who rarely sleeps at home. It's one of those 'be careful what you wish for' situations."

Now, detecting bitterness, she was relieved when he asked a question she did not mind answering.

"So what about your family?"

"Dad is a high school principal. Mom is a nurse. I have two brothers, one younger, one older. I miss my family more that I ever imagined, and I've only been in Texas two weeks."

"A teacher's kid?" His eyes twinkled. "Uh-huh."

"What's that supposed to mean?" She liked his teasingly pleasant smile.

"The worst kids around belong to teachers and preachers. Didn't you know that?"

"Not in my family. Dad was very strict. Loving, but strict. I was an obedient child."

"I'm not too sure about that. I detect a bit of mischief in your eyes. Little demon kid." He held his drink aloft and smiled.

She laughed. "No way. My parents were firm disciplinarians, rigid but fair, and they were very loving. My brothers and I towed the line unless we wanted to see the veins pop up in my father's forehead. The entire family helped keep us straight. My paternal grandmother taught me a few lessons that still keep me out of trouble."

"How so?"

"Mama Em, her name was Emelda, came to live with us when I was around eight. She told me stories about her youth, and in every story, no matter how tough things became, she managed to retain dignity and control. Being in control of my life is my prime endeavor. I want to say when, where, and how much."

"Are you speaking personally or professionally?"

"Both. I've never used drugs, never smoked cigarettes, and I've never been wasted on alcohol. I obey laws and never take unnecessary chances. As Mama Em always said, I don't throw rocks at the penitentiary. I like to have fun and I'm not totally inflexible. I'm willing to bend, but I like who I am. Anyone wishing to share my life will have to accept that."

"Was that a problem for you and Stan?"

She thought about her answer while remembering Stan's anger, hurled accusations, and the clash that could have ended tragically.

"No, the problem with Stan was insecurity. It drove him to hit me, and that is not something I will live with."

"He was violent?"

"Not really. Not at all." The face next to hers in her their wedding photo was the one she preferred to remember. "We were so in love and so happy for the first two years of our marriage. We graduated college, and I started working full-time at Sealand while working on my MBA at night. Stan was recruited by a subsidiary of a big software company. He dreamed of being this innovative software designer who would revolutionize the industry and make a mint. Of course, everyone in the firm had the same aspirations. There were no promotions and few raises. In the meantime, I was promoted from loan processor to underwriter, and then to head underwriter in no time flat."

"And he was jealous of your career."

"Oh, yeah. He was bothered that I made more money than he, and that I had a life outside our home. We had both planned to pursue advanced degrees, but while Stan was sitting around complaining in the evenings, I was in class. He blamed his lack of progress . . . you know the story. He was the victim of discrimination, didn't attend the right college, didn't fit in with the others. My schedule was tight, so he was alone a lot. I guess he had too much time to obsess over what he thought was failure."

"Did you try to get him to stop blaming others and take charge of his life?"

She nodded. "Lots of long sermons, but things went from bad to worse. He would jokingly say that Sealand meant more to me than he did. I started sensing anger under the jokes, so I tried as hard as I knew how to make him see how much he meant to me. We had planned a night out, but I had an unexpected business dinner to attend. He was drinking when I got home. We argued and he slapped me."

"Is that when you left?"

"I left, but not immediately. I just sat there at first, too stunned to react, and he fell asleep. The more I thought of what had happened, the sting on my skin . . ." She shook her head, as if seeking to clear it of a painful memory. "I just went crazy. I looked all over the house for something to hit him with, but a stupid wrench was the heaviest thing I could find. I raised it over my head and came down as hard as I could. When he didn't move, I thought I had killed him. I ran out and drove to my parents' home. He had already called, so they knew he was okay. The blow just glanced the side of his head, but the only thing I saw was blood and lifelessness."

She shivered as she recounted that last, fatal blow to her marriage.

"Then I saw the anger in my father's eyes when I said Stan had slapped me. He calmly asked what I wanted to do. I said I wanted a divorce. He and Mom drove me back to the apartment and Mom helped me pack while Dad listened to Stan slobber on and on about how my job was coming between us and about how much he loved me. After I loaded my things into the van, Dad pulled a pistol from his jacket pocket and stuck the barrel down Stan's throat."

Travis swallowed hard. "Mercy!"

"Yeah, that's what I said. Mom and I were both shocked. I didn't know Dad even owned a gun." She chuckled. "Of course the biggest shock was on Stanford's face. I'll never forget that look."

Her smile vanished. "He called every day for weeks, begging me to come home and give our marriage another try. I almost gave in several times, but I couldn't stop thinking of what could have happened that night, what might happen if he became abusive again. The uncertainty of living in a potentially explosive situation is not my idea of control."

"I can't say I blame you or your father. Any man who would hit a woman deserves to have a gun shoved down his throat. I'm glad you learned to say when, where, and how much. Did your grandmother teach you any other lessons that helped you become the dynamic woman you are?"

"I wouldn't use the word *dynamic*, but I did learn one lesson that has kept me on the straight and narrow. Mama Em was a vibrant woman who became miserable when Parkinson's slowed her down. She walked slowly, usually with a cane, but she continued her daily walks. Daddy was afraid she'd fall. He told me to go with her and I always did, except on the day after my twelfth birthday. I was listening to my new stereo and let her go out alone."

She bowed her head. "I intended to follow, but got too caught up in having fun. When darkness came and she wasn't back, I took my little brother and walked around the block at least ten times without finding her. I can't tell you how scared I was."

"That she was hurt or that you'd get in trouble for letting her go out alone?"

"Both. I was afraid she was hurt and couldn't get home or that someone had harmed her. My imagination ran wild. I remembered a shortcut through this vacant lot and dragged my brother, screaming and yelling, into an overgrown mess between two buildings. We found her, frightened but otherwise unharmed." Her eyes moistened. "She was lucid most of the time, but the onset of senility played havoc with her mind. It saddened me to see her physically and mentally deteriorate.

"I told my dad about it right away, and that became another prelude to one of his many parables. He said 'Mama was close to home but the unfamiliar passage, the change in directions turned her around, confused her, and she couldn't find her way.' I thought of that, and still think of it, whenever I'm tempted to take an unfamiliar route."

She looked at his bowed head. "Did I put you to sleep?"

"No, you didn't put me to sleep. I was just thinking of what you said. That was a nice story. Very profound."

His smile was sweet and his eyes hazy. "I wish I had that wisdom to guide me when I was young. I can think of several wrong turns in my life. In some ways, I'm still trying to find my way back home. I'll have to remember that story for my kids."

"I'm not sure how effective it will be for them. It works for me because I can still see Mama Em's face, walking in circles, so close to home and yet so lost."

He smiled, and this time his smile was for her. "You're a very nice person, Susan Cross. There's real warmth in your soul."

"You sound surprised."

"Just a little. Your work face sometimes appears a little cold and ruthless, but I suppose that's the way it has to be."

She saw herself through his eyes and flinched. "What you see on my face is caution, not frost. I'm as nice as I'm allowed to be. I didn't make the rules, but I am determined to control my life enough to be able to dodge the crap as it goes flying by. As hard as I try, I still sometimes fall short and need a soft place to land just like everyone else. The one thing I can tell you is that I believe in keeping it real. I'm cautious, and I'm not a hypocrite."

They finished dinner and arrived in time to take the last two available seats at the Café Rio. She enjoyed the music and when the band took a break, Travis told her how nice it was to sit next to a beautiful woman who was also a great listener. He drove her home, and held her hand when they crossed the street to her building. She thanked him at her door.

"I really enjoyed the evening. I've never been so alone before," she admitted. "Thanks for spending the evening with me."

She showered and dressed for bed. The evening had been relaxing. She felt less stressed than at any time since arriving in Houston. Travis was a nice man, and she was happy to have found another friend. Sleep came easy, and with it dreams of closeness and total fulfillment. Strong arms held her close. Adoring eyes bore into her soul. She relented to passion that took away her breath. His mouth devoured hers and traveled down her body. Awakening. Igniting.

It was not a dream but a trance where she was lost in the glory of his being. She lay in his arms, enthralled just as she had been when he first walked into her office. There was no animosity between them, only fire. She whispered and then screamed his name. Awakened by the sound of her own voice and the fetching smile of Rev. Willard Cartwright in her head, she clutched a pillow against her body and sighed.

The Monday morning management meeting provided Susan with an opportunity to question the policies she felt were too lax and to give opinions when they were sought. She gladly shared her knowledge, including her views on the need for a unified operation. She watched Price's face contort with disagreement.

"I understand that departments here are fairly independent and segregated. This poses a problem for me. We're a team here at Sealand, and being a cohesive group is the only way to remain tops in our field. "

Price hurled several questions her way, and she responded while thinking that, like Angie, her knowledge was underestimated. She responded with thorough explanations, and Travis watched her with a proud smile.

When Price asked about Cedargrove Heights, she thought before answering. "They have made serious allegations that I hope we can disprove. If not, the parties responsible will have to face the consequences. If Sealand falls, we all go with it. Another reason to remain unified."

Her usually sharp answers became ambiguous and Price began to squirm.

Several employees praised her viewpoints and Susan thanked them, all the while knowing Price would attempt to undermine her whenever possible. She would just have to work around him. She and Angie continued combing through loan files for properties in Cedargrove Heights and comparisons, and Susan scanned the papers for stories, anything she could find, on Rev. Willard Cartwright. When she found an article showing him attending a rally to protest capital punishment, she clipped the picture and kept it in her briefcase. It was not a good likeness, but she didn't need one. His face was indelibly etched in her mind.

She and Travis attended a late-evening ribbon-cutting ceremony for a new branch office, and afterwards, Travis invited her to a dinner. They went to a soul food restaurant that happened to be in Cedargrove Heights. Susan decided to involve Travis in her new project.

"A business acquaintance informed me of an opportunity to increase Sealand's loan portfolio. Winning a bid to share in a large federal housing development will place Sealand in competition with other lenders for a sizable loan commitment. I'm especially interested because the project is aimed at low-income and first-time home-buyers. It might be a purposeful endeavor for this area. What do you think?"

"Are you concerned about this area because of Rev. Cartwright's accusations?"

"Yes and no. No, because I'm not intimidated by his accusations, and yes, because he brought Cedargrove Heights to my attention. Why are you asking?"

"I know he's been in to see you, but I didn't know why until Price brought it up at the meeting. He's always begging on behalf of those people who never make payments on time. Maybe if they dropped a little less in his collection plate, they could pay their bills. Did he question one of my appraisals again?"

His defensiveness came as a surprise, but she had no intention of revealing what she had learned.

"What do you mean—again?"

"Price told me Cartwright had questioned the value I put on a property out there. A foreclosure. I don't know what you've heard about me, but I'm good at what I do. I have every designation the state offers for appraisers, and I take my job very seriously. I also know I have a reputation for being Price's boy, and that's a damn lie. Yes, I'm grateful to him for bringing me to Sealand. Having a set salary each month is better than working extremely hard and still not making as much money. But I'm my own man."

She shrugged. "I just arrived, remember? That makes me a minority in more ways than two. Everyone here knows more about this situation than I do. I shouldn't have mentioned work tonight, so let's forget it."

"I don't mind talking about it. I liked your speech about being a more cohesive group, but that's never been the policy. On more than one occasion, Price has directed us to keep mum about certain things in our area. Since I have no desire to stir the fire, I've stayed pretty much to myself. I don't know much about anything other than my own area, but I do know Price is as self-serving as they come. I say that without reservations."

"Well, if it's any consolation, Rev. Cartwright did not question your appraisal, at least not to me." She had looked forward to a relaxing evening and regretted mentioning Sealand, especially after Travis continued justifying the quality of his work.

"It's hard to explain to people that the house they purchased four years ago isn't worth half of what they paid for it because two neighboring properties were foreclosed. Values are much better than they were in the eighties; they've increased from the nineties, but there are still some soft spots. I don't control the economy. Even the government can't seem to do that."

It was the cue she had been waiting for. "Speaking of government, tell me something about our mayor. He seems to have his arms around most of the city's problems and as large as this place is, that has to be an armful. Crime. Traffic. Unemployment. Schools."

The conversation turned from one generating defensive heat to one focusing on citywide social and political problems. Nevertheless, though Travis was no longer edgy, he remained argumentative and cynical. Susan did not challenge what she felt was a limited outlook on life, but hoped he would regain his composure and relax. She had already determined that he was intelligent and insightful, but each negative opinion made her realize that he was trapped by self-imposed restrictive views. He grew even more agitated. She smiled and nodded at most of his observations and answered his questions without passing judgment.

Wishing she had met him at the branch office rather than riding with him, Susan's concern grew during the drive back to her apartment. His speech was slurred and he walked the short distance from the parking lot to her building with difficulty.

"Come in and have a cup of coffee. I'll make decaf or tea if you prefer."

"Regular coffee is fine." He followed her to the kitchen, constantly complaining about the rigors of his job and not being able to see his children on a regular basis.

Susan didn't dare end the evening until she felt he was sober enough to drive. She listened patiently, but kept her comments to a minimum. He appeared somewhat steadier after a second cup of coffee and a slice of home-made pumpkin bread.

"Tell me something," he said, perching on a stool at the counter. "What do you want out of life? I mean, you can't go much higher with Sealand, so what are your goals? Do you want to marry again? Do you want children?"

"I can see marriage and children in my future, and I am planning to work on a law degree, but I have everything I want for now."

"I want to marry again. I'm seeing someone . . . not exclusively or anything like that. I like her a lot, but she keeps talking marriage and I'm not in love with her. She's very nice but . . . no sparks. Is that a bad thing to say?"

"Not if it's how you feel. Just listen to your heart."

He continued talking and she offered neither praise nor criticism, just an occasional smile. She fully expected him to fall asleep on the sofa, but after walking around the apartment and drinking another cup of coffee, he became alert and his mood lightened. She was greatly relieved when he picked up his coat and walked steadily to the door.

Alone with her cat, she thought about Travis's take on love and marriage. She wanted love, and her need to feel the rapture of a man's arms was becoming increasingly painful. She wanted and needed a man. Only one came to mind. She took the news clipping from her briefcase and stared at his likeness. Every feature on his face was prominently handsome, but his lips were the most inviting she had ever seen. She remembered the touch of his hand and the excitement it had sparked.

"Susan, Susan, Susan." She tucked the photo inside the book she was trying to read. "I can't let any man get to me this way."

She stroked Dino's head and listened to him purr. She was facing a professional challenge and a personal moment of truth. In her heart, she knew exactly what she had to do.

"It is a big city. I think we can both live in it without stepping on each other's toes."

# CHAPTER 4

Susan spent her weekend reviewing files. On Sunday evening she left an answering machine message for the head of Sealand's legal staff and called Angie.

"I've seen enough. The main topic for tomorrow's meeting is Cedargrove Heights, and I want you to be there."

Susan was the first one in the boardroom on Monday morning. Her mind was filled with countless and alarming thoughts that made the soft leather chair at the head of the table a very uncomfortable place to sit. Only her ability to reflect backwards and project ahead eased her panic, so she revisited some of the commendations she had received since joining the Sealand group.

Sealand's office on the west side of Canton was one of the smallest in the lending chain, and any visit from Waylon Deeds invariably sparked speculation. As soon as he arrived early one Wednesday morning, the rumors had begun. He was in town either to promote or dismiss. Susan paid little attention, though she did wonder why he constantly called her to ask for explanations and opinions that seemed outside the realm of her authority. His "how would you handle . . ." ended at three o'clock on Friday when he called and asked her to join him in the boardroom. Fighting rising annoyance, she tapped soundly on the closed door and waited to be invited in. The entire board of directors, including Tom Waverly, smiled at her.

"Have a seat, Miss Cross," Mr. Deeds said, nodding to the empty chair across from his.

She felt her throat closing.

"I've been a constant harassment to you the last few days, Miss Cross, and I apologize," Mr. Deeds said.

"It was no trouble at all," she said, feeling as if he had read her mind.

"It was, but with good reason." He looked around the room. "This company is growing like wildfire, Miss Cross. Sealand is now making mortgage loans in twenty-six states, and we hope to add the other twenty-four. With this rapid growth, there's been no time, and no person, to ensure uniform standards in our branches. We've got one office down in Louisiana, for example, that financed sixty-eight homes, packaged the loans, and tried to sell them to an investor without realizing they were prefab homes. We can't have that kind of thing."

Mr. Waverly nodded in agreement. Susan's hands were damp and her throat felt parched.

"We'd like you to head Sealand's loan production team, Miss Cross. You'd report to me, but everyone here will be at your disposal if need arises. You'll make periodic visits to all branch cities for quality control purposes and make changes at your discretion."

Susan remembered that as a magical moment in her life, and the most memorable in her career. Her father was right. She had been a good student, even in graduate school. When Mr. Deeds had pushed a legal pad across the table showing her proposed salary as head of lending, she had seen concrete evidence that her studies had paid off. Managing a small production office had been effortless. This was her first major challenge, and she would not allow the treachery of others to shorten her stride.

Price walked in the door and her mind was made up. It was possible that Mr. Deeds had learned of Price's unscrupulous practices, feared retaliation, and had sent her in to remedy the situation. Or maybe as a scapegoat? Looking at his deceptive smile, she silently vowed to personally expose him and avenge the citizens of Cedargrove, even though the results could prove painful.

She opened the meeting and introduced the newcomers.

"I'm sure most of you know Angie Edwards from loan servicing, and this is Perry Trask, head of our legal department. As some of you know, the lending practices of Sealand have come under scrutiny by a group of citizens from Cedargrove Heights. Rev. Willard Cartwright and several others met with me and claimed applicants were denied loans with Sealand because they wanted to purchase homes in that particular neighborhood. I attempted to pacify them with contrasting figures, but that didn't suffice, as I was told in a follow-up meeting with Rev. Cartwright. I asked Perry to join us today because I'm afraid this matter isn't going away. Since the loan denials were made before my arrival, I'd like Price to share his knowledge on the subject."

Her words had burned bright crimson paths across his face.

"I know of no such practices here at Sealand. This whole thing is ridiculous. I hope you're not agreeing with this man."

"Whether I agree or disagree is not pertinent. I was blindsided with this situation my first day in this office, so I was unable to respond to their accusations. I don't know the weight of their proof, but I don't think they're making unsupported claims. You were in full charge of lending at that time, and we need to know if you can refute their accusations."

"I was in charge then, but I'm not at this time. Has this already become a legal issue? Is that why Perry is here?"

Susan turned to the others at the table. "I thought of airing this issue with just those involved, but it occurred to me that we're all involved. I was the one who said we should be a cohesive group, so as a group, we have a potential lawsuit. As head of this division, I'm charged with defending Sealand against all allegations, and I will. I already have my answers and, just as good defense attorneys represent clients regardless of their guilt or innocence, I will defend Sealand."

She stood and leaned across the table. "To answer your question, Price, if this matter goes before a judge, you'll be the one on the witness stand, not me. I didn't witness redlining. If I had, there would be different faces at this table. Now, once again, are you certain you can justify the denial of these loans?"

"Do you know what the foreclosure rate is like in that neighborhood?" Price asked, evading her question. "The only loans we've made there and didn't lose our shirt on were government loans. I don't think any of those people pay on time."

Susan fumed. "Let me advise you of something, Price, and I want Perry to correct me if I'm wrong. If you ever utter words like 'those people' in the presence of Rev. Cartwright, you *and* Sealand will end up in deep doo-doo. The majority of the residents there are African American or Hispanic. I'm keenly aware of the performance of loans made in that area, and I want those facts presented here today." She nodded at Angie.

"The delinquency ratio in Cedargrove Heights is currently 52 percent." Angie gave the breakdown of active loans, those loans in foreclosures, and loans already foreclosed. "Would you like a breakdown on months delinquent?"

"No, but I will ask that you update these figures daily and keep the numbers handy should we need them. Thank you for compiling this information so quickly."

She saw joy on Price's face.

"See! It's a bad investment area. I don't know why we have to answer to that man. Any fool would think twice before approving a conventional loan in an area that's already ridden with foreclosures. It has nothing to do with race. This falls under the heading of making shrewd business decisions."

"The fact that this area has a lot of poorly performing loans doesn't give you or anyone else the right to redline it, Price," Perry said, drumming his pen on the desktop. "The issue at hand is one of geographical discrimination. There are people just waiting to haul us on the carpet for discriminatory lending practices."

"If you look at the numbers—"

"If you look at the numbers, why not look at the 40-plus percent that are current?" Perry interrupted. "In defense of your position, you've just verbally incriminated this whole company. Sealand cannot operate under the policy of making loans in only those areas that appeal to us."

"The more pertinent issue is that we, Sealand, made the builder loan for this subdivision," Susan injected. "If discretionary tactics were needed, then that was the time to employ them. I also have figures from two other subdivisions, neither of which is largely comprised of minority homeowners. Both have delinquencies exceeding those of Cedargrove. In each instance, we have continued to make loans that are largely uninsurable and unmarketable. Sealand owns most of them. Sealand will suffer the losses." She closed her file and turned back to Price. "Can you explain that?"

"I don't know what areas you're talking about, but some of those loans were made under a commitment that was issued before we knew of these conditions. I would never make a decision that wasn't good for the company." His face was now beet red and his eyes ablaze with anger.

"Don't get me wrong, Price, I'm not disagreeing with your reasoning," Susan said in a more relaxed tone. "You know as well as I do that you can't simply decide, based on negative collection figures, to discontinue lending in one area. The fact that you overlooked even worse delinquencies in other areas will only serve to validate Rev. Cartwright's contentions. Playing devil's advocate, if I have this information, I'm sure Rev. Cartwright does, too."

"She's right, Price," Perry said. "Any first-year law student could win this case. What do you suggest, Susan?"

"I want every underwriter in this company, branches included, to work overtime and tear these files apart. I want each file re-underwritten and every figure and fact verified." She turned to Angie. "I have a list of properties that foreclosed in Cedargrove. What I need now is a final disposition on each one, including our loss profile. I have a few tricks up my sleeve, but I'll wait for Rev. Cartwright to make the next move."

"Just what do you propose to do? The only way to make these . . . to make the Cedargrove situation go away is to approve all of the denied loans. Give them what they want. It's very hard to go back and remember why certain decisions were made," Price offered, looking around for support from his staff.

Susan met his stare. "That's a lame excuse, Price. No one is trusted to remember why decisions were made. A ton of documentation is needed to close each file, whether the loan is approved or denied. If that file was properly closed, everything pertinent to your decisions should be there."

Susan then presented information on her proposal for the low-income housing commitment, and praised one of the branches for exceptional originations, both in number and quality. As the meeting was ending, a fire alarm sounded and everyone was asked to vacate the building. Fire trucks wailed and employees scampered down the stairs. Passing through the police barricade, Susan learned that a vehicle was burning in the garage and building management was taking the necessary safety precautions.

"Swell!" There had been little time to spend on stripping the Cedargrove files, and she wanted very much to finish. Leaving with as much work as she could stuff into her briefcase, she stopped at the gas station closest to her apartment and began filling her tank. She looked up when she felt a tap on her shoulder. Thinking it was a co-worker who had also been evacuated, she turned, smiling, right into the face of Rev. Willard Cartwright Jr. Her eyes widened, and she dropped the nozzle from the tank, spilling gas on her shoes and his.

"Sorry, I didn't mean to startle you, Miss Cross. I recognized you standing here and spoke, but I realized you couldn't hear me over the traffic noise," he said, flashing his magical smile.

"Hello, Rev. Cartwright. I was just filling up on the way home. We had a car fire in the parking garage at work, and they evacuated the building. I didn't want to leave a stack of work on my desk, but I had no choice." She felt her heart lurch and actually looked down to see if it was visible through her blouse. Aware that she was babbling, she replaced the gas nozzle and waited for him to speak.

"He does work in mysterious ways." His voice was soft and reverent.

"I beg your pardon?"

"Never mind. I'm delighted to see you, Miss Cross. I'm not at all pleased with how our last meeting ended. I know you're new to this area. I wanted very much to meet on neutral territory and begin our relationship on a better note." He smiled and extended his hand. "Hi, I'm Willard Cartwright."

She smiled back. "I also want to apologize for any offensive remarks I may have made, Rev. Cartwright. Can you forgive me?" She accepted his outstretched hand.

"That would be my pleasure, and please call me Will unless we're in the presence of my father. Then he's Will and I'm Willie. Or sometimes when they forget I'm an adult, Willie Joe. May I call you Susan, or do you prefer Sue?"

"Susan. I hate Sue." She grinned. "Willie Joe, huh?"

"My middle name is Joseph," he revealed, still smiling. "So you have an unexpected evening off. Any plans?"

"My only plan is to complete as much work as possible, and maybe drive around the neighborhood. I'm trying to learn my way around the city without getting lost, so I venture a little farther away from my apartment each time I have a chance to roam the neighborhood."

"I'm sure any new city would pose a problem, but Houston is large and sprawling. It's also grown so rapidly that I get turned around myself, and I'm a native." His smile softened as he looked into her eyes.

"We're having our annual Women's Day celebration at the church on Saturday. It's a fashion show and luncheon to raise money for our youth camp. I would be honored if you would join my table as my guest."

Breathing became difficult. "I would love to attend," she said. "As a single man you must dread these events."

"I dread a lot of the social events where my presence is pretty much demanded. Let's just say I do an awful lot in the name of the Lord."

He had the kindest eyes she had ever seen.

"What time does it start?"

"I'll pick you up at eleven, if that's okay."

"That's fine. Let me give you the address. It's right around the corner . . . the red brick building on the left." Pointing in the direction of her apartment building, she felt her hand shaking.

He said good-bye and she watched him stride to the other side of the gas pumps and to his car. She hurried to her building and burst into the apartment with such excitement, Dino went into hiding under the sofa. She went straight to the telephone and dialed her parents' number, praying that at least one parent was home. This was truly a new beginning, and she wanted to share her joy.

"Mom, it's me. Hi. Is everyone okay? How's the weather? I'm sure it's cooler than here, but so are the bowels of hell. Bobby and Charles okay? What about Dad? Did he have his check-up yet?"

"We're fine, honey. We're all fine. It's obvious something is wrong, so please calm down and tell me before my imagination goes to extremes."

"I am excited, and that in itself may be wrong, I'm not sure. Mom, I met this man. The most fascinating man I've ever seen. Handsome, tall, broad shoulders, large dark eyes, chocolate skin that made me salivate, and the most charming smile you could imagine. Mom, he's a minister. Rev. Willard Cartwright Jr."

"Well, I don't know about you dating a minister. I've had to threaten to scrub your mouth with soap . . . did you say Willard Cartwright?" Tammy suddenly asked.

"Yes, have you heard of him? It wouldn't surprise me if you had. He's the most wonderful man, Mom. I didn't like him at first. In fact, I hated him. At least I think I did. He's the one who came in my first day here and pelted me with questions and innuendoes about redlining. I was so angry I wanted to call security. You know it takes a lot to make me lose control, but this man did it. Twice."

"Susan, slow down. How old is this man?"

"I don't know how old he is. I would say mid to late thirties. Mom, he's a minister! Rev. Willard Cartwright." She repeated the name as if it, too, was magical.

Her mother laughed. "For you to be this excited, Rev. Cartwright must be magnificent. I knew of a Rev. Willard Cartwright a long time ago, but he's in his early sixties now. This man is probably his son. The Rev. Cartwright I'm referring to crusaded for civil rights there in Houston and was in a group of young seminary students that marched in Washington with Dr. King. I vaguely remember his face, but I do recall it was a handsome one. And this is the man who upset you?"

"Yeah. Well, he accused Sealand of redlining a particular area. That's where—"

"I know what redlining is," her mother interrupted. "This must be the son of the Willard Cartwright I once knew. He was always marching, boycotting, raising Cain about one cause or another. I thought he would run for public office, but I assume his career in the ministry has been amply rewarding."

"I was told that the senior Rev. Cartwright was, and still is, a crusader, and so is his son. He was downright rude when he came to my office and I soon joined him. Mom, the whole incident was like something from another galaxy. I looked into his face and became totally paralyzed. I couldn't breathe, couldn't think. No man has ever made me feel that way. The second time we talked was even worse. For the first time in my life, I had to search for words."

"Those sure don't sound like reasons to be excited."

"It's not that. I just saw him again, at the gas station. I'm at my apartment now. There was a fire in the parking garage and we were evacuated. On the way home I stopped for gas and he walked up and tapped me on the shoulder. Mom, I have never felt like this about anyone." She saw Dino peeping around the sofa and lowered her voice. "Not Stan, not anyone."

"If he's like his father, I can understand. Does he have the same deep voice? That's what I remember most."

"Yes! That got to me almost as much as his smile. Mom, he just invited me to his church fashion show on Saturday. I am so frightened."

"Frightened? Why frightened?"

"He's a minister, Mom, and as you just said, I have a potty mouth. I'm sure I'll say something to make him think I'm an immoral heathen. I'm already ashamed of the feelings I have for him. I . . . it's inexplicable. I just wanted to jump in his arms and stay there for the rest of my life. I shouldn't have those thoughts about a minister."

"Honey, he's not the Pope. You're not supposed to see halos when you look at him. He didn't take a vow of celibacy. You'll probably have to hold him off with a stick."

"That's the part that bothers me most. I don't think I could hold him off, and you know how I am about being in control. I totally lost it with this man. I couldn't look at him straight. My knees were trembling. My hands were wet. That doesn't happen to me very often."

"I can understand why you feel so flustered, but don't waste your time worrying. He's a man and you're a woman. Whatever happens, happens. He's obviously attracted to you, and in all probability he was just as nervous and as awestruck as you were. You're a beautiful and very forceful woman."

"Well, he did strike up a personal conversation when we first met. He invited me to his church and to their singles' group meeting, which he chairs. In my anger I'd forgotten about that."

Willard Cartwright's smile danced before her. Words could not convey her sudden attraction to a stranger, and she could not fully explain the raw emotion he stirred within her.

"I'm glad you've found a man who excites you. Just don't get too carried away. Take it slow and see how much you really like Rev. Willard Cartwright once you get to know him."

"You're right. If I had been a good judge of character, I wouldn't be divorced. That brings up another point. Before I begin a serious relationship with a man, I'll have to determine if my marriage failed because of Stan or because of me. I know I should put it behind me, but I'm still riddled with questions and . . . a little guilt. Maybe I do tend to overwhelm men, though I certainly don't mean to."

"Only weak ones, honey. Stan isn't a bad person. His insecurities were no match for a strong-willed woman. Your father and I picked up little things that you probably never noticed about Stan, even when you were first married. Things that showed a lack of self-confidence."

She listened, thinking she was not afraid of falling in love, just the pain it could bring. One strike had not dulled her longing for a committed relationship. She wanted everything her life could hold, and she wanted it with Willard Cartwright.

She spoke to her father and found him less than thrilled by news of her new friend. Her mother, on the other hand, had urged caution but had been encouraging.

Her father's advice had been: "Don't worry about saying the wrong thing in this man's presence. I'm sure he's heard everything there is to hear by now."

She thanked her father for his advice, hung up and reminded herself to stay away from hot-button issues—first and foremost was Cedargrove Heights.

Her curiosity was also mounting. What kind of man was Rev. Willard Cartwright Jr.? She envisioned kindness, strength, and gentleness. But could he be a man who could run away with her heart, leaving her stranded in the state of helplessness that she had fought to avoid?

$\mathscr{\infty}$

"What time shall I pick you up tomorrow?" Will asked his father.

"You're not picking me up because I'm not going to that fashion thing. Not this year. I appreciate what the women go through to put this together, but it's one big bore for me."

"A lot of men are involved this year, and quite a few are modeling in the show."

"That's the other reason I'm not going. I respect and love all of God's creatures, and I don't mind men models, but that Sampson boy twisting around like a prancing filly doesn't do a thing for my bad heart."

Will laughed and his mother, who had brought her husband's dinner in on a tray, joined him.

"You'll be there, won't you, son?"

"I'll be there, Mom. In fact, I'm bringing someone. A friend."

"Good," his mother said, looking at his father. "That's the best news I've heard in a long time."

"It's Susan Cross, the lady from Sealand." He spoke quickly.

"Is she pretty?" his mother asked.

He answered without hesitation. "She's perfect."

*❦*

Saturday morning soon followed a restless Friday night. After trying on every dress in her closet, Susan decided that none was quite right for the occasion.

"You're going to a fashion show; you're not in one," she chided herself, and finally chose a lightweight navy knit with an asymmetrical gold stripe across the bodice and gold piping on the sleeves.

She studied her reflection in the mirror. "This is a Baptist outfit for sure," she said to her audience of one. "Wish me good luck, Dino."

She stepped into navy slingbacks, put a linen handkerchief in her matching bag, and added gold jewelry before declaring herself properly dressed.

Rev. Cartwright was late picking her up, which allowed extra time for her nerves to become more frayed. She paced back and forth, rubbing the knuckles of her right hand in her left palm, and thought back to the last time a date picked her up late. She was angry and he was sullen; they saw a dull movie, she refused to kiss him. He never called again.

"It's just as well, Dino. I'm too ambivalent about dating a minister for this to work."

The doorbell rang at precisely eleven-thirty. She removed the security chain and looked, unsmiling, into his eyes, but warmth soon replaced irritation.

"I'm sorry I'm late. I had an emergency at the church. I don't like keeping a lovely lady waiting, but you can count on this luncheon not starting promptly." He said it all in a rush, finally stopping to catch his breath. "You look wonderful." His smile was crooked and utterly disarming.

"Thank you."

Seated next to him moments later, she felt his magnetic pull and sensed the feeling was mutual. As he drove through his neighborhood, he provided her with details about the changing face of the area.

"This is Cedargrove Heights, once a predominately Jewish neighborhood, now predominately black, but with a growing Hispanic population. The older homes to the left were sold when blacks began to move into the area. A few Jewish families remained, but once the older members were gone, the younger generation chose not to keep the properties. Most of them are well maintained, but some were abandoned back in the housing recession of the eighties. Too much upkeep for some and not enough rental income for others. Just about every house along this main street went on the market shortly after tax laws for rental property changed."

She paid close attention to every detail he mentioned and tried to observe as much as she could of his beloved Cedargrove Heights, which bordered a large section of downtown. She knew that if the metro area hoped to expand, bordering property would eventually become prime real estate. The residences changed from the elegant, large brick and wood-framed houses to smaller, cheaply built ones. Wooded areas bordered the east side of the development. Susan saw lots of room for growth.

Will parked in his reserved space and came around to open the door and take her hand. Looking around, she observed several structures situated about the well-maintained grounds. She assumed they represented different eras in the church's history. The original structure was almost hidden behind the austere lines of the newer building. Remembering her grandmother's stories of how the church was the only place blacks could congregate during state-sanctioned discrimination, she felt an immediate kinship to a place she had never been.

Will held her arm as they walked toward the entrance. When he introduced her as his guest to several people in the foyer, she felt special. Heads turned as they entered the room. Susan quickly ascertained that a lot of money had gone into the construction of the large hall and into its elaborate décor. The individual seats were nicely upholstered, video screens were placed throughout, and biblical scenes were portrayed in stained glass on the windows and transoms.

Will introduced her around the table and then placed her between him and Mrs. Whitehead.

"Miss Cross." Mrs. Whitehead beamed a big, welcoming smile. "It's so nice of you to come."

When Will excused himself, Susan learned that Mrs. Whitehead was his godmother as well as his assistant, and met his mother, his sister Terri, and two aunts. Everyone was very cordial, though Susan felt sure they were giving her a critical once-over.

Will joined them midway through the show and apologized for his absence. When the event was over, Susan said good-bye to Mrs. Whitehead and the others and accepted invitations to come again. On the way out, he stopped for "a little church business." She wandered over to the foyer and purchased a purse from one of the street vendors there. On his way to join her, Will described her as a special friend to someone inquiring about her identity.

Susan liked his response.

He drove her around the rest of the neighborhood, pointing out his old high school, the house where he was born, and the house his parents had purchased when he was nine years old.

"I hope you don't mind if I run in and check on my dad. He had a stroke and has recovered just enough to get around in his wheelchair, but he flatly refused to come out for this function, not that I blame him. He's been alone here this afternoon, and I just need to make sure he's okay."

He flashed the smile that she had come to adore.

"I'll only be a minute. You can stay in the car if you like, though I'm sure he'd want to meet you."

"I don't mind coming in. I'd like to meet your father."

They found the elder reverend sitting in a recliner watching a western movie and talking to the set.

Will hugged his father, took the remote and lowered the volume on the TV before guiding Susan over for an introduction. The expression of devotion on his face and the pride and tenderness he displayed toward his father touched her deeply.

"Dad, I want you to meet someone very special. This is Susan Cross. She's head of lending for Sealand. This is my father, Rev. Cartwright Sr."

"Hello, young lady. Welcome to our home." He wasn't as old as Susan had imagined, and there was something enthralling in his smooth face, the same subtle intimidation she saw in his son.

"Thank you, sir. My mother has told me about your gallant efforts on behalf of civil rights. It's quite an honor to meet you."

A smile spread across his face. "Thank you. I appreciate your kind words. Your folks from Houston?"

"No, sir. I'm from Canton, Ohio. My mother recognized your name as someone she's come to respect over the years. I was taught to appreciate the sacrifices made by those who paved the way for the rest of us. My parents were very active in civil rights matters. They still are."

His smile was warm and genuine. "I'm so glad to hear that, and I hope they stay active. Too many people think they've got it made and have become complacent . . . lethargic . . . just plain ole lazy. If we're not careful, we'll be right back where we started." His voice lowered as he took her hand. "You sure are a beautiful young lady. I'm so glad my son brought you by."

The visit was brief, but during that time Susan gained a world of respect for Willard Cartwright Jr. She saw him not as a minister who spouted platitudes in the pulpit, but a man with genuine warmth and compassion. She also knew her views of Cedargrove, its citizens, and their problems had changed. They returned to the car and Will expressed his sentiment.

"I had no idea you knew anything about my father. I'm sure it made his day to know that someone your age remembers the way it was. Thank you."

"There's no need to thank me. I meant what I said. My mother told me of your father's civil rights work during his college years, and that he once marched with Dr. King. I quake in the presence of people like him. I know how much courage it took for them to put their lives on the line to make this world a better place for the rest of us. I'm forever ingratiated to all of them, both black and white."

"The struggle hasn't ended yet, Susan. That's what this whole thing with Sealand is about. This area has been singled out. I'm sure of it. Maybe they hid things to make it look okay to you, but I can assure you it isn't."

Feeling a ton of guilt wrapped in the likeness of Price Bishop, she tried to explain Sealand's position and listened to Will's concerns for Cedargrove residents whose appeals for clemency with delinquency problems had been rebuffed by Sealand's staff. Susan was pleased that they were able to disagree without being disagreeable, but hoped the Sealand and Cedargrove discussions would cease.

He passed a red brick house with white trim, pointed to the driveway, and honked his horn. "That's my house, and my best friend is in the driveway. His name is Rex. Not original, but easy to remember. I'm divorced. The death of our seventeen-month-old son and my ministerial duties drove my wife away. I won't dwell on it. I just wanted you to know."

She waited a few minutes, silently composing her next lines. "I'm divorced as well. My promotions and salary drove us apart, and I left him after a very disturbing physical confrontation. I won't dwell on it, either. It's in the past."

As they neared her apartment she wondered how he viewed their date and how it would end. She liked him a lot. He was jovial and upbeat, yet serious and committed. She unwittingly compared him to Travis, who was bland and deeply connected to bad memories.

They arrived at the door and he took her hand.

"I enjoyed having you as my guest today. You're a very pleasant and very beautiful lady. Thank you for brightening my world." He kissed her hand.

"I had a wonderful time. Thank you for inviting me." She unlocked the door and turned to say good-bye. "I didn't mean to climb on my soapbox, Will. I know the issues of your neighborhood are important to you and I respect that a great deal, even when we disagree."

He nodded. "I'm glad you said that. Yes, the issues of Cedargrove, my church, and my congregation are important to me." There was an amused twinkle in his eyes. "But I'm often reminded that I'm still a man. Mrs. Whitehead, Auntie, says I should pay less attention to my duties and more to my personal life. I plan to follow her advice. Do I have your permission to call you sometime?"

She found his gallant manner almost as thrilling as his crooked smile. "I'll look forward to it."

"How about dinner later in the week? I'm not sure of the day, but I can call you when I get to my office."

"My evening calendar is clear all week, so just let me know when you're available. Thanks again for a wonderful day."

She watched him walk away and realized she had already surrendered more of her heart than she could afford to lose.

# CHAPTER 5

The next week was a busy one for Susan, but she managed to squeeze in a little time for relaxation—and Will. As she feared, she would have to strip the files and underwrite the loans without any assistance from Price's department. The few files his staff did review contained cryptic notations such as "documentation missing" or "unable to determine cause of rejection." When questioned, Price had a ready answer.

"I don't know how to convey this message to you, but this isn't going to work. It's almost impossible to do what you're asking. These underwriters have current files that must proceed or we'll be getting a lot more visits from angry applicants. I simply don't have the manpower to go back and underwrite denied loans, no matter how many ministers cry foul."

The war was on, and she planned to take no prisoners.

She was in the middle of a major problem involving a Dallas branch office when Will called. She kept him waiting only as long as necessary before taking the call.

"I really enjoyed spending time with you Saturday, but I would like to do something next time that wouldn't bore you to tears."

Hearing his voice, Susan imagined his laughing eyes. She wondered if the lack of male companionship could explain her intense response to him, but quickly discarded that theory as she and Travis had been in each other's presence and she had felt nothing remotely resembling what she felt for Will.

"Well, I wasn't bored; women generally aren't bored at fashion shows. I actually enjoyed it, and enjoyed meeting your father. I enjoyed being with you."

"The pleasure was all mine, and I would very much like to see you again. I'm tied up today and tomorrow. Are you free for lunch on Wednesday?"

"I sure am." Wednesday seemed a lifetime away. She wanted to see him now, to touch him, to have him extinguish the fire that was building inside her.

"We're having lunch on Wednesday," Susan repeated to her mother that evening. "I met his mother and one of his sisters at church. He stopped to check on his father when he was driving me home, and I met him as well. He looks much younger than his age suggests."

"Does he . . . is he still handsome?" Tammy asked hesitantly.

"He is. Angie said the stroke happened just after finishing a sermon. He's expected to regain most, or all, of his mobility, but you can see his frustration and impatience. I'll ask Will more about it on Wednesday."

The enormity of Susan's responsibilities became clear as calls for directions and assistance came from the other branches. But even in the midst of erupting crises, her mind kept drifting to Will's appealing smile. On Wednesday, she brushed, flossed, and reapplied her makeup before leaving for Farrell's Steakhouse. Will was waiting at the table.

"I'd figured I'd better not be late twice," he said, smiling as he stood.

She ordered tea and was surprised when he ordered a glass of wine.

"What? We serve this stuff in church. Go ahead, have a glass."

"No, thank you. I can hardly respond to the crisis around me when I'm totally sober. One glass of wine and I just might tell them all where to go and how to get there."

"I'm sure you're very capable, even after a glass of wine." His voice was smoky and smoldering. "Tell me, how did you get in the lending business?"

"Just a fluke. I was headed for law school when I took a summer job at Sealand. A branch manager hired me, and I guess he liked my work. I continued there and went for an MBA instead."

They talked of nothing in particular, but he laughed a lot. Susan found nothing to dislike about him. He was an entertaining, relaxing, and exceptionally handsome man. She remembered her mother's interest, and inquired about his father.

"My mother was excited that I had met your father. He's obviously made a big impression on her. I hope his health is improving."

"Thank you, and thank your mother. Dad is my hero, and it's great to know he is well thought of by others. He was a little surprised that your mother was aware of his summer in Washington. It was a special part of his youth. My appreciation for him, as a father and a minister, is tremendous. His illness was yet another example of just how precious life is. He's getting stronger every day, and I thank God for that."

He walked her to her car, held the door, and asked if she was free for dinner on Friday night.

She said yes, and he said he would pick her up at seven.

"I'll see you then. Thanks for lunch." She wanted a kiss. A hug. Something to take with her. She drove away, aware that he was there with her. He was inside of her.

"Friday is day after tomorrow." She almost sang the words. "I guess I can wait that long."

❦

Work became one long telephone call. By Friday, Susan was exhausted. Knowing she would be seeing Will brightened the drive home. He called as she was trying to decide what to wear.

"Susan, it's Will. I am so sorry, but I'm not going to be able to make it tonight. Another one of those small church emergencies. But I've cleared my calendar for tomorrow. All day. I hope I didn't ruin your evening."

"Ah, no, I understand."

"So you'll forgive me and let me make it up to you tomorrow? Please?"

She tried to hide her disappointment. "Sure. No problem."

"You're an angel. We'll spend the day in Galveston. It's not the beach as you know it, but it is close by. Dress casually. Shorts or whatever. I'll pick you up . . . say ten o'clock? Is that too early?"

"No, ten is fine." She hung up, grabbed her purse, and headed to the Galleria to shop for shorts. The store had a huge selection, and she had a hard time choosing. She ended up with eight pairs, and spent much of the evening deciding which one to wear. She finally settled on khakis and chose a pale pink, very feminine pullover. She fell asleep thinking of tomorrow.

The lump in her throat allowed no room for breakfast to pass, but Susan managed to drink a glass of milk and nibble the edges of a slice of wheat toast. She packed a shoulder bag with tanning lotion, sunglasses, and minimal essentials.

She was holding Dino when she answered the doorbell. "On time again," she said, looking at his khaki shorts, navy shirt, and thrilling smile. "Early, even."

"Yeah, you were my inspiration. Hey, what's that?" He pointed to Dino.

"This is Dino, *my* best friend, and don't tell me you hate cats."

"Hate is too strong a word. I'm just more comfortable with dogs, but I get along with most cats. Hi, Dino."

He reached out and the cat jumped from Susan's arms. Laughing, she said, "Come on in. I'll get my hat."

"This place is fabulous. Decorate it yourself?"

"It belongs to Sealand and came fully decorated. I added a little color and my limited Lladró collection."

"Boy," he said, looking around. "They must like you a lot."

"I wouldn't say that. They own four units in this building. I'm just lucky one was available when they transferred me here." She said good-bye to Dino and followed Will to a red Jeep Wrangler.

"See, I'm also a Jeep fan. This is my runaround utility vehicle. It's usually just me and the dog on Saturdays."

The conversation was easy, and Susan began to relax and enjoy the music on the radio. Will had tuned to a jazz station. He already knew she liked jazz, so she wasn't sure if the music indicated his personal taste or his effort to please. They both smiled a lot, and Susan got her first glimpse of Galveston Island when they crossed the bridge.

"So tell me, how do you like Houston so far?" he asked.

"I don't like the traffic, and I'm fascinated by the size of your newspaper," she answered. "The article I just read regarding twenty cool things about Houston definitely wasn't referring to the weather. Other than that, I like it."

"Ask a question and get a direct response. I like that. We had two newspapers at one time. The *Houston Post* folded many years ago, and *The Houston Chronicle* now rules solo."

He parked in Galveston's historic district, where the island's shops and restaurants were mostly housed in French-styled buildings that reminded Susan of New Orleans. So did the humidity. They window-shopped and toured a museum of Galveston's history before stopping for a snowball. Susan welcomed the pause, but was not prepared for Will's next question.

"If you don't mind my asking, what happened to end your marriage? I know you told me the basics. I'm only asking so I won't make the same mistake he made."

"Nothing is ever one person's mistake," she answered, and sat beside him on a bench in front of a craft store. "Stan was the campus athlete, the one every girl wanted. I'm a big sports fan, especially basketball, so it was a natural match. We dated for roughly six months, had a brief engagement and a wonderful wedding."

"I take it you don't go in for long engagements?"

"I . . . well, I guess I can tell you this. I mean, who better to tell than a minister?" She looked into his eyes. "I'm very old-fashioned when it comes to . . . intimacy. I was a virgin, and was determined to remain one until after I married. And I did."

"Wow! That's not the answer I expected."

"My father didn't expect it, either. His mouth hinged open when Stan asked his permission to marry me and I told him the reason we didn't want to wait."

The memory made her smile. "Stan is not a bad person, but like so many, he was plagued with self-doubt. I didn't realize it for quite awhile, but he craved attention the way some men crave drugs and alcohol. I was fortunate to have found a job that became a career. Stan was supportive and complimentary, but the higher I rose, the lower his ego sank."

Will listened intently and stroked her arm when she finished.

"And I thought you were going to say he cheated."

"Is that what happened with your wife?"

"No, no. She and I were very much in love. At least I was. I was the happiest man on earth when our son was born, but Tracey became restless. We had met when she worked for my accounting firm, so I suggested she return to work part-time and leave Trey in the church's day care, but that was not enough. Her sister is a big socialite in Houston, and I had promised to keep Trey while she attended one of her sister's fancy parties. Dad was out of town and someone at the church needed my help. I called to say I would be a little late and she told me to forget it. I assumed she'd stay home, even though she said she wouldn't, so I took my time with the family. I didn't get home until almost midnight."

Words caught in his throat and Susan felt his pain.

"I saw Tracey asleep on the sofa when I walked into the living room, so I went to the nursery to check on Trey." His head fell forward. "His body was tangled in the bed covers. He wasn't breathing."

"How did it happen?" Susan asked, taking his hand.

"Tracey had brought home a slice of cake wrapped in plastic. I assume she dropped it in Trey's crib when she put him down. He choked."

"Oh, Will." It was her turn to offer comfort. "I'm sure she felt terrible."

"She may have felt terrible, but all I saw was anger. She even told the church that my responsibilities there had caused our son's death. The gap was too wide to bridge. She didn't want the house or anything from it, so we settled monetarily, and she left. I don't really know why I still live there. I shouldn't."

"Probably because, in spite of the tragedy, your happiest memories are there."

He smiled faintly. "You're probably right."

"Well, Rev. Cartwright, or Willie Joe if you prefer, you'll have to create new ones. I'm sure that is what Trey would have wanted."

His smile broadened. "Mind telling me how old you are?"

"Not at all. I'm twenty-seven. How old are you?"

"Thirty-eight as of three weeks ago." He took her hand. "And just how did you acquire so much intelligence and compassion in such a short time? Were you one of those child prodigies?"

"I doubt it, but I did have a wonderful childhood. My parents are both strong, loving people. My brothers and I weren't allowed to watch much television. We had to pick certain shows and watch them together. To this day, I love cartoon heroes."

She saw that the twinkle was back in his eyes, and his full attention was on her. Her attraction to him was more than just physical. She felt him deep inside of her heart.

They finished their snow cones and continued walking into the older sections of Galveston. She was fascinated with the architecture and he seemed fascinated with her. Before the walk ended, she felt comfortable enough to share a few secrets she had never told anyone.

He smiled a lot, and each time her respect deepened and the ripples of passion she felt grew more insistent.

Susan did not think much of the beachfront, which was littered with cars, people and debris. She and Will removed their shoes and strolled along the water's edge. He held her hand and they laughed like kids when the cool waves lapped at their feet. Will took folding chairs from the Jeep after their walk and purchased two bottles of water from a street vendor.

"I'm having fun, Miss Cross," he said, smoothing lotion on her shoulders.

"So am I, Willie Joe."

"I never should have told you that," he said, laughing as he lightly pinched her shoulder. "Now you'll torment me with it forever."

They talked longer, but Susan's thoughts remained on one word—forever.

Susan and Will had dinner at a little restaurant that was owned by someone he knew. He asked for a table on the deck, where the breathtaking vista of a sheltered glen was trapped in the sun's dimming glow. He ordered champagne and raised his glass.

"To you, Susan Cross. Thanks for making my heart feel lighter than it has in years."

He leaned forward and kissed her cheek, and at that moment, she wanted him more than her next breath.

The conversation remained light and entertaining. Unlike Travis, who flatly stated his point of view, Will offered an opinion, asked for her comments, and listened attentively. They clearly had two things in common: they both had a broad and open-minded viewpoint on life, and they both loved their parents.

They finished dinner, shared a dessert, and stared at the moon from the deck of the restaurant that overlooked Galveston Bay. A band played soothing music, and he put his arm around her shoulder.

"This is nice," she said.

"It is. I own a little piece of land near San Antonio. Up in the hill country. It's actually part of our family homestead, but I bought my sisters' interest back when my son was born. I still enjoy going there, especially in the spring and fall."

He placed his arms around Susan's shoulder and looked upward. "It sits high on a hill and just seems so close to the stars."

"I believe you're a big romantic." She snuggled against him.

His face descended and his lips sealed over hers. Her heart throbbed and her knees buckled.

"I guess I am."

In her dreams, Susan was floating, Will at her side, into the sunset. They were removed from their earthly shells, somehow suspended in tranquility, away from all problems and fears. They made love without touching, surrounded by a glow brighter than the sun. She awakened in a deep sweat and looked at the clock. It was almost eleven, and she was expected at Angie's by three.

She hurried through the rest of the morning, read the paper, and finished her laundry before leaving. With her own heavy workload and a family at home, Angie could volunteer her time only in the evening and Sunday afternoon. Her postal worker husband left for his evening shift at six during the week and at four on Sundays.

Susan's respect for Angie grew after she told her story as they dug through reams of paper.

"I envy you and your lifestyle. I got married in college, and we moved here when Dawes Petroleum recruited Dwayne. My life has changed a lot since then. I learned of Dwayne's affair and knew I could not live that way."

"Good for you."

She frowned and shook her head. "People say a woman can tell when a man is fooling around. I know exactly when Dwayne started drifting away. I asked him about it, but he said it was the strain of his job and trying to achieve a more stable position. I'll skip the seedy details, but my painful discovery came one evening when Jessica developed a temperature and I called Dwayne at work. When I said it was an emergency, the woman answering the phone said he had left two hours earlier and gave me an address."

Hearing the pain in Angie's voice took Susan back to her final episode with Stan.

"I don't have to tell you what I found. Dwayne knew me well enough to assume I came armed with the revolver I kept in my closet, so he just stood there swearing nothing happened even though he was half naked when I arrived. I was so angry that I lost all sense of reason. Still holding Jessica in one arm, I kicked and trashed that place until I was exhausted."

"I admire your backbone," Susan said. "How awful! I don't know what I would have done in that situation, but I'm sure it would have been something close to what you did."

"I can't tell you how much it hurt, but I was too proud to cry. I went back to that apartment and packed his clothes. I had them waiting on the little porch when he came home. I didn't want an explanation. I just wanted him gone."

"Good for you," Susan said, and lifted her frozen margarita.

"Then, I had to figure out how I was going to take care of my daughter and myself on the money I made. But you know what, Susan? I felt so good about myself. I felt too much pride to stay with him even if I had to beg to survive. When you speak of being in control, I know exactly what you mean. I admire you for sticking up to Price Bishop. We're going to fight him and we're going to win, and not just because he's a hateful idiot, but for all the times innocent women have been left holding the smoking gun."

Angie was adamant about reviewing every file from Cedargrove Heights and all corresponding approvals.

Her mood lightened when she talked of her present husband, Carl, whom she described as down to earth, sweet and kind.

"Carl is a nice man. Some women mistake kindness for weakness. That same sweet man that women say they want is the one they drive their cars over. Carl had been taken advantage of more than once. I could tell he was cynical and mistrusting when I met him at a political rally. I didn't have family or close friends to keep the baby, so I seldom went anywhere without her. We sat next to Carl, and Jessica reached out as if she had known him all of her life. She fell asleep in my arms and he carried her to my car when the rally ended. He asked for my phone number and called later that evening to make sure we got home safely. We went out a couple of times, and he fell in love with my daughter. There was no real engagement; we married in a civil ceremony. It seems like yesterday in some ways. Everything was new, including most of Houston."

"It still is," Susan said. "I can't get over the Galleria. It's like shopping in New York or Chicago."

"This city has grown tremendously in the last ten years. There was a soybean field across the street from my first apartment in Southwest Houston. Now it's a high-income neighborhood with large homes, shopping malls, and a golf course every few blocks. We've got a nice zoo, pro basketball, football, and baseball—and each team has a new, state-of-the art arena."

"Travis said there's a great theater district."

"Oh yeah. And the museum district is wonderful. We take the kids whenever we can. Carl and I thought about relocating after we married and Dwayne started giving us hell about seeing Jessica. Thank God for Carl's sister, Kathleen. She's an attorney. By the time she finished filing for back child support and money for his half of the bills I struggled to pay, he was glad to leave us alone. After Jenna was born, we decided to stay in Houston, and I've never been sorry."

"Well, you're a great mother. You have a wonderful family, and I've never seen anyone in this house look unhappy."

She felt the beginnings of maternal tugs on her heart-strings. She felt love and happiness in Angie's home. The girls were pretty and well behaved, and the two-story brick home was delightfully decorated in a creative style befitting a growing family.

They set up shop at the breakfast table. Angie unlocked the wheeled file cabinet Susan had bought to safeguard the loan documents, they sipped Angie's famous frozen cocktails, and Susan finally shared her feelings.

"I enjoy having a career, but I would give up part of my salary, the big office, and having to deal with dopes like Price in a heartbeat for what you have. The girls are adorable, and I see the look in Carl's eyes when he's with you. That's what I want—the love and security of having a wonderful, supportive man in my life."

Thinking of her parents, she said, "I grew up in that kind of family. My parents are happy together. They raised us and now they're enjoying their first grandchild,

courtesy of my brother, Bobby, and his wife, Jennifer."
She sighed. "I guess it's only natural for the oldest child
to have the first grandchild, though I was the first to
marry." She felt more disappointment than bitterness.

Putting the subject of family and marriage aside, she
returned to the matter at hand. "I'll never be able to
repay you for your help. I just know we've not heard the
last of this mess, and I have to be prepared for whatever
the good folks of Cedargrove toss my way. I promise you
that if I go down, I will not divulge to anyone that you
helped, but if I win this fight, I'll make sure Deeds knows
what a valuable employee you are."

"Have you heard any more from them?" Angie asked,
separating loan documents from her daughter's school
project.

"Not exactly." Susan hesitated. "I'm going to tell you
something that I've only confided to my parents and my
best friend Barbara. I'm not sure where it's heading, but
I've been seeing Rev. Cartwright socially."

"What!" Angie screamed, staring at Susan. "You . . .
and Willie Cartwright? Girl, tell me you didn't?"

"It's not serious, at least not yet." She spoke casually,
but in her heart she knew seriousness was her goal. She
wanted to fall in love again, and there was no one she
would rather love than the Rev. Willard Cartwright Jr.

"Susan, Willie Cartwright is one of the most eligible
men in this town. Every woman I know would like to get
her hands on him. I felt it was such a shame that the two
of you were at odds with each other. He's perfect for you.
Handsome, well respected, and rich as cream."

"Rich?"

"He owns an accounting firm. Didn't you know that? He employs something like two hundred people. His firm has a big hospital contract as well as some with the city of Houston. He also owns an apartment building in the newer section of Cedargrove, which he reserves for low-income families. From what I've heard, he a heavy investor in several commercial projects in the city." She threw up her hands. "I can't believe this. You and Rev. Willie! I don't know what to say."

"I knew he has an accounting firm but I didn't know . . ." Susan was mildly surprised at Will's accomplishments. "I did notice that his clothes are very expensive. Obviously tailored. Of course, I doubt those wide shoulders and that magnificent body would fit in anything off the rack. Tell me the truth, Angie. I've been afraid of my feelings for him, partly because he's a minister and partly because of this mess," she said, pointing to a stack of files. "I feel like I'm in heaven when we're together, and that's without intimacy. Should I proceed, and if I do, will it jeopardize my career?"

"The only advice I can give you is to forget this mess and go for it. Being a minister doesn't make him any less a man." Angie wagged her finger. "And a fine man at that."

"He is fine, isn't he? I'm so glad to be able to talk to someone about this. I think I'm falling in love with him, Angie. We spent the most wonderful day together yesterday. Every time he smiles at me, my heart just melts. We drove to Galveston and browsed in some of the shops, walked along the seawall, and talked about our childhood, our hopes and dreams. Then we ate dinner at a restaurant overlooking the water. I could feel myself falling in love."

"Oh, that sounds so romantic. Willie Cartwright!" Angie squealed with delight. "Don't be afraid to fall in love. I don't think he would ever do anything to hurt you. So what if something happens at Sealand? You're educated, smart as a whip, and connected. You could get another job in a wink. That man is sweet."

"Angie, we sat there after dinner sipping our coffee and talking, and I've never felt so alive in my life. I would have married him on the spot if he had asked."

"How long has this been going on?" Angie asked.

"These terrifying feelings began the first day he walked into my office. That was the reason I had such a hard time keeping my wits about me."

She felt a deep bond with Angie and felt comfortable telling her how it all had started.

"Remember the day we were evacuated? I stopped for gas, and there he was. We apologized for rudeness during those two encounters in my office, and then he invited me to a church fashion show."

"So you've been out with him twice?"

"No, three times. We had lunch on Wednesday, planned to have dinner on Friday, but he was tied up. Yesterday was his way of compensating. He was a perfect gentleman at all times. Angie, I just feel so wonderful when I'm with him. Just talking, holding hands, my heart felt like it would explode. When we got back to my place, he stayed just long enough for the most thrilling kiss I've ever had. After that, I had a fierce inner struggle. My practical heart wanted assurance, my liberated spirit resisted the strength of our connection, and the rest of me just wanted Will. Wanted him as I have never wanted any man."

"I'm sure he felt the same. His wife left him a long time ago and women have been after him ever since. The ones I know of didn't get far, and it wasn't for lack of trying."

"How do you know all this?"

"For one thing, he dated Barbara Patton in accounting. She's a real broom-riding witch. Always talking loud and saying nothing. She dated him until about four months ago. She'd sit in the lunchroom every day talking about getting him bedded and wedded, but it sounds like she didn't do either one. We all got sick of listening to her. I think everyone there shouted when the bragging ceased."

"What happened?"

"I'm not sure. First she bragged about having him close to the altar, and not for a sermon. Then she just stopped talking about him. Someone asked why, and she said things didn't work out. I know someone else who dated him. She said it didn't work out because of his responsibilities, but she's a real society maven. Her first husband was a pro football player and she's involved with several big social events. I don't think Willie had time for all of that. Either that or he was bored to tears by that bunch, the same way I am."

Susan felt sympathetic. "I'm sure it's not easy dating or being married to a man who is constantly on call. Of course, right now my social life is nonexistent, so I don't expect any conflict." She put the file aside and looked at her new friend.

"Angie, he's the first man I've been attracted to since Stan. Heck, my attraction to Stan wasn't like this. Just watching Will walk in my door turns my knees to jelly. I keep thinking if he can rattle me this much just by walking into a room, I could find myself totally helpless if I fell in love with him, and then my control alarm sounds."

"I understand what you're saying, but we all take chances with our heart when we fall in love. A powerful man like Willie Cartwright showers you with his masculinity just by being there. You know who he reminds me of? That guy on TV. He stars in that show, *The Unit*, and he was the president on *24*. They even look a lot alike."

"Dennis Haysbert. You're right. They do look a lot alike. There's just something thrilling about a big guy, especially his walk. Confidence and masculinity. Takes your breath away. My dad is a big man. Rugged and robust. He made me feel safe when I was growing up— he still does. I won't tell Willie that, or he might think I'm looking for a father substitute. Believe me, that's not what I have in mind."

After a good laugh, Angie became serious. "No matter what man you fall for, I doubt you'd ever be a doormat. You're not a weakling." She gave Susan a sisterly pat on the shoulder. "I'm so happy for you. For a minute

I thought you might be falling for Travis Polk. He and one of my collectors went to a ballgame together and Travis spent the whole evening talking about what a wonderful person you are."

"I like Travis a lot, but we're just friends. He's a nice man, but he's seeing someone, and I'm not attracted to him. I didn't plan to fall for Rev. Cartwright." She spread her hands. "It just happened."

"Just take your cue from him and don't be afraid. I know how a failed marriage can make a woman extra cautious. Men have the same problem. I was gun-shy and so was Carl, but when he asked me to marry him, I felt it was right. He's been a great husband, the best thing that ever happened to me. I can't imagine my life without him. Quit worrying and enjoy yourself."

Angie's straightforward advice eased most of Susan's fears. She should focus her thoughts on the time she spent with Will and how much she enjoyed his company; how she admired his calm, mature outlook on life and life's curveballs; and how his wonderful dancing eyes dazzled her. Even when they disagreed, her tremendous admiration and respect remained. She felt a deep connection with him, both spiritually and emotionally.

"I enjoyed that sermon, son," Rev. Cartwright said, adding, "Seems I've heard it somewhere before."

Will laughed and helped his father from the wheelchair to the sofa. "Okay, I pirated most of it from one of your sermons. But, hey, that's the highest form of flattery."

"Cop out," his sister Terri said. "Where were you all day yesterday?"

His response was brief and dismissive. "Galveston."

"Galveston? What were you doing down there?" she asked.

Will shrugged, hoping his non-response would end the inquisition. "Trying to relax."

Rev. Cartwright smiled up at Will. "Did you take that pretty woman with you?"

Mrs. Cartwright sat next to her husband. "I knew you wouldn't want to eat out today, so I cooked a pot roast last night. I just popped everything in the oven. We can eat soon." She turned to Will. "What pretty woman?"

"A friend, Mom. Susan. You met her last Saturday at the fashion show."

"Your father wasn't at the fashion show." Mrs. Cartwright nudged her husband. "What do you know that I don't?"

"I know she's pretty, and she must be intelligent or she wouldn't have that big position. Willie brought her by after the fashion show. She said her mother remembers me from years ago. I like her, and I think she's a good fit for Willie. I can tell he likes her a lot."

Will grinned shyly. He could not contest such an obvious truth.

He sent Susan a bouquet of red roses on Monday, and they had lunch on Tuesday. She mentioned her love for tennis and racquetball, and he saw this as another link in solidifying their relationship. They had lunch again on Friday, and Susan broached the subject she had avoided.

"I know we shouldn't talk about Cedargrove Heights, but I've been thinking about something. Since you're also an accountant, I'm sure your church has a credit union. Sealand offers several benefits, including special interest rates when monthly payments are debited from a Sealand checking account or from a credit union account. We also offer financial counseling, and I will personally volunteer to conduct workshops for prospective homebuyers."

His face lit up. "It's funny you should mention that. We do have a credit union, but participation has been lagging lately. Two minority auto dealers just offered set pricing for credit union members, and will make donation to Cedargrove Baptist each time a member purchases a new or used vehicle from them. I gave the executive board my pitch last night.

"I won't go into details, but there are some trouble-makers in our midst. Also, a lot of them just can't stand to hear the truth. They don't listen when they're told how to manage their money, but they come running when they're about to lose their homes or their cars."

"Then they want the big guns to plead their cases," she answered with a smile. "Many people want riches without responsibility."

"So true. My problem is that I never learned to say no."

"Can't say no, huh?" she asked teasingly. "Let's see. What can I ask for?"

"Come on now. If I figure you right, you wouldn't ask for help even if you really needed it. Not that I would ever be able to say no to you." He wanted to kiss her right there in the restaurant. "No matter what you asked of me."

He walked her to her car and held her loosely against him. He looked into her eyes and caught a glimpse of her soul. Words were not necessary.

Her jumbled emotions were taking a toll on Susan's nerves. Will was right about the redlining. She knew the Cedargrove situation was miniscule compared to other news-making incidents. Still, each time she heard or read of an injustice of any kind, she would feel guilty. When she thought of Rev. Cartwright Sr. and the millions of brave people who put their lives and those of their families in peril to try and right the wrongs of the narrow-minded, she would feel even more ashamed.

While Will was out of town, and with Angie's help, she was making significant progress on the files. There were many fires to extinguish and her phone rang constantly, but regardless of her workload, Cedargrove and Will Cartwright were foremost in her thoughts. She had found a man who thrilled her to the bone, but as gratifying as that was, she knew the connection could prove destructive. She trusted Will, but there were too many unknowns floating about. Even Angie acknowledged that a relationship with such a public figure could lead to major complications.

Travis was an added worry, as her time with him was becoming increasingly unsettling. Even at lunch, he drank too much and constantly complained. The next time he invited her to dinner, she searched for a way to say no.

"What about the woman you mentioned who wants to marry you? Is she comfortable with our friendship?"

The question caught him unaware. "Our friendship has nothing to do with her. If you don't want to go, just say so."

"I don't want to go out to dinner, mainly because you won't let me pay, but I would like to fix you dinner at my place. How about that?"

She called home for her mother's stewed chicken and corn casserole recipes. She added green beans, rice, and sweet rolls to the menu and made her grandmother's famous sweet tea. Travis raved over the meal and had third helpings of the chocolate cake made with buttermilk and eight eggs.

After dinner they relaxed on the balcony and listened to music. Travis became comfortable enough to remove his shoes.

"That was a great meal. I don't know many women who can cook, certainly not like that. My mom isn't a great cook, but she can stretch a meal further than anyone I know." He looked at her admiringly. "You have it all. You're beautiful, successful, and a damn good cook.

Any man would be lucky to have that combination in a wife. Your ex-husband is an idiot."

"Thanks for the compliment, but I'm far from perfect." She tilted her head to the side and made a face. "I can't prove this, since I'm asleep when it happens, but Stan said I snore."

After a hearty laugh, his expression turned serious, and she again asked about the other woman.

"I'm not trying to pry into your personal life, but I am interested in knowing more about that special woman you mentioned. I'd like to meet her. You didn't even tell me her name. Friends share, you know."

"Her name is Lucy. She lives down the street from my mother. She's a nurse. We went out last night. The movies. She loves movies and television, which I always find boring. Or maybe I'm just boring."

"You're not boring. I so enjoy your friendship."

"That's probably because you haven't made friends here in Houston."

She was slightly offended. "I have other friends, both male and female. I've met two guys in this building, but I wouldn't call them friends. In fact, I think the one downstairs is stalking me. Either that or we have the same schedule. I see him practically every time I leave here."

"Seriously?" He frowned. "Shouldn't you report that to the police?"

A slight breeze blew her hair in her face, and he brushed it back.

"It's not serious. He's older. I can outrun and outfight him if I have to. I just don't want to date him, and he keeps asking me out. Yesterday, he offered to take out my trash. He also told me that his wife died a few years ago, so I think he's just lonely—and he constantly brags about his wealth."

"I don't think a lot of poor people live in this building. I also know it's hard for a woman like you to find a man who is on an equal footing, so maybe you should consider someone from this building."

"I can't believe you said that." She slapped his leg. "Why don't I just ask for a copy of his tax return?"

"Hey, I'm just thinking of you. I see you married to a high-powered dude, certainly not a lowly brother like me."

"I wouldn't have a problem with your salary, but I'd have a problem with anyone who thinks of himself as a lowly brother. I'm happy with my life the way it is. I don't need marriage or wealth to be happy."

He stretched and bopped his head to Kirk Whalum's saxophone. "But it sure does help."

Susan was glad when the evening ended. She saw a lot of Stan in Travis, and that made her even more uncomfortable. Her father was right about relationships in the workplace, she thought. Dissolving their friendship would be a snap if they didn't work together.

She began the workweek by thinking of possible ways to ease Travis from her personal world, but before she could formulate her first course of action, Will called with an interesting proposition.

"I've been back almost a week and still can't find time for myself. I've missed you, but I've got a plan."

She had missed him, too, more than she cared to admit, but his offer caught her completely off guard.

"Seems the only time I have any control over my schedule is when I'm not in Houston. I'm taking a trip to Atlanta this weekend. It's a minister's convention. I'll be leaving Friday around three and returning late Sunday evening. I took the liberty of purchasing two tickets and reserving a room for you. Can you make it?"

Her heart almost stopped. "Sure!" Feeling that her answer had come too quickly, she added, "I just told my friend Angie that I would like to get away for the weekend. How should I pack?'

"There's a reception Friday night. Cocktail dress, I would say. Saturday will be a workday for me, but I'm planning to make it a short one. There's a big gala Saturday night. That's a formal affair with dinner, awards, and dancing. That sort of thing. Is that a problem?"

"Not at all." The slinky dress she had just purchased would be perfect.

She floated through the rest of the week. Her mood was so light that even Price noticed. Travis stopped by her office to ask her to dinner on Saturday night and became inquisitive when she said she would be away for the weekend.

"Are you going home?"

"No, I'm taking a short trip that I hope will allow me to get some things straight in my mind."

"Some things seemed to have straightened out already. You're glowing. Is there a man in your life that you failed to mention when we were sharing the other day?"

"I told you I made a couple of friends since I've been in Houston. Remember?"

She smiled, but he did not.

"Hey?" She flashed a concerned grin. "What's going on?"

"Nothing." His anger was visible. "You said you made friends. You didn't say anything about dating."

"And you don't tell me about your dates. I said friends share, not elaborate."

He leaned over her desk and spoke softly. "I lied about my feelings for you, Susan. I even lied to myself, but I can't anymore. When we're together, I never want to leave you. I come to work happy because I know you'll be here. You say you don't want a physical relationship without an emotional one, so why can't we have both?"

She didn't answer; she simply could not think of anything to say.

"I guess that means you're not attracted to me at all."

"We're friends, Travis. What about Lucy? You even bragged about the numbers in your little black book and the women who had your number."

"I'm not in love with Lucy and I don't see that happening but . . ." He stopped. "Look, if marriage is important to you, I'm prepared to take that step."

She was shocked. "Well, gee. Don't put yourself out. If that's a marriage proposal, I'll have to decline." His woeful expression touched her heart. "I value your friendship, Travis, but I can't allow myself to be pushed into something before I'm ready."

"I meant what I said. I'll marry you tomorrow. I can't see spending the rest of my life waiting for the perfect person and the perfect circumstances."

"That is even more insulting. Just how imperfect am I?"

"That's not what I meant. You're my boss. You make more money than I do. I'm just saying that this is not a perfect world. We have to make adjustments. I'm not like your ex-husband. I'm content with my position here. I have over two dozen rental properties and other investments. I can offer you a comfortable life, even if you decide not to work. If you continue here, I will not resent the difference in our positions or in our salaries. I will love you as much as one person can love another and try my best to make you happy."

Deeply touched, she reached across the desk and placed her hand on top of his. "You are so sweet, and I really do care for you. I'm not trying to be difficult, and I wish I could offer a more palatable explanation. It's just that we seem to be at different points on the spectrum."

"Is this one of those things you talked about?" he asked, his mood lightening. "Does this have to do with control?"

She smiled. "Not really. It has to do with love. One of the things I plan to do this weekend is sort out my personal life, explore my feelings. You should do that, too. If you've dated Lucy for several years, you must have feelings for her. I've enjoyed your friendship, but I think you should consider this other relationship. There is a man in my life, but that relationship is in the formative stages, and it's certainly not physical."

"So that's the kiss-off? You're breaking up with me?"

Veins popped out on his forehead, and she saw Stanford the night of their confrontation. She thought of how life would be if she accepted his proposal. Simply miserable; of that she had no doubt. It was obvious that Travis was not as secure as he believed himself to be. She was glad they were just friends.

"Travis, let's not make more of our relationship than it is. You haven't even dated me exclusively. Your offer of marriage seems like a concession on your part, and you know that's wrong. This other woman is probably in love with you, and I'm not. I don't think you're in love with me, either. Lust and love are not the same."

He hung his head.

"Okay, go on your weekend trip, but promise me you'll think about us." He turned to leave, but then stopped and looked over his shoulder. "Don't be so sure I'm not in love with you, but I can take a hint."

She watched him walk away and knew the feelings she had for Will could never be duplicated.

The rest of the week was not nearly as productive as she hoped it would be. She spent an undue amount of time trying to shake her guilt for allowing Travis to fall for her. By Thursday night she was more than ready for the Atlanta getaway. She packed and then called her parents to inform them of her expected weekend plans. She gave her mother the hotel's phone number and waited for the expected reactions—her mother's delight and her father's litany of precautions.

"My little girl has fallen for a preacher man," her mother declared. "That's the best surprise I've had in years. I trust you completely, but I was a bit worried that some pretty boy would sweep you off your feet. I imagined having to take your father's gun and run the snake out of town, but you've just shocked me beyond belief."

"Don't, Mother. I'm torn enough as it is. I want this to work, but the memory of my first mistake makes me want to end our relationship right now. Suppose I had fallen under Stan's spell to the point where I wouldn't have reacted when he slapped me? Can you imagine what kind of life I would have had?"

"Susan, Susan, Susan. You're fretting over nothing. I'll be willing to bet money that no matter how taken you are with Willard Cartwright, if he so much as steps on your toe, you'll have a six-shooter in your hand and murder in your eyes. I raised you to have self-respect, and to the best of my knowledge you've never let me down. Go on to Atlanta. Enjoy yourself."

Her father put in his piece. "What's so special about this preacher? Your mother says he's good-looking. Don't let that fool you."

"You know me better than that, Daddy. It's more than just his looks. He's strong yet gentle. He's attentive, dynamic even. I'm comfortable with him. I find it so strange that I can be comfortable and excited at the same time. He talks. He listens. I trust him. We haven't known each other long, but I feel that we've shared so much. I even told him about Uncle Ollie."

"What about Oliver?" Tammy asked.

"It's something I've never told even the two of you. He tried to . . . to touch me inappropriately. I was around eleven or twelve."

"What!" Ralph shouted. "Why didn't you tell me this, Susan? I would have kicked Oliver's old ass all the way across Ohio."

"That's what I told Uncle Ollie. Talking with Will led me to reflect on everything in my past, my childhood in particular. All those experiences together have made me the person I am today. Having two strong parents made me confident and forceful enough to protect myself. I told Uncle Ollie that if he touched me my dad would break his neck. I feel that same kind of protection with Will. I guess he reminds me of you, Daddy."

"Can't argue with that," Tammy said.

"I understand, but I still want you to be careful."

"I've given myself that same advice." She placed her hand over her heart. "I just don't know how to stop myself from falling in love."

Susan went to work Friday morning planning to leave at noon. Will said he would pick her up at one o'clock. As the minutes ticked away, her apprehension grew. She finally went to Angie for a pep talk.

"I'm so excited. I don't know how I'll react if this weekend is a disappointment. I think I'm in love with him."

"And what's wrong with that? You're beginning to sound like those new age women who complain because they're educated and self-sufficient but still can't find a good man. I don't think most of them have any concept of what a good man is all about. They find reasons to shy away from the decent men. As they age and start thinking they'll never find anyone, they run out and drag home some dope user and try to turn him into their dream man."

"Gee, Angie, don't try to cheer me up."

"No, you just listen to me. You like Travis as a friend, but he's not the right man for you. No bells ring. Then you meet this Adonis and you get uptight because he's a preacher and because you think you might fall too hard and lose control. I don't think you got to the top floor of Sealand's office building by being afraid. Loosen up and give the relationship a chance. If you don't, you'll end up in one of those Prozac trances like a lot of other women I know."

Susan thanked Angie and then returned to her office. Travis was waiting.

"I thought you had gone until I saw that your door was still open. Are you driving or flying?"

"Flying. I'm leaving in a few minutes. I have to go home first."

"Well, I hope you have a great time. I just wish we were going together, then I know I'd have a good time."

The heat of his stare burned into her skin. *Why didn't I see this coming?*

"Isn't this your weekend with your kids?" she asked. "You and I never do things together on those weekends."

"Does that bother you?"

"Of course not. Your time with them is limited. I wouldn't be bothered even if we were in a relationship."

She kept the conversation light, refusing to let him impose his misery on her.

"You guys do something fun this weekend. I'm sure you'll have a great time."

He met her smile with a frown, but she remained firm.

"I have to take care of two things before I leave, so I'd better get to it."

"Okay. Have fun."

She wondered why it was so hard to have friendly relationships with members of the opposite sex. She returned two phone calls to branch managers and then called to thank Angie for her advice. She drove home, checked the timers on her interior lights, and waited for Will. She also had a pep talk with her conscience. *A man offered his friendship and I accepted. There's no reason for me to feel guilty.*

The doorbell rang and she walked into the warmth of Will's outstretched arms.

"Thank you for making this an exciting trip," he whispered.

"And how do you know it will be exciting? We haven't left Houston yet."

"Because each second I'm with you is more exciting than the last. Just knowing we'd be together has kept me on a natural high. Auntie asked if I'd been drinking."

After they were settled in their first class seats, he ordered a glass of white wine and she ordered a Coke. When the drinks arrived, he switched. "I knew you wanted wine," he said. "Please don't feel that you have to change your habits for me. That would make me very uncomfortable. In fact, I would have ordered wine, but I took a decongestant before leaving home and I don't tolerate the mixture very well."

She was not sure whether he was trying to accommodate her, but she liked what he said about not changing her habits. After he checked in at the hotel, he gave her a key to her room. It was separated from his by a nicely appointed living room. She was as impressed by the luxury as she was with the man who was going out of his way to make her feel at ease.

Having little time to spare before the evening event, she showered and dressed right away. Angie had suggested she wear the slate-blue cocktail dress she had purchased during one of their outings. The neckline was high and the back was cut low. In addition to black and beige, she had evening shoes in silver, gold, and different metallic patinas in her wardrobe. She and Angie had agreed that silver best complimented the dress.

She checked the mirror one last time before going into the living room. Will was waiting by the bar.

"I hope you don't think I'm being silly, but I have to say that I've never seen anyone who could make clothes look so good."

She smiled, and he frowned.

"You're usually a virtual chatterbox when we're together. You have been quiet and reserved today, especially in the cab. Do you regret accepting my invitation? Have I said or done something to offend you?"

"No, of course not. I'm sorry if I haven't been good company. I enjoy being with you but I'm just not sure . . . okay, here goes. I love being with you. I guess this whole weekend thing and your profession have made me a little nervous. I'm attending a function with a bunch of ministers. I don't want to say or do anything to embarrass you."

"Susan, I'm a minister by profession, but I'm still very much a man." He looped her arm around his. "I promise not to make you do penance for having human traits."

They were at the reception for four hours before he was able to break free.

"Are you tired?" he asked when they were on the elevator.

"Not really," she answered. "I enjoyed the dancing. I can't recall a gathering of African-Americans that didn't involve that Harlem shuffle. A woman with an extra large caboose and gigantic feet kept stepping on my toe. Damn, that hurt." She clamped her hand over her mouth as he unlocked the door. "Oops."

"Stop that," he laughed. "You're allowed to say damn in my presence anytime. I'm thirsty. What about you?"

"Ditto. Perrier is fine. Is there any foot soak in that mini-bar?" She kicked off her shoes and sat on the sofa.

"No, but I'll be happy to rub your feet." He unscrewed the cap and handed her the bottle and a glass. "Give me a minute to shed this coat and tie."

She went into the bedroom and put on her slippers. She finished the bottle of water and recalled Will saying that he enjoyed a good brandy after dinner. She took two bottles from the mini-bar, rinsed two glasses, and waited.

Will sat on the edge of the bed, deep in thought. After being alone for so long, he had found the perfect woman. One look at her and he went limp in both knees. Now, all he had to do was find the right words to express his feelings without sounding like a tongue-tied adolescent. His biggest fear was that she would freeze him out. If that happened, he knew it would be hard for him to find the courage and the time to begin another relationship. And he knew he would never find anyone as beguiling as Susan.

He kept telling himself that she must have felt something or she wouldn't have come on the trip but found it hard to believe that she felt as strongly as he did. He never believed in love at first sight, but she had become imbedded in his heart the second he walked into her office. She was intriguing in a wholesome but wickedly sexual way. He knew when their lips met for the first time that he would never be whole outside that kiss. When they were together, he didn't want to be anywhere else. His eyes followed her. He was afraid to blink for fear of missing a second of her wholesome charm.

The pain of losing his wife and son was lodged in his heart like fishhooks under the skin. The more he tugged, the more intense the pain became, but Susan had a zest for life that could help him outdistance the bad memories.

He decided to go out and face her, hoping the right words would come.

Susan was about to knock on Will's door when he reappeared.

"I remembered you liked brandy after dinner." She offered him the glass and saw that his brow was furrowed.

"Will, is something wrong?" she asked, feeling more tension between them than she had felt the first time they met.

He half smiled and kept his eyes averted. "No, nothing is wrong." His smile broadened. "Nothing at all."

He settled on the sofa next to her. "You haven't said anything about your job lately. How are things going?"

Having promised herself not to talk about Cedargrove Heights, she focused on a positive aspect of her work.

"I'm packaging a proposal to snare a large loan commitment for Sealand. It's one of those participations aimed at assisting low-income homebuyers in the inner city. Federal funds are included. The overall project is designed to promote pride in ownership, replace some of the dilapidated complexes with single-family dwellings, and remove eyesores from the fringes of downtown."

"That's great. Is this aimed at a specific area of downtown?"

It was difficult reading his thoughts. He still seemed preoccupied. She took that to mean his thoughts were serious. She didn't want to talk about her work or his. She wanted to talk about their relationship.

"I'm sure some perimeters have been established, but we haven't gotten that far into the negotiations. I've offered my proposal, so the only thing I can do now is wait. I probably shouldn't say anything to jinx it, but if Sealand wins the bid, I'll make sure Cedargrove Heights gets a share of the funds."

"Can you do that?" Seeing her frown, he quickly clarified his question. "I'm not questioning your authority or anything like that. I just thought . . ."

A smile tiptoed around her lips.

"You're playing with me, aren't you? That's okay. I deserve it."

She laughed and took his hand. "I guess we both feel a certain amount of eggshells under our feet when we're together. I understood what you meant. The program would be administered under firm guidelines, but I don't see why they wouldn't approve some or all of the monies going to an old, established neighborhood with room for growth."

"I can't tell you how much this means to me. I can't wait to tell the others."

"Don't tell them yet. I wouldn't want Deacon Roosevelt Jones condemning my soul to hell for misrepresentation. He's one scary old dude."

They both laughed, and he tightened his grip on her hand.

"I'm so glad you're getting settled in your new position. I admire you, Susan."

They looked into each other's eyes. He started to bend toward her, but abruptly moved back.

"Is Houston starting to feel like home yet? I'm sure you miss your family."

She was hoping he could see her need, but she answered his questions and they chatted about Houston's sports teams, city growth, and religion. She let him do most of the talking, especially about religion. But her heart was crying out; she hoped he would hear.

"It's getting late. I'd better get to bed. I have a break-fast at seven-thirty. What are you going to do tomorrow?"

What she wanted to do tonight was more to the point, she thought. "Oh, I'll just browse around, go to the mall. I have to update my entire wardrobe to adjust to the Houston heat. I may also spend some time here in the spa."

He stood as she gathered the empty bottles and glasses from the table. "I probably shouldn't have invited you on this trip, since I'll be tied up for most of the day. If there's something you'd like to do, I can always slip out early."

"Don't worry about me. I'll be fine. I'm glad you invited me. I needed a break from . . . everything." She smiled and waved her hands.

"This is my treat, so whatever you want to do—spa, beauty salon, not that you need any beauty enhance-ment—just charge it to the room."

"I'll be fine. I'm not someone who needs constant attention. Go to your meeting and enjoy your day. I'm glad you invited me along."

"So am I, and I hope you have a good night's sleep." He kissed her lightly on the cheek, but she wouldn't let go of his arm.

Standing on her toes, she tilted her head back, her eyes heavy with desire. "Will I have to do penance if I ask for a real kiss?"

His mouth came down softly on her parted lips and lingered until she tightened her grip on his arm. He seemed to read her silent expectations. His kiss became urgent and fiery. When he moved away, her entire body was hot and needy. She leaned against him and he traced her mouth with his tongue.

His lips devoured hers. His tongue explored the recesses of her mouth. He raised his mouth from her and silently gazed into her eyes before brushing his lips against her face. Breathing an intoxicated sigh, she loosened her grip and he took her face in his hands.

"You won't have to do penance, but I will unless we stop right now."

They said goodnight, she turned off the lights and went into her bedroom. Throwing the pillows from the bed was not enough to vent her frustrations. She thought of Travis, putting his feeling out there, even offering marriage. Why couldn't Will tell her how he felt? He might as well have. She read it on his face and felt the pressure of his arousal. She turned out the lights and listened to the stillness. In the midst of her torture, she vowed she would learn Will's true feelings for her before the weekend was over, even if she had to ask.

# CHAPTER 6

The next morning, Susan found Will gone and a note on top of the ice bucket telling her that his meeting should conclude by four o'clock and that he would miss her. She checked her cell phone, and found a message from Travis.

"I didn't express myself very well yesterday, so I'll try once again. I'm madly in love with you. I want to marry you, not so we can be intimate, but because I want you in my life forever. I love, respect, and admire you. I want to hold you in my arms and make love to you more than I've wanted anything in my life. As far as work goes, you and I aren't competing. I respect your position as much as I respect you as a woman. Think about it, Susan."

She felt close to tears. It wasn't that she didn't find him attractive. If she had been the kind of woman to give in to sexual urges, she would have pulled him up to her bedroom that first night, but that was not her way. She had to make Travis understand. She had been honest with him. Knowing that did not lessen her guilt, but it did make her determined to end the game she and Will had been playing. *It would be much simpler if he weren't a minister.*

She had seen pure lust on his face. His self-control made her respect him even more. She knew he had dated since his divorce, remembered Angie describing two short-lived relationships, and wondered if he was against premarital sex. If he was, she felt their relationship would soon fizzle. She was not strong enough to hold out. She also had no intentions of rushing into marriage as Travis had proposed.

Not wanting to spend the day lounging around, she dressed and took the hotel shuttle to the shopping mall. There was nothing she wanted to buy except the gift she wanted to get for Will. The night before he mentioned that he had forgotten his cufflinks for the formal dinner. She found a pair that she thought he would like. They were gold and in the shape of clasped, praying hands.

After buying a few intimate items and three light-weight blouses for herself, she browsed through some of the more exclusive shops in both Lenox Square and Phipps Plaza. Her only great find was a CD by an old college friend that she dug from a 60 percent off bin in one of the music stores. It was still too early to return to the hotel, so she took a cab to Peoples Street. Her mother had suggested she view the art collection at Hammonds House Galleries. She purchased a large painting entitled "Rush to Freedom" for her parents. The offer of reduced shipping rates prompted the purchase of a small, unframed print for her apartment. She took a cab back to the hotel.

The memory of Will's goodnight kiss was still fresh. She thought of ways to seduce him, immediately followed by a sharp jab of conscience.

The hotel lobby was crowded with guests and conventioneers. Looking around, she recognized some of the members of the minister's convention and picked Will out of the crowd by his distinctive stance. She stood watching him and feeling all the admiration and pride a woman should feel for the man she loves. Several of the men noticed her, prompting Will to turn and come to her. She smiled when her eyes met his.

"Susan," he said, his delightful grin in full display and his arms outstretched. "Hello, gorgeous. I missed you today," he whispered when he got close.

She had missed him, too. Spiraling tension and passion filled her body with the kind of heat that evoked memories of the early months of her marriage to Stan and how they used to run to each other at the end of the day. She would always cherish those memories, but she wanted new ones. It was Will's lips she wanted to remember—sleeping and waking up together and making love until their passion was spent and she was too weak to stand.

Will went back to his seminar, telling her that it would disperse at four. She went up to the room, but stayed in the living area to wait for him. She ate her room-service lunch and turned on the television for distraction. Slipping into a nap, she dreamed of his hands on her body. She opened her eyes and he was sitting in the chair next to her. It took a few seconds to realize she was no longer dreaming.

"It's not even three yet. Is your meeting over?"

"No, but I couldn't concentrate," he said, lacing his fingers and leaning slightly forward. "There's something I want—need—to say to you, and I've been trying to build up the courage to accept a rejection should your feelings not match mine. I'm sorry to wake you, but I knew if I didn't say it now, I'd lose my nerve and spend the rest of the day telling myself what a coward I am," he revealed, his lips quivering.

"Will, I think it would be a good idea to say what's on your mind. Watching you squirm is making me nervous."

He forced a smile. "I won't bore you with the details of my life. I would like to tell you enough so that you'll understand my feelings."

He took a deep breath and she braced herself, her heart pounding wildly.

"Finding myself alone after Trey died and Tracey left was devastating. I missed what we once had—or at least what I thought we had. I loved her very much. I wasn't sure I could comfortably trust my heart to anyone again."

Excitement and fear closed around her. She wanted him, needed him.

"I tried to heal, and later started dating, but nothing ever clicked. I'm sure I caused pain to some of the women who offered me affection, but I couldn't make myself feel what wasn't there. Physical passion was all I could manage, and even that was dim. My heart didn't respond. I began to wonder if I had anything left to give. I wondered if I could ever feel for any woman what I had felt . . ."

His voice trailed off but not before his sincerity and obvious pain stirred her greatly.

"I stopped dating. Stopped accepting personal invitations. I cautioned family and friends against fixing me up with some poor unsuspecting woman I could not possibly love. Physically, it's been hard. Emotionally . . . I felt dead inside—that is, until I walked into Sealand and met the most desirable woman imaginable. Nothing in life prepared me for the feelings I had that day. Auntie, Mrs. Whitehead, said I babbled on like a scared teenager."

He paused and smiled.

"I'm not a teenager, but I am scared—scared, excited, and more in love than I thought possible. Everything changed for me the day I saw you, beautiful, even in the midst of extreme irritation."

Her apprehensions, every negative thought living inside her, began to fade.

"After I left your office, I hummed to myself and smiled a lot. I felt light, like a weight had been lifted from my life. If I wasn't afraid of frightening you away, I'd ask you to marry me right here, right now. Please tell me I'm not making a fool of myself."

"If you asked me to marry you right now I would be scared, but not of making a commitment. Becoming a minister's wife never occurred to me until I met you. When I think of it, I'm frightened beyond belief—I'm frightened of the unknown, frightened by my feelings for you. I'm at my best when I'm in full control, and my biggest fear is that loving anyone as much as I already love you will take that away. You lead a life that makes extraordinary demands on your time and your heart. I don't know how that would affect our relationship, but I have seen a few happily married ministers." She tried to break the tension with a smile.

His nervousness subsided and his eyes shone with wonder. "I don't know all there is to know about love, but the feelings I have for you are amazing. I don't want to control you. I just want to love you. You're right; my time is in great demand, but I would always make time for you. For us."

He stood and pulled her up and into his arms.

"Please don't think my invitation had ulterior motives. I'm not asking for anything you're unwilling to give."

She wanted to give him everything, and more. Her body trembled with excitement and anticipation.

"I sensed uneasiness between us yesterday, and I wanted to say these things last night. I'm just a man, Susan. A man of the cloth, yes, but also a man with needs and desires. Don't be afraid to touch me. To love me. I will try to keep anything from coming between us or making you unhappy. If problems arise, I think you and I can deal with them."

"I want to love you. I do love you." She settled against him without hesitation. Cedargrove, Sealand, and the need for control were forgotten. She tilted her face toward his in complete surrender.

His mouth covered hers. It was not the sweet goodnight kisses they had shared in Houston. It was compelling and urgent. She gasped when their bodies aligned and she felt the whole of his desire.

Her mouth was wet and wonderful. Firm breasts pressed against him. No woman, not even Tracey, had excited him so intensely. He thought of his position in the church and the community, of the emptiness that filled his heart. Susan could fill that emptiness; she could make his life whole.

"Susan," he said, moving close to her ear. "Are you sure you're ready for this?"

She took his hand reassuringly. "I'm not promiscuous, but I also have needs. I can't think of living another day without you. I can't think of not having you in my life."

Emotions flooded her heart. Their fingers interlaced, and just as his fingers filled the spaces between hers, his love filled her soul. She led him to her bedroom. He moved behind her when they reached the bed, his fingertips kneading the ridges of her shoulders. The friction of his hands ignited fires within. His arms enclosed her body, completely erasing all doubt. She wanted to stop time. To freeze the splendor of the moment.

She started to unbutton her blouse, but he took over. He tenderly fumbled, staring wide-eyed as her body was slowly unveiled.

Susan needed him to hurry, but wanted it to last forever.

He placed her blouse on the chair and deftly unhooked her bra. She wondered if he was losing his uneasiness and if he wanted her as much as she wanted him.

He wondered if she could hear the pounding of his heart. She dropped her arms and he slid the bra straps down her shoulder and kissed the slope of her back. She turned, and her breasts rose to meet him. He hesitated, wanting to behold the magnificence. Her body was perfect. Her breasts were full like ripe fruit, with buds that were invitingly erect. She unzipped her skirt and shimmied slightly until it fell, in a heap, at her feet. She sat on the bed and he picked up the garment from the floor and placed it next to her blouse.

When he turned back to her, she was lying across the bed, clad only in her panties.

"You're breathtaking," he whispered.

She devoured his body while he retrieved a foiled square from his wallet and came to the bed.

His eyes were dilated pools of passion when he kneeled over her. "I love you, Susan. Knowing I can say that with certainty leaves no doubts about our relationship. I love you so much."

He covered her mouth with his. His tongue slipped between her lips and his eyes closed slowly. Tasting the sweetness of her nectar, he moaned and continued down the contour of her neck. With his head nestled between her breasts, his tongue made firm sweeps over her nipples. She moaned his name and arched her back for more.

His mouth circled the globes of her breast and she became woozy and heated in ways she had never known. He did something indescribable with his hands and mouth, and the air around her became thin. She gasped as he soothed away the pain of neglect.

The heat of his body burned away all memories, making everything new and different. He peeled away her panties and kissed the inside of her thighs. Her legs fell apart, and he moved between them. When their bodies merged, Susan felt his soul move into her soul.

Her softness tightened around him. He swallowed the scream that was building in his throat. Susan met each thrust like a smoothly choreographed dancer. It was new and intense. The excitement shadowed their first time, but there was also comfort and familiarity, as if his body had known hers many times before.

Susan knew she could not hold out very long. Feeling his body tense, she accepted and gave until their moans ruptured into a combined roar of ecstasy. Their bodies crested and then fell in total fulfillment.

They remained locked together, body, mind, and soul. Her head was on his chest and his arms held her in place. Susan heard the thunder of his heart but did not realize there were tears in her eyes until Will touched her face with his fingertips.

"Are you okay? Did I hurt you?"

"No, I'm great."

"I didn't mean to rush that way, but it's—"

She stopped his words with a kiss. "It was wonderful. You're wonderful. It's just that . . . I felt something I've never felt before. I know that sounds sappy, but it's true. I was in love before, but nothing came close to what I feel with you."

"I feel it too. You feel right in my arms. I don't know if I can let you go."

"You don't have to." She kissed his lips repeatedly. "Your evening function is hours away."

They made love again—slowly this time, but with the same frenzied passion and fiery contentment. She hated to leave his side.

"I know you have to attend this function tonight, and as much as I want to stay right here next to you, one of us has to move, so I'll make that sacrifice."

"I'll just add bravery to my growing list of your admirable qualities."

He caressed her face, his eyes flowing with love.

She was running water in the shower when she heard him call her name.

"Susan! You didn't have to do this," he said, coming in with the jeweler's box in hand. "Thank you, but I wish you hadn't spent so much money. Are you trying to spoil me?"

"Do you like them?"

"I liked them enough to circle them in a catalogue that's somewhere on my desk. That's how I know they're expensive. You really shouldn't have."

"I'm glad you like them, and yes, I am trying to spoil you," she declared firmly. "I can only imagine the hurt you endured when you lost your son and your wife. I want very much to spoil you, to make you happy, to keep you happy. I want our love to occupy every inch of your heart, making it impossible for pain to enter. I want to satisfy you. I don't want you to ever need anyone else."

He drew her into his arms. "That's one thing you will never have to worry about. Just knowing you care, knowing you want to be with me, is the greatest gift you could have given me. I'll never be happier than I am now unless . . ."

"Unless what?" she asked.

"The only thing that could make me happier is to have you for my wife, to come home to you each day, to love you forever."

"Well, you already know I don't believe in long engagements," she said, trying to contain her excitement and surprise. She kissed him and went into the shower. Afterwards, she dried her hair, finished her makeup, and dressed. She was getting a bottle of water from the minibar when he entered in formal wear. Her heart skipped lightly with happiness.

"You are without a doubt the most irresistible woman I've ever laid eyes on. I'll be the envy of every man there tonight."

"And I'll be the envy of every woman."

Will had not told Susan that he was president of the ministers' association or that he was an honoree. Her heart swelled with pride when he accepted the award for excellence in leadership and went to the podium to speak. She was once again struck by his strength, his humility, and his self-possession. He was a man, she thought, who would not need to prove himself or take control. He was the man she wanted to love forever.

He eloquently expressed his concerns for unity in the church and in the community, health awareness, and intervention for at-risk teens. After dinner, the gospel choir that had performed before the invocation sang a few standards from the big band era. He held her loosely and they swayed in harmony.

"I'm so proud to be here with you. I enjoyed the evening so far, but all I can think of is snuggling in your arms."

"If you are feeling half of what I feel, we'd better head for the exit fast. I'm almost afraid to look around, afraid everyone will see on my face what I feel inside. We are being watched, you know. I'm usually solo at these functions, and now the most beautiful, most wonderful woman is with me. Stay close to me."

After the dance, he went for punch and his best friend, Robert Wise, joined Susan at the table. "My buddy Will has been holding out on me. We talk at least once a week, but he never told me he had something going on with a very lovely lady."

"And what makes you think we have something going on?" Susan asked, smiling as Will joined them.

"I know this dude pretty well; we bunked together for years. But even a blind man could see there's something special going on. Sparks flew between you two last night, and this afternoon in the lobby, but tonight . . . your glow lit up this joint."

Will smiled sheepishly. "Go easy, my friend. You're embarrassing Susan."

"Susan isn't the one embarrassed, but I'll go easy on you," Robert said, holding up his glass for a toast.

Susan was happy when Will said goodnight to his colleagues. "Okay, excellent leader," she teased when they were in the elevator. "Lead the way."

"You like teasing me, don't you?" he said, toying with the curls that softly draped her shoulder. "That's okay. Robert started teasing me as soon as he saw us together. He's been a good friend for a long time. His wife is pregnant with twins, so I'll have fun teasing him now."

He unlocked the door and she walked ahead of him. "Did you order this?" she asked, looking at the bottle of Dom Pérignon chilling in a bucket on the coffee table.

"I thought it would be a good way to end this special evening."

He filled two glasses and joined her on the sofa. "I love you, Miss Cross. I love you with all my heart, and I want you to be my wife."

She took the glass and smiled through her tears. "I love you too, Rev. Cartwright—more than I ever thought possible, and I want to be your wife. Forever."

They kissed, and the sparks Roberts had described exploded around them. Claps of thunder almost drowned out the softly playing music, and rain beat insistently against the windows. But Susan and Will were oblivious to nature's angry sounds, as they were lost in their own intimate world of newfound connections and astounding pleasures.

After they made love, he folded her into the contours of his arms. Sleep came quickly and peacefully.

When Susan awakened, Will was looking down at her as if he had been committing her face to memory.

"Good morning, beautiful," he said, kissing her forehead. "At the risk of sounding like a lovesick puppy, I just have to say that you are the most fascinating woman I've ever known, asleep or awake."

"Good morning. For a minute I thought I was waking from a dream. Tell me it's for real. Tell me we're here together and in love, and that we'll have many nights like the one we just had."

"It must be true; I could never dream anything this wonderful. I love you. I want to have many such nights with you . . . for the rest of my life."

Drawing her closer, he said, "There is something we should talk about before going down to the prayer breakfast. I know a lot of the ministers here, some of them quite well. Robert Wise has been my best friend since college, so he was the first to notice my happiness, even before he knew I was here with someone. When he met you yesterday, he asked if we were engaged, and I'm sure some of the others were probably wondering. Would I be speaking out of turn if I said we're unofficially engaged?"

"I'll say we're engaged if you promise it will be a short engagement. I'm not going to be able to stay away from you, and I don't think it would look right for a minister to live in sin, so we'll just have to get married right away," she said playfully.

She enjoyed listening to him describing their relationship to his friends.

"We haven't known each other very long," he would say, "but we'll have an announcement very soon."

Later, they packed and sat in the living room, sharing more details of their lives; only this time they were looking into the future, not the past.

"As much as we've talked, I never asked if you want children. I'm not suggesting we start the minute we're married; I just want to know your thoughts on the subject. It's taken for granted that most women do, but you have a great career. Motherhood interferes with that, so the decision is yours. I'll still love you no matter what you decide."

"My mother would be happy to answer that question. I spoiled my younger brother Charles so much that Mom and Dad threatened to make me come home from college to care for him. They couldn't do a thing with him after I left. But he was such a wonderful little boy. I wanted to spoil him even when my parents were home. So yes, I very much want children. Of course my older brother, Bobby, spoiled me when I was a kid. He was a big athlete in high school, and I rode the wave of his popularity my first year at JFK High. I would introduce myself as Bobby Cross's sister."

"Is there a big age difference between you and Charles?"

"Only six years," she answered. "Bobby and I are two years apart and were always close. We did just about everything as a family, so the three of us spent a lot of time together. When my parents were busy around the house, they made the oldest child responsible for the others. When Dad took Bobby to his Little League practice, I cared for Charles while my mother prepared dinner. I helped him with homework until I left for college, made his favorite sandwiches, and shot hoops with him at night when he joined the basketball team."

"I have a picture in my head of you holding our baby in your arms. I can't wait for that to happen. I know your career is special to you, and I'll respect that, but I hope we don't have to wait too long."

"I'll be twenty-eight in January. I certainly would like to have a child before I'm thirty, but we should make sure we're okay together before we decide on something so important. I like to think I'm strong and self-reliant. I want to become a part of your life—not change it— to share the things that are important to you. But I do need to know there will be time for the two of us, and then the three, four, and five of us."

"Are we having that many?" he asked, laughing. "I'll make time for us; I'll make time for family. I promise."

As the weekend came to a close, thoughts of Monday morning and the situation at Sealand crept into Susan's head. And then there was Travis. She dreaded having to tell him she was involved with someone else.

"Nickel for your thoughts," he said when they were seated on the plane.

"Nickel, huh?" she answered. "Isn't it a penny?"

"Not for the thoughts that put that pensive look on your face."

"The look only means I have a lot of thoughts to process. Everything happened so fast. We just met. We've talked a lot, but how much do we really know about each other?" He frowned, and she added, "I'm not having second thoughts about our relationship. I feel a little . . . overwhelmed, but in a good way."

"So do I," he admitted. "And I'm not trying to rush you into marriage. If I'm being overeager it's because each second I've spent with you, even when we disagreed, had a big impact on my heart. I love you, Susan, and I'll wait for you to set a date for our wedding."

"I don't want to wait. I want to come home and not have to say good-bye to the man I love. I don't need a long engagement or a big wedding. Thanks to my parents, I already had a fabulous wedding. Now I want a fabulous marriage."

She enjoyed his closeness during the plane ride, and he held her hand as they waited in baggage claim. When they arrived at her apartment, she did not want him to leave. "It was a wonderful weekend, Will. I know you have to go, but I'm so going to miss you."

"I'll miss you, too. I don't understand what happens when I'm around you. I want to hold you next to me forever and never let you go. Does that frighten you?"

"No, I like my space and my independence, but I know without reservation that I'm ready to share it with you, completely and without end."

They kissed and he promised to call her before she went to sleep.

She picked up the newspapers that had been left by the front door, and noticed the flashing button on her answering machine when she placed them on the desk.

"Ten messages," she noted, stooping to pet the cat. "Who's been calling us, Dino? Everyone I know in this city knew I wouldn't be home. Have you been receiving calls from some slinky feline? Well, you handle it. I'm going upstairs and unpack."

She carried her two bags up the steps, with Dino close behind, and put them next to the window seat. Unable to ignore the red light from the answering machine on her nightstand, she sat on the edge of the bed and pushed the machine's play button.

The first message was from Price. "Susan, I've been calling your cell phone all morning. Call me immediately. Mr. Deeds is on his way back. This is serious. Call me." The message was recorded at 9:55 that morning.

She and Will had agreed to turn off their cell phones during the weekend. Will had called his parents and Mrs. Whitehead on Saturday, and Susan had called her parents, Angie, and Barbara. She hurried back downstairs and took the phone from the bottom of her purse. There were six missed messages. The first was from Price.

"Susan, I know you're out of town, but I need to speak with you about that article in the *Chronicle*."

She sat in the desk chair and frantically forwarded through the messages on her cell phone and then the ones on the answering machine. Most of them were from Travis and Price—same messages, different tones. There were two from Mark Chestnut, a reporter she had met at the ribbon cutting ceremony, requesting her comment on allegations of redlining leveled by a group of citizens from Cedargrove Heights. The last message on both phones was from a request from Angie. "Susan, don't talk to anyone until you call me."

She took the Sunday edition of the *Chronicle* from the protective cover. It was folded with section two on top. The caption under a photograph of four men standing in front of Cedargrove Baptist Church brought a sickening pain to her chest: *Local Civic Group Lodges Serious Complaint Against Lender.*

The story alleged that Sealand, and Susan Cross, head of lending, failed to investigate their complaints and had participated in discrimination against their neighborhood. Susan's chest heaved in anger. Before she could dial Angie's number, the phone rang again. She saw that it was an Ohio call and grabbed the receiver.

"Mom, I'm here."

"Hello, honey. You sounded so happy when you called on Saturday. I can't wait to hear details of your weekend with Rev. Wonderful."

"It was fabulous, Mother." Her deadpan delivery reeked of bitterness. "He told me I was beautiful and wonderful and special. He said he loved me and he asked me to marry him. He said I was the most provocative and fascinating woman he had ever known . . ." Her voice wavered; she struggled for control.

"Susan, what's wrong? What did he do to you?"

"Mom, I believe he invited me out of town so his people could plant a story in the paper, and I wouldn't be available for comment. He used me, Mother. Every sweet word that came from his lips was a damn lie. I found my answering machine filled with messages, including some very ugly ones from that snipe Price Bishop insinuating that he has my job."

Joining in, her father said, "I thought this whole redlining thing had gone away. That is what it's about, isn't it?"

"Yes, Dad. They're claiming Sealand targeted that area for discrimination, and when the matter was brought to my attention, I failed to take action. Those slimy bastards made it appear to be my fault."

"Susan, I want you to calm down and put this whole thing in perspective," Tammy cautioned. "Are you sure Rev. Cartwright was behind this?"

Before she could answer, her father chimed in. "Susan, do you want your mother and me to come down there? We can leave right away—"

"Absolutely not," she interrupted. "I'll deal with it. I just walked in and found urgent messages from Travis and Price, and then saw the article in the paper, so I'm mad as hell right now. I'll be okay as soon as I calm down and catch my breath."

She went to the refrigerator for a bottle of wine, popped the cork, and drank from the bottle.

"Have you asked Rev. Cartwright about this yet? Isn't it possible that he was as unaware of this as you were?"

Her mother's voice was calming, but each time Susan thought of the way Will had talked to her, constantly reassuring her of his love, she went into a rage. With the phone cradled to her ear, she walked back to the desk.

"I didn't see the article before he left. He lives about fifteen minutes from here. I'll have to wait until he gets home to ask him about it, but I think the article speaks clearly enough." She tipped the bottle with both hands.

"Susan, I want you to promise me that you'll calm down before you confront this man," her father said, his voice filled with obvious worry. "I remember when you found that boy you dated in high school with another girl. You attacked his car with a piece of iron, broke the windshield and the windows. Scared the devil out of both of them. And now that I think back, you sounded a lot calmer then. And we all know what you did to Stan. I think we should come down there. I don't want you to face this alone, and I don't want you to do something regrettable."

"Your father is right. I want to see Houston, anyway. It's been—"

"Mom, Dad, I love you for your concern, but I'll be fine. I promise not to do anything rash or regrettable, though at the moment I can't imagine regretting chopping Will Cartwright into tiny pieces of vermin. I feel used. Used by Sealand, by that prick Price Bishop, but most of all, by Will. I'm okay now. Don't worry, Daddy. You won't have to bail me out of jail. I'll call you later tonight." She hung up and called Angie.

"Girl, I don't know if Will had anything to do with this, but I want to see some bastard fry. I want to ask about your weekend, but I'm sure it's spoiled now."

"Angie, I've never been this angry in my life. He deliberately got me out of the way to allow this to hit the papers. You should hear the message Price left. He has probably already planted his sorry butt in my chair. 'Be in my office at nine.' Who the hell does he think he's talking to? One way or another, I'll mop up this mess with his ass, and that's a promise. How far did you get on the files?"

"I had four more, but when I read this I just dropped everything and finished them. Did you see the part about that Rev. Otis? He said he discovered this problem . . . oh yeah, with the assistance of Rev. Cartwright. As it turns out, his file was one of the last rejects. I've been calling all over the city to get the 411 on him and got it. It's all here."

"Thank you, Angie. Now all I have to do is find someone in the media, preferably TV. I wish I could do it tonight. I'll start—"

"Wait, wait, wait!" Angie yelled excitedly. "I know someone. You tell me what to say and I'll do my best to get your comments on the ten o'clock news. I also know the reporter who wrote the story—not personally, but he has covered a lot of stories involving Sealand."

"Yes, I know," Susan said. "I gave him my business card at the ribbon cutting for the Memorial Drive office. He called my cell phone to get my side of the story, but I was in Atlanta with Rev. Charm."

"Listen, Carl is at work. Why don't you come on over here and spend the night?"

She was touched. "Thanks, Angie, but I need to collect myself and make some calls. Guess whom I'm calling first? He said he wouldn't turn his cell on until he got home. Angie, you should have heard him telling me how much he loved me. He even asked me, unofficially of course, to marry him. Mom called a few minutes ago. I'll have to call back tonight so they won't worry. If things get too hairy here, I'll let you know. I can never thank you enough for your help with those files. You're a true friend."

"Don't worry about it. We're in this together. I don't even care anymore if they find out I'm involved. We'll get all of them. Be sure to call me later."

She opened the sliding glass door to the balcony and was almost pushed back by the heat. *It's October. It's blistering even when the sun is down.*

She sat on the patio, blowing hot air into hot air, and looked at the thermometer hanging on the window. *Ninety-two! At seven o' clock?*

*Seven o'clock. He's home.*

She stopped and held her head, telling herself to calm down before calling Will or anyone else. She placed the CD she had purchased into the machine, collected her wits, and dialed his number.

Will stopped by to see his parents before going home. He smiled when he saw both of his sister's cars in the driveway. He could deliver his good news to everyone at the same time.

He almost ran into the family room, where his father and brother-in-law were enjoying dessert and the football game. "Hey, everybody. How was service today, Pop? Tell me what I missed."

"Nothing special," Rev. Cartwright said, looking up. "But you sure seem happy. Did something happen in Atlanta?"

His mother and sisters came in from the kitchen. He could hear the children playing upstairs. One day, he thought he would be hearing that sound from his own children, and felt happy all over.

"You could say that. I just got sort of engaged to the most beautiful woman in the world."

"That must be Miss Cross. I didn't know she went with you. Congratulations, son." Rev. Cartwright let out a hearty laugh. "She sure is a looker."

Everyone began talking at once until his sister, Eugenia, yelled, "Will someone please tell me what's going on here? Who is this Miss Cross, and why does everyone know about this but me?"

"You would have met her if you'd been at the fashion show, Jean," Terri said. "She's very pretty, but don't you think you're moving too fast, Willie? You just met this woman a few weeks ago."

"And it was love at first sight. I know she's the one. She's beautiful and wonderful and bright, and she loves me. Be happy for me, please."

He took his cellphone from his pocket and switched on the power. It rang before he could slip it back into his pocket.

"Hello, Reverend." Susan's voice was dry, colorless. "I'm sure you're not surprised to hear from me, so don't bother lying. You're done quite enough of that already. 'I love you, Susan, I want you in my life.' What you wanted was to get Susan out of the way so your conniving band of devils could plant your seed."

Each time he tried to speak, she cut him off with another angry outburst. Pain and humiliation punctuated her accusations.

"I can just hear you and the boys sitting around the pulpit and making your plans. 'Use your charm to get the broad out of town. She likes you.' Well, let me boost your ego a few notches higher, Reverend."

"Susan, baby, whatever you're talking about is making no sense to me. Please calm down and tell me what's wrong. Tell me—"

"I'm about to tell you. I'm going to tell you the whole story. See, Reverend, from the moment you walked into my office that first day I was hopelessly gone on you. Doesn't that make you feel mighty? I have never had such feelings for anyone. I was blinded by my feelings for you, but it's all clear now. Crystal clear. I let my guard down, Rev. Cartwright. I allowed you into my life and allowed myself to care for you."

"Susan! Please—"

"Shut up and let me finish. I'm no minister, and right now I don't feel much like a Christian, but I would never stoop so low as to use someone the way you used me. Bask in your glory, Reverend. Ride high so you'll have a long way to fall when your house of deceit crumbles. And it will. That's a promise."

The phone clicked in his ear. He first looked at his father, who did not seem surprised.

"Can someone please tell me what's going on?"

"That bastard Rev. Otis," Terri answered, holding a folded copy of the *Houston Chronicle*.

Will read the headlines. "Why would he do this?" He dialed Susan's number. "Why would he sabotage . . . don't hang up, please! My sister just showed me the article. Susan, I swear to you that I didn't—"

"Oh, you naughty Reverend, you even swear. I don't think I've ever felt the rage and loathing I now feel for you, but I'll live through it. I have a debt to pay."

The phone clicked again, and flashes of pain shot through his heart.

"I can't believe this. She thinks I deliberately got her out of town so she couldn't respond to this. I've got to convince her that I knew nothing about it."

"You didn't, but that snake Clyde Otis did." Mrs. Cartwright shook her head. "He'll get his. God will get tired of this. He's take Clyde by the neck and wring the evil out him like a soggy dishrag."

Will threw his hands up. "That man tries to undermine everything I do. He's done it before, but I've never had so much to lose."

*ᕱᒉ*

Using the repeat button on the CD player, Susan sat on the floor and listened again and again to words of passion, love, and loss, that aptly described her pain and disappointment. Stroking Dino and trying to keep a clear head, she resisted the urge for more wine. She needed to relax, but was afraid of dulling her senses.

She looked around her first solo apartment, her first attempt at housekeeping alone. She believed in home ownership to the point of never even imagining spending top dollar for a rental, but she did enjoy the ambiance. The richness of the material on the sofa and chairs, the dining table that she had only shared with Travis, the fresh-cut flowers she bought twice a week. It had been home only briefly, but she did not want to lose it. Not this way.

"I could have had a relationship with Travis, but no, I wanted Rev. Cartwright." She stared at the wine bottle in her hand, feeling her heart shatter anew as she realized how much Will had come to mean to her in a very short time.

The tone of Price's messages and the fact that Mr. Deeds had been summoned suggested they were planning a hasty exit for her. She was not shocked that she was being used as a scapegoat for the company, but the fact that Will had used her was unimaginably painful.

"Betrayed, Dino. Mighty Will, a little branch from the Judas tree. I'm fighting this, Dino. I may go down, but I'll go down fighting. I'll take him and . . . " The doorbell interrupted her declarations.

She thought it was Travis and, despite the risk of sending mixed signals, she would have welcomed a shoulder to lean on. "Yes?"

"Susan, it's Will. I need to talk to you."

Her heart raced. Taking deep breaths to stifle the screams that were building in her throat, she cracked the door and spoke slowly. "We have nothing to talk about, and I would greatly appreciate it if you would just leave."

"Just give me ten minutes. Please let me explain. Please."

She stood behind the door and tried to calm her anger. Smoothing back her mussed hair, she fumbled with the security latch and let him in. He reached for her but she moved back and pushed his hand away.

"I can't imagine what you could possibly have to say now, but go ahead. Tell me some more lies, Will."

"Susan, I know how this looks, but believe me, I had nothing to do with that article. I had no idea the media had been contacted. I swear . . ."

The telephone interrupted his attempt to explain. She let the machine pick up, and then held her finger to her lips to tell him to keep quiet.

"Susan, this is Travis again. I want you to call me no matter how late you get in. Price called Deeds, and now he's acting like he already has your job. Call me."

She turned to Will; his face was a mass of frowns.

"Did you hear that? My job is on the line. I don't really care to hear your defense. Now please leave."

"Why is your job on the line? You weren't even in the city when this happened."

"Forget the logistics! My job is on the line because the rest of the world is just as crooked and manipulative as you are. Did you think you and your little bunch of trou-blemakers had a monopoly on deceit? There are people out there waiting for me to fail in this position, and guess what? You just helped them reach their goal."

"I swear to you, I had no knowledge of this. I invited you away with me because, for the first time in a long time, I thought I had found someone to love. I never lied to you. I love you, Susan. You've got to believe me."

"It doesn't matter now. One way or another, my days in this sweatbox are numbered. Even if our relationship survived all of this, it would soon become a long-distance one. From what I understand, most of those don't work out. It—"

The phone rang again. She picked up when she heard Angie's voice.

"Hi, how did it go?"

"There's nothing to worry about. I was able to reach my friend at the TV station, and they're going to air your rebuttal. I also called the newspaper. It took a while to get to the right person, but I said that I was you and told them how shameful it was that they had printed such a one-sided story. Mark Chestnut called me back. He will be at Sealand in the morning, and so will a TV reporter and camera crew."

"I don't know what I would do without you. You're the only true friend I have in this place," she said, looking at Will. "Angie, I have a guest right now. Rev. Cartwright is here. I'll call you back. If you don't hear from me in ten minutes, that means one of us is dead, so please call the police."

Angie giggled. "Got you!"

Will shifted his weight from one foot to the other, his pained expression growing more pronounced by the minute.

"Susan, I don't know how to make you believe me. I love you. I would never hurt you. I thought this matter was under control. I would do anything to relieve you of this burden. Anything. I didn't use you, and I love you beyond words. Please believe me. At our last meeting, one of the members questioned my handling of this matter and suggested I might have a conflict of interests. He had seen us together at the church. I advised them to wait until my return and we would find a solution, but obviously they didn't. I'm not lying, Susan."

"Don't sweat it, Will. One way or the other, there's nothing between us now." She looked at the floor, trying to remain cool, but feeling as though she was going to faint. Walking over to the stereo, she said, "I have a lot of things to do before morning, so please leave."

"For heaven's sake, Susan. Don't let this happen to us. This is tearing me apart. I love you. How can you doubt that after the last few days? I did nothing to—"

She held up her hand. "Let me give you the gospel from my side of the fence, Will. I received this promotion to head Sealand's production staff less than a year after I was made branch manager back in Canton. I'm qualified. I sacrificed my time well beyond normal work hours. When they promoted me to branch manager, Sealand revised its ad campaign. Guess who made the cover of every piece of printed material? We had a little uprising of black activists there, too. I accepted that maybe I was the new black poster child. I didn't particularly like it, but I accepted it. When offered this position less than a year later, I would have been crazy not to question Sealand's motives, don't you think?"

"You think they promoted you to this location because of Cedargrove?"

"I think it's quite possible that someone on high felt a black face was needed here, too. I was probably sent here to be the scapegoat. This alone would be hard to deal with. Now I find that in a moment of weakness I allowed myself to care for someone, thus creating an opportunity to be deceived again. As we speak, a slack-jawed weasel named Price Bishop, who doesn't have enough brains to come in out of the rain, is questioning my job performance. He was next in line for the position I was given. So please excuse me if your words sound a bit hollow to me right now."

"I understand how you feel, but you're wrong. I would never do anything to harm you."

"It doesn't matter anymore. I have some calls to make. Please see yourself out." She picked up the phone and dialed Travis's number, not waiting for Will to leave.

"Travis, I'm home. I got your messages, and I got four from Price. I assumed from the tone of his voice on the last one that he does have my job, but thanks for your concern."

He indeed sounded concerned. "Do you want me to come over there? I can try and help you sort this out. I don't want him to do this to you. I want—"

Not wanting his pity, she cut him off. "Thanks for your offer, but I'll see you in the morning, and don't worry, I'll be fine. I may be down, but I'm not out yet. We'll talk about it in the morning."

Will was still there when she hung up.

"Susan, I'm sorry for everything you're going through. I know you're angry and hurt, but I also know

I love you, and I had no part in this. Think about this weekend, because all of it was real. You make me happier than I've ever been, and I don't want to even think of losing you. I'll call a meeting and see if I can defuse this mess. I apologize from the bottom of my heart."

She held the door open. "Please don't do me any favors. I want to meet you on the battlefield, face to face. Don't get any ideas of redeeming yourself by having them go away. You just worry about your own hide, Rev. Cartwright, and have a nice life."

She watched his broad shoulders droop and her heart cried out. He turned to face her. His lips formed words that remained unspoken as he turned and walked away. Her heart shattered. She closed and locked the door before answering the phone.

"Hi, Angie, I'm glad you called. I almost let him get to me."

"How did he defend what he did?"

"He claimed to have no knowledge of the story. He said that his last advice to the group was to wait until he returned to take the next step."

"You know, Susan, he's probably telling the truth. The paper did quote Rev. Otis, not Will. Willie Cartwright doesn't appear to be the kind of man who would do something like that. Now, on the other hand, that Rev. Otis is a slime bag if ever I saw one. Did Will seem sincere about his feelings for you, or do you care to discuss it?"

"Only with you. He said he loved me and wanted to spend the rest of his life with me. I really thought he meant it, Angie. There was this little voice inside of me saying that I was rushing things, but I really believed him. I know for a fact that I'm in love with him."

"Don't you think you should find out if he's telling the truth before dismissing him from your life? Even if you wait until this is over, I think you should explore your relationship. That man is too good to let get away. That is, if he was sincere."

"I don't think I care to find out. This whole thing has caused me more pain than I should have allowed. I spent a wonderful weekend with a man I was sure would be the last and greatest love of my life. Everything was perfect. We talked about our future. Children. Now I feel like a damn fool."

Anger and pain fused.

"Angie, I need to call home. My parents are probably going nuts worrying about me. I'll see you in the morning."

Yearning for comfort from someone whose love was never in question, she dialed home.

"Mom, it's me. I just wanted to let you know that I'm okay. I'm still fuming mad and more hurt than I've ever been, but I'm in control."

"Honey, does Willard Cartwright mean that much to you? Are you angry because of the problem at work or your personal feelings for him?"

"Both, I think. I was falling in love with him, Mom. No, that's not true. I am in love with him. Just standing next to him, holding his hand. Just hearing his voice, watching him walk into a room was more thrilling than any experience I've ever had, but so much for that. I have a career to save. I'll plot my revenge on Rev. Cartwright at a later date."

"Have you talked to him yet? Did he admit to this?"

"He claims not to have any knowledge of it. He said that one of his members was responsible."

"And you don't believe him?"

"I don't know, Mom, but even if I did, I don't see a relationship with him now. I don't feel an iota of trust in him, and I don't trust myself in his company."

# CHAPTER 7

Susan's head throbbed so intensely that even the tick of the clock was annoying. She lay awake and tried to think of other things, but Will's smile would not go away. After flipping channels on the television, she finally turned it off, pushed back the white sheet with lime and yellow butterflies, and went to the kitchen.

Dino hopped off the bed and followed her down the steps.

"Oh, Dino. Why aren't humans this loyal?" she asked as the cat purred against her legs.

She made a cup of warm milk, found it tasteless, and poured it down the drain.

"No use going back to bed, Dino. There's no way I can fall asleep tonight."

She made a pot of coffee and turned on the stereo. After a short doze on the sofa, she showered and dressed. Hearing the paperboy downstairs at six o'clock, she hurried, picked up the tri-folded newspaper, and tucked it under her arm.

"Okay Susan, let's go in and get this over with."

Feeling skittish and very much alone, she made her way into the darkened, eerily quiet building. Once in her office, she sat on the edge of the desk, opened the newspaper, and found the article Angie had hoped would be there. The caption was all she needed to read: *LENDER CRIES FOUL.*

She was sitting at her desk reading the full story when she heard footsteps approaching.

"I thought you might be here. I couldn't sleep either," Travis said, coming in with outstretched arms. "I'm sorry you had to come home to all this. I talked to Price several times last night. He is trying to make it appear that you knew about this story. He told Deeds that he had advised you to satisfy Cartwright by approving the loans in question and that you refused."

"I don't see that it would have made a difference if I had been here. I knew the matter would not go away, and I've been working to build a defense. I couldn't let Cedargrove, or anyone else, bully me into going against my responsibility. Those loan applications were incomplete. If I had knowingly allowed them to slide past guidelines, I might as well admit that I'm not good at my job."

"Maybe you should have approved them. It certainly would have saved everyone a lot of trouble, especially you."

"You know as well as I do that Price Bishop redlined that community. The people of Cedargrove know it, too. If, in reviewing those loans, I had found no problems, I would have approved them and let the chips fall where they may. I agreed to process the loan applications once the necessary documents were provided."

"Price said the underwriters had reviewed the files and couldn't find sufficient reasons for the denials. He claims time lapse made it impossible to successfully fight their charges. In that case, how can you possibly fight it now?"

"In my own way, Travis. I'm not backing down for Price, Rev. Cartwright, or those people in Cedargrove."

She saw his eyes darting back to the credenza behind her. From the corner of her eyes she saw that she had set her purse on the edge of the credenza instead of inside the drawer. The airline stub was sticking from the outside pocket.

"You went to Atlanta this weekend? That's where the papers said Rev. Cartwright was." His face contorted in angry comprehension. "You were with him."

Susan watched his face contort in anger as he slapped his palm against his forehead. "You were in Atlanta with Willard Cartwright. Oh, I may be slow, but I'm getting the picture now. The paper won't run a story without trying to get comments from both sides. He took you out of town so you couldn't rebuke their claims."

He stood and smiled. "You and Cartwright have been . . . how could you?" he asked.

She waited for his next rhetorical outburst.

"When did you start sleeping with him, Susan? Is that how you planned to make their charges disappear? I guess you underestimated yourself, pretty Susan." He exhaled and leaned forward, placing his palms on the edge of her desk. "While you were playing me, he was playing you."

"I didn't lie to you, and I didn't play you. I accepted friendship and gave it in return. I asked you not to expect anything beyond that. Maybe I should have anticipated your feelings, but I certainly didn't encourage them."

"Of course not. It was the perfect set-up. Well, the joke's on you, now, isn't it?"

His spiteful laugh filled the room. Susan stood and walked around the desk.

"Travis, I told you over and over that I wasn't ready to make a commitment, and that was the truth. Maybe I should have realized you were getting serious and ended our friendship sooner, but I honestly didn't see it coming. I'm profoundly sorry if you feel misled."

He grabbed her shoulders. "You couldn't make a commitment to me, but you didn't tell me you had made one to him." He let go of her and bolted for the door, literally running into Price. "I need to see you in my office, Price. Now! It's urgent!"

Susan slumped down in her chair. She had not led Travis on, but felt guilty just the same. She half expected Price to come storming back at any minute, and then realized it was nine o'clock. She filled her travel cup from the coffee bar, tucked her leather portfolio under her arm and walked across the reception area, past the boardroom, and into Price's office.

The office was empty. She looked around the room that was similar to her office but much smaller. *This is what it's all about. Well, you don't have my office yet, you despicable reprobate.*

She started back to her office and heard someone call her name. Waylon Deeds stood in the boardroom door.

"Come on in, Miss Cross. We're about to start the meeting."

"I was informed that today's meeting would be held in Price's office."

"Price was a bit too hasty in his presumption. I'll be using the boardroom as my office until the renovation is complete, but our meetings will still be held here. I'll officiate this morning. Regular business will be postponed so we can get down to the issues at hand. Here, have a seat," he said, pulling a chair back from the table. "Unless someone has a pressing issue, we'll skip the usual discussions and go straight to this Cedargrove Heights matter."

Price came in soon after and sat on the other side of Mr. Deeds. Travis walked in with the same grimace on his face, followed by three production managers, the head of secondary lending, and the accounting manager. Mr. Deeds called the meeting to order and suggested dispensing with regular business, and asked if everyone had seen the paper. Susan focused on Price's gloating face.

The room quickly cleared, and Mr. Deeds spoke to Susan and Price. "I would rather discuss this matter with the two of you, and Perry Trask from legal, before involving the others. Needless to say, I'm greatly troubled by the article in yesterday's paper. Sealand has worked hard to avoid this kind of publicity. Now we'll have to work even harder to make it disappear. We're waiting for Perry to get here and see what course of action he thinks we should take."

"Mr. Deeds, I would like to continue handling this matter until such time as it becomes a legal issue." Shaky at the beginning, Susan's voice evened out as she spoke.

"This is already a matter for legal, Miss Cross. I left here with the understanding that you and Price would handle it. Now he tells me you refused to inform him of how the case was progressing until it came down to this," he responded, slapping the newspaper on the table. "I don't want this to evolve any further than it has already. It's out of hand. Let Perry handle it."

"It's not out of hand, sir. I had a plan in place in the event something like this happened. I would like to follow it through."

Price cleared his throat. "Your plan failed. I told you it would, but you didn't listen. These people want blood. There's nothing to do but turn it over to legal."

Not bothering to look Price's way, Susan addressed Deeds. "My plan will still work, Mr. Deeds, especially now. With the media looking over our shoulders, we have to disprove these charges or this institution will lose its place of distinction in the lending community."

"There's nothing we can do now," Price interjected. "Let Perry handle this and let us get back to our jobs. Those people can't make a single payment on time, but let them think they can get money by filing a lawsuit and they all line up, especially that big-mouth Rev. Cartwright."

Facing Deeds, Price continued. "If we had let Perry handle this in the beginning, as I advised when I first called you, we wouldn't be here now with egg on our faces."

They waited for Deeds to respond.

"I think it's a legal matter now, Miss Cross. We need to cut our losses and move on."

Susan felt the blood rushing through her body. She knew she could not buckle; could not weaken, and could not let Price see the tiniest crack in her resolve. "With all due respect, Mr. Deeds, I have already gone over my plan with Perry, and he approves. You hired me, sir. You put me here to manage this operation. As long as the allegations are procedural and not legal, I should be allowed to continue with my plan."

"Oh, give it up, Susan!" Price said impatiently. "You had a chance to defuse this mess and you blew it. If you keep handling things your way, we'll all end up in jail," he added with infuriating smugness.

Susan had been pointedly ignoring him, but not this time. Her voice thick with contempt, she said, "I don't recall addressing you, and I was not aware that I needed your permission. Mr. Deeds mentioned that he expected the two of us to handle this. But you never discussed this problem with me when I arrived, and you lied repeatedly when I questioned you. You will recall—unless you selectively choose not to—that the Cedargrove situation was thrown at me on my first day here when you directed Ann to send Rev. Cartwright and his delegation into my office. You knew I had no idea what they wanted. When I asked for your assistance and that of your department, I got zilch. You have overseen this travesty, and I will not be your scapegoat."

She turned to Mr. Deeds. "I will not be a scapegoat for anyone. I was apprised of this situation, not by Price, but by Rev. Cartwright and the people from that community. After reviewing the allegations, I requested the assistance of all underwriters to review those files and validate the denials. To date, neither Price nor his department has lifted a finger. I've handled this to the best of my ability, and with Perry's cooperation and approval. The only way to clear this up now is my way. Anything less would be an admission of guilt and a tremendous loss of credibility for Sealand."

"I totally agree." Perry had arrived in the middle of her statement and taken a seat by the door. "I've reviewed Susan's plan, and I concur with everything she suggested. Price feels we should go back and approve the entire stack of previously denied loans, which would make us look guilty as sin. You do that and Cedargrove Heights will be a small ripple in the wave of damage lawsuits that I know will be filed. Every loan that has been denied since this company was founded will come under scrutiny."

Before Mr. Deeds could answer, Price spoke up.

"I don't think Miss Cross should be anywhere near this situation. As a matter of fact, I think she should resign and save herself the embarrassment. It has come to my attention that she has a personal relationship with Rev. Cartwright. I don't see any of us trusting our jobs to her—not under those circumstances."

Susan was steaming and looking from one to the other. She decided she might as well risk it all. Turning to Price, she pointed her right index finger at his chest.

"You listen to me, you weak-kneed coward, this company wouldn't have to wade through this pile of crap if you had one ounce of sense or courage. I don't know how many people were in on this, but I know that no underwriter worth his or her salt would have rejected a loan based on the reasons you gave to the applicants. You denied those loans for your own personal, racist reasons. If you'd bothered to scrutinize the files, you would have discovered that each file was missing pertinent documents, but you didn't take it that far. You didn't do your job, and I'm not taking the blame for your screw-up."

Laura knocked and entered. "Excuse the interruption, but there are reporters and cameramen in the lobby asking for Miss Cross. It's a Mr. Warring. I thought you might like to know."

"Miss Cross?" Mr. Deeds turned to Susan and she turned to Perry, who was holding the morning paper with her rebuttal exposed on the page.

"Perry has the morning newspaper, Mr. Deeds. That will explain."

Perry pushed the paper down the table. Mr. Deeds glanced at the article and pushed it back.

"I wish you had consulted me before you did this, Miss Cross. You have—"

"She consulted me," Perry lied. "After her initial contact with the citizen's group, Susan anticipated that media involvement was inevitable and prepared to take it head-on. I'll be right by her side to answer any legal concerns, not that she will need my assistance."

Mr. Deeds looked unconvinced. "I'm thinking we should treat this as a legal matter and proceed from there. Having a war of words in the media is not going to help. If this firm lied to borrowers about their creditworthiness, we might as well face the heat now."

"Mr. Deeds," Susan said, standing. "I was brought into the middle of a brewing controversy without any warning. You're asking me to step aside, but you haven't considered the consequences Perry mentioned. I did not deny these loans. If I had, you can bet I would have done it properly. As Perry said, backing down now would open the floodgate for a class action lawsuit that I'm sure would be devastating for Sealand. The accusations have been publicized. There is only one way to handle this. My way."

Mr. Deeds's face was now a deep crimson. Stroking his chin, he looked at Perry, who shrugged his shoulders.

"Very well," he said disconsolately. "Send them in, Laura."

When the cameras were in place, the reporter began his questioning.

"We're live in the boardroom of Sealand Prime Financial to get their response to the allegations of redlining that were leveled by a group of citizens from Cedargrove Heights. Production manager Price Bishop, legal advisor Perry Trask, and the company's president and CFO, Waylon Deeds, joins Susan Cross, head of production. Miss Cross, after your meeting with this group, did you assume the matter was settled?"

She carefully weighed her words. "I informed Rev. Cartwright of problems with each of the loans in question. I've sent letters to all applicants, informing them of the specific problems that hindered approval on their loans, and now I'm prepared to explain all denials from inception of this housing development to now. The article in yesterday's paper simply expressed the unilateral view of the group from Cedargrove. Sealand is ready to respond publicly to all allegations."

"Are you proposing a forum of some kind?"

"I invite Rev. Cartwright, Rev. Otis, and all persons involved to meet with me and Mr. Trask. The meeting will be open to the media, and I especially invite the journalist who wrote the first article."

"When and where will this meeting take place?"

"The logical site is here because the files are here, and we can accommodate a fairly large number of attendees, but I'm quite flexible."

At the end of the briefing, Susan was more confident than she had been since returning from Atlanta. No one was going to take away what she had earned. She still said when, where, and how much.

*☙❧*

Susan and Price left when Mr. Deeds said he wanted to speak with Perry alone. Price strutted back to his office and Susan waited outside the boardroom. Perry emerged, appearing preoccupied and a bit unsteady.

"Thank you for your vote of confidence, Perry. I know you went out on a limb, and I appreciate your support. I won't let you down."

"Nonsense. I do agree with your plan. I also support your guts in taking a stand. If everyone was as knowledgeable as you about the legalities involved in managing this end of the business, my end would be a hell of a lot easier and the company's expenses would be cut in half."

"Thank you, Perry. I want you there with me, and I need your advice."

Travis stopped and smiled when they passed in the hallway. He had told Price about her personal connection with Willard Cartwright to get back at her. However, for the time being, Susan chose to stay focused. She could not afford to be sidetracked.

She was not surprised that the usual interruptions from Price's staff had stopped. As far as they were concerned, she had been relieved of her duties. She didn't mind; she saw it as the break she needed to make sure everything was handled the way she needed it to be.

"I feel like I'm preparing for a day before the Supreme Court," she told Angie. "I won't let us down on this."

Sitting at her desk, her mind kept going back to Willard Cartwright. Even in her anger, he was there with her. She missed waiting for his call, missed the sound of his voice and the effect it had on her heart. Her wandering mind got a much-needed break when Perry called at noon.

"I'm about to go to lunch and wondered if you're free to join me?"

She gladly accepted, and for more reasons than one. Though Perry had supported her stand, his voice now lacked some of its earlier confidence, betraying concerns she was anxious to hear.

She and Perry met at the elevator, and she had the pleasure of seeing Price do a double take when he saw them get on together. She knew it took very little for her nemesis to see a conspiracy behind every door. Deceit and lies were his weapons of choice, and he no doubt assumed others shared his twisted approach to human interactions. *Well, chew on this, little man,* she thought gleefully.

As she expected, Perry headed down Kirby Drive to the little pocket of restaurants where the lunchtime crowd consisted mostly of legal professionals. They settled on one that was not crowded and were immediately seated. They ordered tea and made small talk before Perry turned serious.

"I had an ulterior motive for asking you to lunch, Susan. Price is an idiot and I'm glad you stood up to him, but I do have concerns about your relationship with Rev. Cartwright. I need you to tell me that your personal relationship with this man did not prejudice our position."

She took a sip of tea and gathered her thoughts. "The first time Willard Cartwright came to Sealand with his allegations, the two of us went for each other's throats. By his second visit, I was openly hostile. On the day we were evacuated from the building, I ran into him at a gas station. It was a purely chance encounter. We both apologized for our prior behavior and he ended up inviting me to a fashion show at his church. That was the beginning of our relationship." She paused to let him digest scene one.

"We went out several times, and he invited me to accompany him to Atlanta this past weekend. Travis Polk and I had a friendly relationship that never advanced past friendship. That was my call. This morning, he spied the airline ticket folder from Atlanta in my purse and added two and two. He became enraged because he felt I had rejected him in favor of someone else. He charged Rev. Cartwright of simply getting me out of town so his cronies could plant that story. I had already come to that conclusion, and having done so, wasted no time in saying good-bye to Rev. Cartwright."

She turned and looked directly into Perry's eyes. "At no time did I say or do anything that would compromise Sealand's position in this or any other matter. When the subject of redlining came up, Will and I disagreed so sharply we decided it was best to make it totally off limits. We never discussed it again."

"Good. Do you feel you can prove we were within our rights to issue those denials?"

"We were and I can. My response to Rev. Cartwright was an honest one, but I lied by omission. Now I'm going to tell you the truth. I found legitimate reasons to deny each of those loans, but not for the reasons Price's under-writers cited. Price redlined that area, Perry. I have not divulged this to anyone who didn't already know it, and in the presence of Rev. Cartwright's group, I'll continue defending Sealand, but only if Deeds allows me a free hand to make amends."

He smiled. "When did you study law?"

"With a few more hours, I can get a law degree. I considered law school after college but went for the MBA instead. I had taken a few basics, but most of my classes were taken after I became a Sealand employee. There was a wonderful old man in Canton who encouraged me to learn as much as I could about every aspect of lending, and I did. He chose the classes, and Sealand agreed to pick up the tab as long as I maintained a B average. My lowest average was ninety-two."

"Do you think Cartwright was trying to distract you?"

"I'm not sure, Perry. Even though we began on the wrong foot, the attraction was there from the beginning. Once we got past the initial insults, he asked me to marry him. But I can't say for sure that it wasn't part of some ploy. As it stands now, I'll probably never find out."

"That's too bad," he said with genuine regrets. "From what I hear, he's a complex man. I'm sorry you're caught up in this, and I'll do everything within my power to help you through it."

Having no doubt of Perry's sincerity, she thanked him again for believing in her and for his concern. His trust was one more reason she knew she could not fail.

After bringing Angie up to date on the latest moves, Susan spent the rest of her workday alone in her office, receiving only a sprinkling of calls from other branches. Her mind rambled back through her childhood and to the daily doses of pride and self-confidence that she received. *I will not fold.*

Soon after arriving home, she called her parents and listened to their tales of dissension in their church and tried to dissect Will's claim of innocence.

"I'm not defending this man, but don't discount what he says. Your mother thinks the sun rises on the elder Cartwright. I just know that any man would be a fool not to fall in love with my daughter. I'm being biased, and that's my prerogative."

"Thanks, Daddy. I needed that. As far as Will is concerned, I don't feel like sorting through that pile of garbage to find the source of the stench. I can't make another mistake, and I can't let any man control my life."

She took a long bath, lay on the sofa and fell asleep with the TV on. When she awakened and the news was on, her press briefing was being aired.

"Susan Cross, executive vice-president and newly appointed head of the lending division, has invited citizens of Cedargrove to present their complaints in a public forum."

After watching, Susan pronounced herself pleased with her confidence and her delivery. She also studied the faces around her: Waylon Deeds wore a half smile, as if in deep prayer; Perry displayed the ever-brave assurance, and Price Bishop had his ever-present smirk. At the end of the interview, Tony Warring delivered his commentary.

"Sealand holds the distinction of being the largest privately owned lending institution in the country. Headquartered here in Houston, the company has enjoyed a prominent position in our lending community. With offices in twenty-four states, Sealand offers a large array of lending and banking services. We will keep you abreast of the developments in this controversy."

"I hope you saw this, Rev. Cartwright," Susan said, stroking Dino's back. "I want to meet you face to face and show you what I'm really like." She fell asleep again, this time not waking until morning.

She went into the office early, hoping to avoid contact with either Price or Travis. The secretaries had not yet manned their positions when her phone rang.

"Susan Cross."

There was a moment's silence before he spoke. "Susan, Will. I'm calling about the news piece. I have contacted the complainants, and we are prepared to meet with you at your convenience."

"That's kind of you. How about Friday morning at nine, room 212 of our building facing Voss? Approximately how many will join you?"

"When offered a chance to expose this matter, some of them feared going on television and backed down. To the best of my knowledge, there will be twelve, plus Mrs. Whitehead and myself. Is that agreeable?"

"Quite agreeable."

"And may I ask who will represent your company?"

"I'm the spokesperson. Perry Trask of our legal department will be with me. I'm not sure how many others will attend, but be assured you will not be outnumbered. I would also advise you to bring a legal representative for your group."

"Are we moving toward litigation?" he asked, his voice now dry and a little sharp.

"That's strictly up to you and the people of Cedargrove. I'm bringing legal counsel because I want to make sure I'm on solid legal ground when I answer your allegations. I suggested you do the same in case someone wants to challenge the facts as they are presented."

"I understand. Thank you. I'll see you on Friday, unless there is something else you want to discuss."

She wanted to scream, *Yes!* Instead, she said, "Nothing on this end, Reverend," sounding overly cheerful.

"Thank you."

She thought she heard him say her name as she hung up, but it was only his voice echoing in her head. Frustrated, she gathered a stack of loan commitments and went down the hallway to secondary lending. Passing Travis in the hallway only intensified her anguish. Her face was still stinging when she finished her business and headed back to her office. Price called her name as she passed his door.

"Yes?"

"I was just wondering if a meeting has been scheduled with your friend from the church."

"I'll give you plenty of notice, Price."

He leaned back in his chair, a look of spiteful jubilation on his face. "I'm sorry you got yourself into this mess, Susan. I don't know how you can defend your position, but I wish you luck."

She started to walk away but changed her mind. The undisguised elation in his voice was more than she could swallow. She slammed his door shut and swung around to face him.

"I'll just bet you do."

Walking closer, she placed her hands on his desk and assumed an in-your-face stance, feeling a barely controllable urge to smack his face.

"You had better pray that I take flight and leave here, because you are in no way prepared to go toe to toe with me. In addition to being disloyal, you are weak and stupid, which accounts for your lack of judgment in choosing your sparring partners. Save your good luck for yourself. You just might need it."

As she sped from his office, she again bumped into Travis. She wondered if he had been eavesdropping on her and Price, or whether he'd been waiting for her.

"Susan, wait. I need a second of your time."

She continued toward her office, the sound of her heels clicking against the floor. Travis was close behind. Rounding her desk, she turned abruptly and asked, "What do you want?"

"I did something yesterday that I knew was wrong. I was hurt and angry. I'm sorry for your troubles, and sorry that I may have added to them. Please forgive me."

"I don't have the power to grant absolution, Travis, and I try very hard to avoid the need to seek it," she said, her voice tightly controlled; her face all but devoid of expression.

"Was your need to hurt me greater than everything else, or did you hope to add a star by your name for helping Price?" She almost felt sorry for Travis, but her heart was in no condition to register pity. "Unless you have business to discuss, leave my office immediately."

"Susan . . ."

"Go to hell, Travis! Go straight to hell and take your boy Price with you."

He very wisely walked away. She was less than thrilled to have him caught in the crossfire, but it was his own doing. He had made two disastrous choices: betraying her and aligning himself with Price. But she had no time to waste thinking about Travis and his self-imposed hell. She had work to do.

She closed her door, dictated a memo for distribution, and then called Perry. "It's on for nine on Friday. You'll get a memo, but I wanted to alert you personally. We're meeting in the training room."

"Are you okay, Susan? You sound distracted."

"I'm fine. I spoke with Rev. Cartwright. I told Price what I thought of him. Lastly, I threw Travis out of my office. What you hear is probably the sound my soul winding down."

"If you need me for anything or if you just need to talk, please feel free to call."

She thanked him and hung up. Her plan was to keep busy for the rest of the week. Wednesday was a quiet day with no interruptions and a moderate amount of work. On Thursday, she was informed that Sealand had been selected as one of the lenders for the low-income housing initiative, but she was still too emotionally shaken to feel elated. She had finished dictating a memo announcing the commitment when Deeds poked his head in her door.

"Miss Cross, are you all set for tomorrow?"

"Yes, I am. The files are in the training room, the seating arrangements are complete, and I've instructed Laura to have the large coffee urn from the boardroom filled and in place."

"How many do you expect?"

"One newspaper reporter, a TV reporter and his crew, Rev. Cartwright, his assistant, and twelve or so from his group. I suggested they bring a legal representative. I assume it will be the four of us?"

"Yes," he confirmed. "But I'm not following you on this. Why did you suggest a legal representative?"

"Mr. Deeds, those people are coming in here tomorrow without an ounce of trust in me or my word. I want them to be able to have one of their own at the meeting to verify that what I say is true. When they leave tomorrow, I want this matter to have been put to rest once and for all, whether I'm here or not." She thought of Angie.

"I see. Did you advise Perry that you had taken this initiative?"

"Since finding this pile of manure, I've not made a move without Perry's knowledge and consent." She calmly waited for his next question.

"I talked with Perry earlier, and he thinks you have the situation well in hand. It's obvious that you're not liable here. I don't want you to feel this battle is yours alone. Is there anything I can assist you with, or any questions I can answer?"

"Yes, but if you don't mind, I'll reserve them for after the meeting. Right now I am focusing on successfully completing a task that I find most distasteful. I will defend these charges and I will win," she said, confidently. "And then we can talk."

She double-checked everything, including the sugar and cream for the coffee. She locked the door to the training room but remained in her office until she was sure Price had left for the day. Travis joined her as she walked toward the elevator.

"Susan, no matter what you think of me, I do care what happens to you. I did a selfish and stupid thing, and I'm eternally sorry for having done so. Good luck tomorrow."

"I was happy to have you as a friend, Travis. Falling in love with you would have been nice, but that didn't happen for me. All in all, I never purposely hurt you and I never would have, but you knowingly tried to hurt me, and at a time when the deck was already stacked against me. Right now the only feelings I have for you are ones of contempt, so please don't wish me well." She spoke with finality and continued on her way.

At home, there was a message from Angie inviting her over for a pot roast dinner. Feeling the need for company, she gladly accepted. She stopped at the liquor store for two bottles of Angie's favorite merlot. She was surprised when Carl opened the door and welcomed her with a protective hug.

"I traded shifts with a coworker to give you another shoulder if you need to lean," he explained. "Don't let them get to you, Susan. A lot of men are afraid of strong women and will try anything to take them down. You've done nothing wrong."

"Carl is right," Angie said. "You met a man who appeared to be upstanding and honest. A minister. If he used you to further his agenda, then he's the one who should feel ashamed. I wish you'd let me come to the meeting. I want to be there for you."

"You'll be there in every one of those files. You're the reason I can walk into that room tomorrow with confidence. It's best if no one knows what we're up to. The element of surprise—a sneak attack—is our best defense."

After dinner, she sat on the sofa and talked about what was eating at her. "I'm not nervous about facing them. I have my ammunition, but Angie, I'm going to stand there in front of those black people and justify what that little viper Price Bishop did to them. I feel like such a traitor. I couldn't face Will now even if I wanted to. Sealand screwed that up."

"Susan, if you don't squash this mess, you'll lose your job or at least a significant measure of respect from the people you manage. If that happens, Price Bishop will be able to continue doing what he did to them. Some things have to be sacrificed in order for bigger and better things to come about."

Before going to bed, Susan chose her outfit for the next day: her favorite black suit, gray shirt, and black pearls. As she moved about the apartment, she kept reassuring herself that she would not fail.

"Those people think I'm made of plastic, Dino, but they're wrong. I'm Susan Cross, Bobby's little sister. I'm the daughter that Ralph and Tammy taught to be resilient. I can't let them break me. I say when. I say where. I say how much."

Her self-help pep talk apparently worked because she slept surprisingly well that night. She arrived at work early, and went directly to the training room for one final check, but decided to wait in her office. She wanted to make a grand entrance. She wasn't sure why, but it seemed important at the time.

Laura came to her door to fetch her. "Miss Cross, the people from the church just arrived; I had someone watching out for them."

"Thanks, Laura."

As she headed down the hall, the trim brunette with efficiency stamped on her forehead called after her: "We're rooting for you, Miss Cross."

She smiled, gave Laura a thumbs-up, and headed into battle.

She heard voices when she stepped off the elevator, and she knew one of them belonged to Will. She paused at the door to the training room and girded herself for what lay ahead. The ball of fear in her throat grew larger. She took a deep breath and warned herself that this was no time to freeze. She had to give the best performance of her professional life. Regardless of the pressure, she could not let them see her quake. She fixed her face into a faux smile and entered the room. She saw Will immediately. There was no smile on his face and no excitement in his dark brown eyes, just discomfort and anxiety.

"Good morning, everyone. My name is Susan Cross."

There were at least thirty people in attendance. Looking at the sea of black faces, she wanted to take the microphone and go over to their side. They looked to be average, hard-working people, some of whom may have never owned a home. She wanted to tell the whole ugly story and sink Price Bishop's boat, but that was not possible, since she was on the same vessel. She remembered Angie's words: The only thing standing between those people and the likes of Price was someone who cared. She had to retain her position and still remain on the side of justice.

She scanned the room, looking for the reporters and the other members of her team. Sealand's table was at the front of the room, facing the crowd: Only Perry was seated. He managed a weak smile, which she sort of returned. After waiting a few minutes for late arrivals, Susan asked everyone still standing to take a seat.

"I'm sure the media would like to wrap this up quickly and so would I, so let's please get started." Looking around, she asked, "Where is Price?"

Just then he slunk into the room, waited for Mr. Deeds to sit, and plopped into the chair next to him.

Susan tapped the microphone. "Are we ready?" she asked, praying her emotions would not spill over into her voice. "Before we begin, I would like to introduce the Sealand representatives here today. I'm Susan Cross, head of lending for Sealand Prime Financial. Next to me is Perry Trask, head of Sealand's legal division, and next to him is Waylon Deeds, Sealand's president and chief financial officer. Next to Mr. Deeds is Price Bishop, our production manager.

"Now I want to introduce the spokesperson for the Cedargrove residents, Rev. Willard Cartwright. Next to him is his assistant, Mrs. Whitehead. I would like the following individuals to please stand." She glanced at her notes. "Rev. Frank Otis." She felt a deep loathing for the short balding man, who stood and took a quick bow.

"Is there a legal representative in the group?"

Will stood and said, "Our legal representative is Marcus Paxton."

A tall, eminently calm man of about thirty-five stood on Will's left.

"Thank you." She could not look at Will. She needed to be focused and work around her feelings for him. She took a deep breath and began.

"We're here this morning because serious allegations have been leveled regarding Sealand's lending policies. For the record, the term redlining is used when a certain area is targeted for lending discrimination. In such cases, qualified borrowers are turned down for loans simply because of the area in which they have chosen to purchase a home. Financial institutions operate under strict guidelines, and I intend to prove that each decision regarding loans in Cedargrove Heights was made with those guidelines in mind."

The tremor in her voice disappeared as she continued. "Having recently relocated to this office, I had no knowledge of this matter until Rev. Cartwright brought it to my attention."

She spotted Deacon Jones and felt encouraged. He was smiling.

"After hearing the concerns of Cedargrove residents, I investigated their allegations." She pointed to the stack of files at the end of the table. "I'm now prepared to answer any questions you may have, but let me first make you aware of a very important issue. Sealand is the interim lender for this development. We believed in the project enough to finance it for Block Builders. If the homes do not sell, Block cannot pay off the construction loan to Sealand. Therefore, it is clearly in our best interest to approve each loan application that crosses our desk."

She stood erect and looked directly at Will. "Rev. Cartwright's concern for his community is duly noted. Redlining is a serious charge, and since such an allegation was put into the public via the press, I'm especially pleased to have Tony Warring from Channel Two and David Chestnut, the newspaper reporter who wrote the initial story, here today."

Everyone looked at the reporters and camera crew, but Susan's eyes helplessly settled on Will. For a brief moment, his pained expression tore into her heart. She quickly refocused and continued.

"Now I ask each of you who has a comment to stand, one at a time, state your name, and give your verbal consent for me to discuss your personal file here in this forum."

Two men stood at the same time.

"Okay, we have two gentlemen. May I have your name, sir?" she asked, addressing an overdressed man in a crimson hat.

"My name is Randy Watson."

She remembered his file. He was probably a scam artist, not someone she wished to protect. "Thank you, Mr. Watson. And you, sir?"

The other man appeared very nervous. "I'm Craig Williams."

She turned to Price. "Mr. Bishop, would you kindly pull the files on these two gentlemen, Randy Watson and Craig Williams."

She thumbed through the files Price handed her, and then looked at the man in the crimson hat. "Mr. Watson, there was a problem with some of the assets you listed. Are you sure you want to go into this in front of a crowd and the media?"

"Yes, I wanna go into it. That's why I'm here," he growled. "You people kept asking for the same information on my income properties, and then you denied my loan. I guess it's hard for you to believe that I own five rental houses and had assets to pay cash if I chose. If that's not discrimination, I don't know what is."

A slow smile crept across her face. As much as she dreaded taking a combative position with the black people in front of her, this one was clearly a jerk.

"No, sir, it's not hard to believe that you own five rental houses. The problem is the length of time that you claim to have owned them. If what you say is correct, then there are other issues at stake that could have serious ramifications for you. I'll ask you again, are you sure you want to—"

"Listen, lady, I don't know what you mean about 'claim to have owned.' That's exactly what your people kept asking me before. Two of those houses were paid off in '99. One was paid off in '03, one in '04, and one last year. I gave you copies of the notes, stamped 'paid in full.' I should file harassment charges against you for the way I was treated. I'm not a poor man. I applied for a

$200,000 loan. I can afford twice, three times that amount."

"Let me ask you once again, Mr. Watson, are you positive that you want to proceed with this matter here in front of the media and two attorneys?"

"Are you deaf? I just said I did, didn't I?"

Someone snickered and Susan's courage grew stronger, as she knew Mr. Watson would pay a stiff price for his heedlessness and his ignorance. Her hands were steady as she held onto the file she had red tagged. "My records show you filed Chapter 7 bankruptcy two years ago. For the benefit of those unfamiliar with this procedure, Chapter 7 is a court-supervised liquidation of assets. The proceeds from the sale of said assets are used to pay outstanding debts. Balances not liquidated and unsecured are forgiven and become losses for the creditors. In other words, the debtor walks away without paying his bills and the creditors, particularly the unsecured ones, have to absorb the loss. Mr. Trask, Mr. Paxton, am I correct on this?"

Paxton nodded and Perry responded with a very loud, "Yes, you are."

"Mr. Watson, you failed to list the houses you owned outright and the equity in the other properties in your bankruptcy proceedings. Your debts of over $87,000 were forgiven. The reason I continued to question your willingness to proceed is that both Mr. Paxton and Mr. Trask are attorneys, officers of the court, and duty-bound to report this oversight. You committed perjury, Mr. Watson," she said, shaking her head and looking at him with pursed lips.

"That's a lie! If Sealand knew all of this, why didn't you report me before now? Because you're lying, that's why!"

"Sealand employees were not duty-bound to apprise the court of your misconduct, sir, but these two gentlemen are. As far as loan approval is concerned, once you have cleared this matter with the court, please feel free to re-apply."

"I don't want your loan! I wouldn't take it if it were free. I knew you people would do this. Get here in front of the press and try to humiliate us."

Susan smiled to herself. He had given her the perfect opening. "Mr. Watson, we people, as you say, did not choose this forum. I would have preferred to speak to each of you in private, but your group brought the press into this. You just called me a liar, sir. For the record, please state which part of my explanation you feel to be false. You just acknowledged, very proudly, that you owned the real estate in question. Do you deny filing for bankruptcy? If you do, I've got a copy of your petition and the exhibits right here."

"You're just trying to trick me. Don't worry about me. There are still a lot of people here that you have to answer to."

"I'm prepared to do just that, Mr. Watson. For the sake of clarity I'll ask your counsel, Mr. Paxton, to address the validity of my comments."

Paxton hesitated. "I would feel better speaking to my client in private."

"I would have preferred to do that as well. Did you read the article in the newspaper that contained certain allegations made by this group?"

"I read the article, Miss Cross."

"Then surely you recall the line charging that Susan Cross refused to rectify this blatant injustice. The injustice is that such an allegation was printed. Susan Cross allegedly refused to take action to satisfy the people, so now we're here to do just that. Now please, sir, address the validity of my earlier statement. Was this a legitimate rejection or an act of discrimination?"

"Presuming your facts are in order, there were sufficient reasons to deny the loan."

"Thank you, Mr. Paxton. Before we proceed, which one of you will take this matter to the bankruptcy judge?"

Perry spoke up. "I will, Miss Cross."

"Thank you." She looked at Mr. Deeds, who nodded and smiled. She then turned to the other man.

"Mr. Williams, the rejection of your loan was a simple matter of debt to income. Your current obligations exceed your stated income, which would render you unable to repay this loan." Her jitters were completely gone. She was in charge.

"You are named in a paternity suit in the Harris County courts. A Cynthia Stiles has obtained a judgment against you for support of a minor named LaShea. Once the monthly child support of five hundred and fifty dollars is deducted from your current earnings, there will not be enough disposable income to qualify you for this loan. I'm sorry. Do you have any questions, sir?"

He mumbled no, and took a seat. Susan did not want to gloat, but she was once again grateful to the man who had taken the time to explain every facet of lending to her.

"Next, please. Who is next?" She looked and saw only lowered heads. "Rev. Cartwright, what's going on? I thought you had at least eleven applicants who came to question Sealand's practices. We have press coverage, which your group was seeking, so where are the complainants?"

Will stood and asked Rev. Otis to also stand. "He is the one responsible for the newspaper article, and he's still planning to purchase the house he applied to buy. I'm sure he would like to have a definitive answer from you as to his eligibility."

"Certainly. Mr. Bishop, would you get the file on Frank Otis? Please remain standing, Rev. Otis, and give your verbal approval for me to reveal the reason your loan was denied."

He glanced sideways at the woman next to him. "I give my permission."

"Rev. Otis, I'm prepared to give an in-depth account of this denial, but simply stated, this is also a matter of debt-to-income ratio. Your credit check proved satisfactory, but your income didn't support an additional debt of almost fifteen hundred dollars per month."

"Explain yourself, young lady. This is my wife, Aretha. She's a postal employee and makes a good salary. We have few debts. I'm also a postal worker and a servant of the Lord. Together, we have a good income, so go ahead with your explanation."

His trim, tidy wife rose and stood at his side.

"Rev. Otis, your loan had been approved until it was discovered that you co-signed an auto loan that has a very large balance. The other maker on the note is Millie Hampton, and the balance is over $40,000."

"Millie Hampton! You co-signed a loan for that tramp?" Mrs. Otis's hands went to her hips, her eyes blazed. "Now I'm the one who wants an explanation!"

"With all due respect, ma'am, that has nothing to do with my personal qualifications. That was just helping a friend."

"This debt is a contingent liability, meaning you are liable if Ms. Hampton fails to pay. The past pay habits and the status of the loan at the time you applied with Sealand indicated that you were going to be called upon to help satisfy this debt. The auto loan was delinquent back when we checked your credit. I had someone update the records twice, and that loan has now been turned over to Apex Adjusters. I believe that's a repo firm. Now unless that car sells for the balance owed, you and Ms. Hampton are liable for the difference to Banner Bank and Trust. You were advised of this action several times."

She held up copies of letters addressed to Rev. Otis. "Of course the bank sent your mail . . . let's see . . . the address you listed was the same as Ms. Hampton. Do you reside there, sir?"

"He does now!" his wife said, slinging her purse over her shoulder and storming out of the room.

"I'm sorry for any embarrassment you have endured here today, but, again, this was not my idea. Now, I would like for Mr. Paxton to affirm that each reason given for rejection of these loans was legitimate."

"Miss Cross, you have covered some very subjective areas here today. Some of the decisions could have gone either way."

"I beg to differ, counselor," Perry said, standing. "No lender would make a loan to a borrower with an outstanding delinquency of $40,000, unless that amount represented only a small fraction of his income. If you or anyone in your group considers these matters subjective, then let me suggest that we take this to mediation."

The room became hushed. Susan noticed an approving smile from Mrs. Whitehead. A woman stood and raised her hand. Susan had no problem with the likes of Rev. Otis or Mr. Watson. They were clearly not upstanding men, but it was the honest face standing before her that touched her heart.

"Yes, ma'am? May I have your name and your consent to discuss your file here today?"

"My name is Eunessa Parker. When I went to buy the house, the man in the office looked at my information and said I would qualify with no problems, but your company turned me down. My husband was permanently disabled in Desert Storm, but he gets a good pension and I have a good job. I just want my family to have a nice home."

Accepting the file from Price's hand, Susan knew that somehow she had to make this right. She knew that for each Frank Otis in the room, there were two honest individuals who had been wrongfully denied credit.

"Mrs. Parker, you have excellent credit, job stability . . . you've worked for the same company for fifteen years. That's very commendable." She closed the file.

"You applied for a FHA loan, but the amount of your purchase exceeded the maximum FHA loan amount. That's the only reason your loan was denied. Sealand's loan personnel should have fully explained that to you, and if they did not, I apologize on their behalf. Your loan was reworked under conventional guidelines. It will be approved, but will require more money down. Are you still interested in purchasing this property?"

"Yes, I am."

"I'll hold your file and personally assist you with the paperwork. I'm pleased to say that Sealand will participate in a program designed to assist borrowers such as yourself with their home purchase. Because you have such good credit, I'm sure you'll qualify, even if Sealand has to assist with the down payment. I'll give you my card before you leave. Call me at your convenience and we'll work this out."

Turning to Will, Susan said, "Rev. Cartwright, there were quite a few files, sixteen I believe, for which additional information is needed to secure loan approval. The program I mentioned will offer the assistance to enable some of the others to qualify as well. The ceiling for this program is $160,000, and the requirements parallel those of FHA. I would be happy to provide information on this and other programs that could benefit many of you in purchasing a home."

Will stood, smiling for the first time. "Thank you, Miss Cross. We would appreciate any information you can share with us."

"I'll gladly hold a home-buying seminar here or at your church on any Saturday. On behalf of Sealand, I offer my services and those of our lending division to help each of you obtain the loan for which you applied. I can assure financing for most of you if you still want to purchase a home in Cedargrove or elsewhere. Letters were sent that should clarify the information needed. There is no need to reapply. Just call a member of our lending team, or call me, and we will be happy to assist you. I previously offered to waive the origination fee, and that offer still stands."

She returned Will's nod and he sat down.

"Would anyone else in this group like to come forward at this time?" she asked. "Then I am assuming that all questions have been answered to your satisfaction. In conclusion I should add that, as Sealand's representative, I deeply regret this meeting becoming necessary. Sealand is an old and very reputable institution. We're in the business of making loans and, yes, we have to make money as well, but it is now my responsibility to ensure that we do so in ways that are mutually beneficial to all citizens, regardless of where they've chosen to live. As long as I'm in charge of lending, any denials of credit will be fully explained and each applicant given ample opportunity to respond. If I can answer a legitimate question or assist any of you with a problem, simply pick up the phone and ask." That was her final word to the man she deeply loved.

When he stood to speak, her heart quivered.

"In view of the events that unfolded here today, I wish to offer you an apology, Miss Cross. When I return to my office, I will make that a formal apology to you and to Sealand."

"Thank you, Rev. Cartwright."

The room emptied quickly. Afterwards, Mr. Deeds came up to congratulate Susan. He wanted to know if he could be of further service.

"I would like to meet with you later, in private." Susan was still filled with anger each time she thought of the possibility that she had been the intended scapegoat for Price's mistakes.

Price, who had kept his head mostly down since he was introduced, moved to leave, but his exit was blocked when Perry stood to congratulate Susan.

"If you don't mind, I plan to speak with Deeds about giving you extra help in lending so you can branch across to legal. You were magnificent. Just magnificent."

"Thank you, Perry."

Unable to escape the huddle, Price mumbled, "Yeah, congratulations." He pushed past Perry and hightailed it for the door.

"Thank you, Price. I'm sure you mean that from the bottom of your heart."

As he stormed away, Perry laughed and squeezed her shoulders. "It's lunchtime. What say you and I go grab a bite? This whole ordeal took a lot out of me."

"Sounds great," she said, following him out of the room. Rev. Cartwright and some of his group were waiting at the elevator. As he disappeared behind the closing doors, she felt that she was seeing him walk out of her life forever, and that thought brought back her pain.

Perry let out a loud yell as soon as they were in the car. "I've been in many courtrooms, and I must say that was one fine display. If you had an axe to grind with Rev. Cartwright, you pulverized him today. How did you get so much information? You know most of that would not have been picked up on a routine credit check."

"Most of it would have if I was the one checking the credit application, but I owe a lot to Angie Edwards from collections. She looked under stones that no one else could have known about."

"Get her a raise. Deeds has to be receptive to anything you say right now."

"I have to admit I'm not nearly as gleeful as I would like to be. Perry, I don't stand around whining, but something is dreadfully wrong here. I'm also careful in my work. I cross each 't' and dot every 'i,' but for the sake of my career, I stood there today and defended a blatant act of discrimination."

"I'll never believe you did it just for the sake of your career. Besides, it all comes out in the wash. You can now do things to help the honest people in Cedargrove. So far, you are in full control. No doubt about that."

"Yes," she replied, smiling. "I suppose I was."

After the meeting, Will left with the others and went to see the only person he could rely on to understand.

"I wasn't wrong, Pop. She really is incredible. It just hurts to know how angry and disappointed she feels toward me. I'd do anything to get her back."

His sister Jean had been listening.

"Sounds like you never had her in the first place, or she wouldn't have turned on you that way. Why would she think you did this, and why would you lie about it? This woman doesn't know you at all, and in spite of your strong feelings, I don't think you know her, either."

"I don't know her that well," his father rejoined, "but I know she's special. Put yourself in her place. She felt she'd been deceived. If you love her as much as I think you do, go to her and apologize for Otis. Say whatever you have to say to get her attention."

He looked around at Mrs. Cartwright. "That's what I did with your mother. I begged, and I'm not ashamed to admit it."

Susan was not surprised to find a message from Laura on her desk when she returned. Mr. Deeds wanted to see her in the boardroom.

"Come in, Miss Cross; have a seat." He answered her knock. "I can't tell you how proud I was of you this morning. Now what would you like to discuss?"

She took a chair. "First of all, I need to stress that the information I used today was factual. If I had underwritten those loans, I would have handled them as I did today. The original underwriters never cited those factors. In other words, the loans were denied for the very reasons alleged by the people of Cedargrove."

"I suspected as much. How were you able to make such thorough evaluations?"

"I'll be happy to answer that question, but first I have one for you. Obviously, Price had apprised you of the Cedargrove Heights situation. Did that necessitate bringing in a black face? Is that why I'm here?"

If Susan expected him to be at least momentarily startled by the question, she saw no such indication in his expression. He just looked at her thoughtfully before answering. "I went to Ohio to review the annual budget and overheard a discussion about the woman who was head underwriter. No one in that discussion mentioned that you were black. Later, I accepted a branch manager's resignation and his recommendation for a replacement. He did say that you were black, and he also used adjectives such as knowledgeable, capable, and trustworthy. Now I admit I heard a few other adjectives, such as well-dressed and beautiful, but they did not sway my decision, and neither did the fact that you're black." He smiled tensely.

"I then took the liberty of scanning your personnel file, knowing at the time that I needed to cover some bases here." Looking faintly bemused, he continued. "I have a daughter at UT, a junior. She's a good girl, but spends most of her time attending sorority parties and worrying about the latest fashions. I sat there listening to you today. You are knowledgeable, confident, and driven by conviction. The only thought in my head was how much I wish my daughter were more like you. Your race was not a negative or positive factor in your promotion. You were simply the best person for the job."

She believed him.

"There has been a change in your responsibilities. From now on you will have double duty. Perry wants you to act as litigation liaison for lending and servicing. You will continue your regular responsibilities with the help of an assistant of your choosing. I'm offering you a $10,000 salary increase as compensation for your added responsibilities—and for that commitment you secured. It will put Sealand over the top. Well done."

She wanted to thank him and just leave, but knew she had to finish what she had started.

"I must remember to thank Perry again. Based on what he told me earlier, having someone review potential problems on this end could reduce his workload as well as save the company a fortune annually. My math puts that somewhere in the neighborhood of, say, twenty thousand?"

He laughed. "You have a deal, Miss Cross."

"Thank you very much. There are a couple of things I'd like to discuss. To answer your questions regarding my assessment of those files, I had help from a highly qualified and hard-working woman in collections named Angie Edwards. It was her research that saved Sealand."

"I'll be happy to compensate her, but I don't think I'll negotiate amounts with you."

She smiled slightly, indicating that she had not finished. "To compensate for the unfair decisions Price made, I would like to offer some kind of special financing to those who legitimately qualify. I have already offered to waive origination fees, but I would also like to offer, when available, maybe special rates. I also suggest you set up a quality control department. It's not a cure-all, but it will help prevent situations such as the one we just had. People tend to act more responsibly if they know they're being watched."

"Are you suggesting Angie Edwards for this position?"

"I've not spoken to Angie about such a position, but she might be interested. She does have the qualifications. For openers, a manager and maybe two clerical assistants can do the job. They would do random reviews, one department at a time. That kind of safety net is also very industry impressive."

"It's a good idea. I'll get rolling on it right away." He paused. "On second thought, why don't you roll with it? Work up the guidelines." Then he said, matter-of-factly, "By the way, Price handed in his resignation this afternoon. You'll need to interview for his position as well. Narrow your candidates down to three and let me see their files."

She was tempted to ask if Price had resigned voluntarily, but knew he hadn't.

The day had been tiring but exhilarating. As she cleared her desk to leave, Travis appeared at her door.

"Can I help you?" she asked without looking up.

He walked in and closed the door. "Price has resigned. I suppose you want my resignation as well?"

Still not looking up, she asked, "What makes you think that?"

"We both know the answer to that. Look, I was in your corner all the way until I found out about you and Rev. Cartwright. I had no right to get angry, but I did. I also had no right to strike out as I did and spill my guts to Price. I'll understand if you want me to leave."

She finally looked up at him. "Do you want to leave?"

"You know I don't, but I'm sure you'll be uncomfortable working with me now."

"I don't feel that way at all. To the best of my knowledge, you did not compromise this company's credibility. That is why Price resigned. I only want your resignation if you want to offer it."

"I'll think about it." After turning to leave, he hesitated, his hand on the doorknob. "For what it's worth, I'm glad it turned out this way. Deeds said you were superb this morning."

She simply smiled.

# *CHAPTER 8*

Susan went shopping for groceries after work. The Friday evening traffic was heavy, but having only Dino waiting at home, she was in no hurry. Maneuvering out of the slowly moving vehicles, she stopped at Kroger for fruit, a couple of steaks, chicken breasts, cat food, and litter for Dino. Her evening was set. She would call her parents, oven-grill a steak, and enjoy a glass of wine and some music—alone.

After storing the groceries, she poured a glass of wine and went out to the balcony with the phone and her laptop. A phone call interrupted the scolding she was giving herself for allowing Will's memory to continue dogging her thoughts.

"Susan! Girl, I'm so happy for you. You tore into them this morning." Angie was practically screeching. "Travis heard about it from Mr. Deeds and spread the word to the rest of us. There were more people on your side than you could imagine. They knew Price was a jerk. How did he respond to this?"

"He resigned."

"You mean you ran the little bastard off? I knew you could handle yourself in a fight. I don't remember ever being so proud of anyone." Settling down, she said, "Deeds called me in and offered me a raise and a promotion to quality control manager. I know that was your idea. I'm grateful."

"No, I'm grateful. You saved Sealand, and me, and I'll never forget it. Now tell me what you decided."

"I thanked him for the raise and told him I would get back to him Monday about the position. He said the duties were not yet defined."

"That's because I haven't defined them yet. The position reports to me."

"He didn't tell me that. He offered me a $10,000 pay increase for the new position, and gave me a bonus for—his words—outstanding performance. How did you manage that?"

"Oh, I beat up on him a little about my salary increase. He offered me a raise and I raised his raise. I'm sure he knew that unless he offered you something decent, I'd challenge him again. I also convinced him to allow me to offer a form of compensation to the Cedargrove borrowers who were unjustly turned down. I have a new responsibility. I'll be working closely with Perry, and as I soon as I can, I plan to resume classes and get a law degree."

"I can't tell you how much I admire you. That's why I wanted you to stay. You can help a lot of people just by being here and being you."

"Hold on, Angie, there's someone at the door." She put the security chain on and cracked the door. It was Will, head slightly bowed, standing uncertainly before her. She undid the chain, stood back, and told Angie she would call her later. "I have company."

"Is it who I think it is?"

"You got it."

"Girl, no! Before you go, we want you to come to dinner tomorrow evening, and I won't take no for an answer."

"In that case, the answer is yes, I'll be there. We'll talk later." She turned and faced Will. "What can I do for you?"

"I've been so worried about you, Susan. Judging from the way you handled yourself today, I suppose my concern wasn't necessary, but I did worry."

"You have enough people counting on you as it is. Save your concern for them, Will. I'm fine."

"What I wanted to offer you was my love, but I guess it's too late for that. Susan, I never lied to you. Frank Otis brought this matter to the media without my knowledge, and certainly without my approval."

The phone rang again.

"Excuse me. I'll make this brief."

It was her mother. Will went to the patio door and stared out as she talked.

"Hi, Mom. I'm fine. No, I'll be here until I decide to leave. No, Mom, the meeting went well." Her mother then told her that Charles was getting married on the Saturday after Thanksgiving.

"Thanksgiving? Why the rush? Of course I'll be there. I could never miss my baby brother's wedding. How long have you and Daddy known about this, and why didn't you tell me? Mom, I've been there, remember? I'm not upset to be the only one in the family who is unmarried.

I'll call that little rascal and congratulate him. Mom, I have a guest right now. Can I call you later?"

She hung up and turned to Will. "Mom thought I would be upset that my baby brother is getting married. I can't believe that."

"And you're not, I assume."

"I'm not upset at all," she said, emphatically, looking directly into his eyes.

"Susan, I love you. I didn't lie to you. Please believe me. I'll marry you today. I want to spend the rest of my life with you."

She said nothing, but was thinking of how desperately she wanted to say yes. He was the answer to her every prayer, but she could not see past the pain in her heart.

"Will, I deeply regret that our relationship has become a direct casualty of Price Bishop's machinations and those of his unwitting accomplice, Frank Otis. But you should know that I requested and received special compensation for the applicants that I feel should have been given more consideration. I would have gladly done that from the beginning."

"I know. You have every reason to be angry and hurt, but you are wrong about one thing. At no time did I attempt to exploit our relationship. I invited you to Atlanta because I wanted to be with the woman I loved, and still do. Is there a chance for us to get past this?"

"I don't think so, Will. I can deal with problems, but you have too many people involved in your life. I'm happiest when I'm in control, and there are too many things about your life that can chip away at that control. There are no hard feelings on my part. I wish you the best of everything."

Silent screams filled her head and became deafening. If he loved her, he would fight. He would try to convince her they belonged together.

But without another word, he walked to the door. "Good-bye, Susan."

She locked the door and went to the kitchen. She was in control. She had her dignity and her job. So why was she feeling such pain and emptiness?

Susan spent most of Saturday shopping at the Galleria. On Sunday, she watched Carl burn steaks and listened to Angie's advice regarding her love life.

"Willard Cartwright is an exceptional man, Susan. You might want to rethink crossing him off your list until you're sure about your feelings."

Susan carried that thought home. There was no denying her feelings for Will, but the weight of her earlier caution had intensified.

Back at her apartment, she took her heart to a different place and called her brother, Charles. Only slightly doubtful that he was marrying four months after his twenty-first birthday, she remembered the feeling she had for Stan and was thankful for her brother's happiness. He asked her to be a bridesmaid, and she gladly accepted. When they finished talking, she called her mother.

"He sounds so happy, Mom. I know he's young, but Charles always knew what he wanted. Just listening to him made me feel good."

"Did you agree to be in the wedding?" Tammy asked.

"Of course. I would never let my problems diminish my happiness for him."

Her spirits remained high through Monday morning. The atmosphere at work was refreshingly different. Everyone was friendly, and there was no Price Bishop to make waves. Susan was finally able to relax in her new position, even when Travis rapped on her door.

"I've thought about our last discussion, and I don't want to resign. My family is here. My kids are here. Most lenders no longer have staff appraisers, so I would have to hustle hard for less money. I want to stay, but only if you're sure we can work together without conflict."

"Our relationship is obviously a little strained right now," she said, making no promises. "But I'm willing to give it a shot."

"Again, I'm sorry for everything that happened, and I wish you well in your relationship with Rev. Cartwright."

"My relationship with Will is over, but thanks anyway." Wishing to end the conversation, she opened a file before continuing. "I'm glad you decided to stay. We need good employees."

It was slightly awkward for the next few days, passing Travis in the hallway with only polite smiles, but that was all she required. When she requested time off to attend her brother's wedding, Mr. Deeds threw in a bonus.

"Take that week off. You've earned it. I have very few travel plans for the rest of the year. I can't handle crises as well as you, but I'll try and fill in."

She thanked him for everything and hummed through the rest of the day. She felt good about her life. Perry was easy to work with, and the interaction with his department was an interesting change of pace, but Perry's attempt at matchmaker proved less than spectacular.

"One of my colleagues read the Cedargrove story and wants to meet you. I wasn't sure you wanted a fix-up date, but since you like basketball and I have four tickets, I thought you might like to accompany Jan and me to a Rockets game, and I'll invite Josh along. If you two hit it off, fine, if not, no harm done. What do you say?"

Against her better instincts, she agreed and met the three of them at Toyota Center for a Thursday night game. Josh personified everything she most abhorred about men since her divorce. He was of average height and build; in fact, everything about him was average—except his conduct. He yelled at the players and referees, voiced loud opinions about each call, and argued with another fan over a player's potential.

At halftime, they went for beer and popcorn and he managed to remain civil, though not particularly appealing. At the start of the third quarter, he yelled, "Sit down, all six of you," to a very large man two rows ahead. Mortified, Susan turned away in disgust, and Josh remained silent for the rest of the game.

Perry was apologetic the next morning. "I don't know what happened. I conferred with Josh on a couple of cases just after he passed the bar. He's usually the life of the party. He was trying too hard to impress you and came off as a boorish clod. I hope you weren't too miserable."

"There is no need to apologize, Perry. You've been a friend to me since I arrived here, and that means a lot. I enjoyed meeting Jan. She certainly has a wonderful sense of humor."

"That accounts for her ability to put up with me," he said with a smile. "Well, I won't attempt another match. Jan is sending you an invitation to our annual Christmas party, and I'll invite every single guy that I feel is potentially suitable and see if anything happens. How about that?"

She laughed with Perry. Every phase of the job was now going well. She made an official announcement of Price's resignation, but skirted discussing the reason. With Deeds's approval, she hired Price's replacement. She and Angie set up the new quality control department; hired two employees, including Angie's replacement; and promoted one from within.

Weekends were spent with Dino or at Angie's house. In her attempts to include Susan in her active social life, Angie enticed her to attend a mortgage banking dinner by promising the best peach cobbler in the world. Susan met a few members of the lending community that she had spoken with by phone. She and Angie drifted in different directions during the reception, but Angie hurried back to Susan's side before the meal began.

"Look over my left shoulder and tell me what you think."

Susan had no trouble spotting the subject. She allowed her eyes to travel the considerable length of his body. "That's Marcus Paxton, the attorney who came to the meeting with Cedargrove. I think he's gorgeous. What's his story?"

"Never married, bright, very sweet, and I'm sure you'll like him. I'm sorry I didn't think of him sooner. He did a lot of work for Sealand before it had a legal department. His specialty is family law. He still handles some of our probate cases. Follow me." Angie moved sideways, balancing her glass in one hand and guiding Susan with the other.

Feeling like a wanton female stalker, Susan allowed herself to be propelled through the crowd. Angie stopped close to the unsuspecting man, began a loud conversation, and deliberately backed into him.

"I'm sorry. I wasn't paying attention. Marc! I haven't seen you in a while. Where have you been keeping yourself?" she said, smiling.

Susan stood silently by her side.

"Hey, Angie. I've been around. Working like a dog mostly. What about you? I heard about your new position. Congratulations."

Susan watched his face while pretending to look past him. Deep-set hazel eyes luminously highlighted a rich, butter-smooth complexion.

"Thanks. I've been working hard, but I enjoy it a lot more than I did before. Here's a card with my new extension. I'm still close by. Sealand is growing and improving, in spite of the aggravations."

"I know. I was at the meeting with Cedargrove. I didn't want to, but it's hard to say no to Will."

Susan silently agreed.

"I also followed the story about your new program."

That was the opening Angie needed. "Then you must remember Susan Cross." She pulled Susan in front of her. "She's the best thing to happen to Sealand, and she's a dear friend."

Angie turned and winked. "Susan, Marc Paxton handles the family law division of his father's firm. He's bailed me out of quite a few messy probate cases."

"Hello, Marc," she said, extending her hand. "Nice to see you again."

"The pleasure is all mine," he replied, his lips stretching into a wide smile. "You were magnificent in that meeting. What law school?"

"None, actually. I have a few classes under my belt, but went for a MBA instead."

"I never would have guessed. How long have you been with Sealand?"

"I've been with the company since college, but I recently transferred to Houston from Ohio." Finding him enormously handsome, she began to fidget and prayed Angie would not leave them alone.

Angie not only stayed close during the reception, she invited Marc to join their table for dinner. The speaker was not interesting enough to take Susan's mind off Willard Cartwright, and neither was the good-looking man at her side, but she did find him quite interesting.

He was three years her senior, graduated Harvard Law School, and had never found time to marry.

After the luncheon ended, Angie hurried to catch another attendee who was leaving ahead of them, and Marc made his move.

"So, Susan, what do you think of Houston?"

"I haven't seen a great deal of the city, but I'm not too fond of the heat and the terrible traffic."

He laughed. "Please allow me to acquaint you with some of our more favored attractions, beginning with our superb restaurants. This weekend, if you're free."

"I'm free and I'd love to see a little more of the city." She scribbled her cell phone number on the back of a business card. "I'm staying at the Executive House."

*୫ଧୁ*

Susan's first date with Marc was a quick lunch on Tuesday, but the second was an enjoyable dinner on Friday night. She learned he was a wine buff with a big appetite, and she delighted him with details of her kitchen skill.

"You make biscuits from scratch? I don't know anyone who does that. I'd love to have breakfast at your place." The lilt of his voice when he said the word *breakfast* suggested his intended direction for their relationship.

Susan was on guard when he took her home, but was almost persuaded by his probing goodnight kiss.

"I enjoyed dinner." She eased from his arms. "See you tomorrow."

She dressed in jeans for a concert in Herman Park on Saturday. Marc was laid back and humorous and Susan enjoyed the outing. This time the goodnight kisses continued until his hand snaked under her top.

"It's a little late, and I'm a lot tired," she said, removing his hand.

"He's slightly aggressive, if you know what I mean," she told Angie the following afternoon. "He's entertaining and has a high level of confidence, but he's not a braggart. He plays classical piano and violin and competitive chess. I'm a pretty good chess player myself, so we do have a great deal in common."

"I'm glad," Angie answered. "See, there are a few good men in this city. I found one, and I'm sure you will, too. Maybe you already have."

By the time of their lunch date on Tuesday, Marc spoke with ease about his life.

"My ancestors were able to prosper in spite of the obvious obstacles. My great-grandfather owned a cotton gin, my grandfather acquired a lot of property and owned a general store in the Fifth Ward, and my dad was the first attorney in the family. I followed his lead."

Susan told him of her initial goal of pursuing a legal career. "I'm not taking any classes now, but I fully intend to continue, hopefully, next semester. I enjoy law very much."

"You also must enjoy a good battle if you took on Willard Cartwright. Most people shake when he walks into the room."

"Are you speaking from observation, or are you acquainted with Willard Cartwright?"

"We're well acquainted. My father and the senior Rev. Cartwright are good friends, and I dated Will's sister Terri years ago."

Susan was completely attentive. "Are you members of his church?"

"No, we're Catholic, but my dad has a lot of admiration for Rev. Cartwright as a minister. They're very nice people. Will is a genuinely concerned and compassionate man, not a grandstander. He's also a damn good racquetball player. Beats me every time we play."

Her relationship with Will was over and she had vowed not to second-guess her decision, but soon realized she was more interested in Marc's conversation now that Will was the subject. Hoping that Marc would be more than a distraction from her memories of Will, Susan met him for lunch on Thursday and accompanied him to a poetry reading at a club in the trendy Westheimer section of the city on Friday night.

In a conversation with her mother, she defined him as a bohemian intellectual with highly refined tastes. "That's a contradiction, but a nice one," she told Tammy.

She met Marc for Sunday brunch and he described himself as an odd duck.

"My mother was the disciplinarian in our family. She is Asian and very strict. I enjoyed things from my parents' world. Even as a child, I liked classical music and theater, which made me somewhat of a social outcast among my peers. I had a close-knit family, so it didn't bother me too much. I still find it difficult to find dates with similar interests."

"I understand. I've always been told that humans are paired by nature, and it's a simple matter of crossing paths with your predestined mate. I think that concept worked better when there were fewer people in the world. With the population of Houston alone, we might have a very hard time connecting, but I think we finally meet the right person." She smiled sweetly.

Marc was relaxed and enlightened, and easy to be with. Susan also relaxed and prepared to be swept away by his charm, but hesitated about taking the big step. He took one she didn't expect and invited her to his parents' home for dinner.

"They really liked you," he said when were back at her apartment.

"I like them, too," she answered, smiling. "And I like you."

"But?"

"But what?"

"You know what I mean. There's some kind of wall between us when it comes to intimacy. I'm not looking for a quick roll in the hay, but I sense hesitation on your part. Is it me?"

She knew what he meant and searched for an acceptable answer. "No, it's not you. I like you a lot; I'm just not into casual sex. I like moving slowly so I can sort of see where I'm heading."

He reluctantly accepted her answer and invited her to a gospel concert the week before her trip to Canton. He was on time and, as usual, very complimentary.

"You're beautiful. If our relationship doesn't work out, you're going to be a hard one to forget."

Susan wanted to want him, but Will was still very much on her mind. A determined Mrs. Whitehead had sent her photographs taken at the convention. At first she placed them in a drawer, but after rethinking her decision, she framed one of them and placed it on the nightstand next to her bed. She reasoned that she had to forget him with his face in full view, or suffer each time she saw him or his likeness.

They met Angie and Carl at the concert and the two couples sat in the center orchestra section of the theater. Susan's eyes almost immediately fell on a pair of broad shoulders sitting in the front row, two seats ahead. Shifting a bit to get a better view, she saw that it was Will. Sitting next to a handsome and refined gentleman should have been enough, she thought, but seeing Will made her realize anew that she was not close to forgetting.

The crowd turned when the opening act walked down to the revolving stage, and Susan's eyes collided with his. He nodded and smiled, lifting his eyebrows when he recognized the man at her side.

Susan did not enjoy the concert. It was difficult enough putting him out of her mind with no contact, but seeing him rekindled every vestige of the feelings remaining in her heart. And there was no escaping him at the end of the show, as Will's party blocked their exit.

She smiled and gripped Marc's arm for support.

"How are you, Will? Hello, Terri." She felt strangely relieved that he was not with another woman, even though she was holding another man.

"Hello, Susan." His smile was clearly forced. "It's good to see you again, Marc. How are you, man? How's your dad?"

"As ornery as ever. How is Rev. Cartwright? Dad said he's recovering nicely."

"He's much better, thank you. I'll tell him I saw you." His words were directed at Marc, but his misty eyes were fixed on Susan's face.

Marc greeted Terri, and Mrs. Whitehead came over to Susan.

"Hello, Miss Cross. How are you?" she asked with a motherly smile.

"I'm doing well, Mrs. Whitehead," she replied, accepting a quick embrace.

Will's eyes had not left her face. She blushed, wanting desperately to go to him.

"I know things are hectic this time of year, but after the holidays, if you're available, I'd like to plan that home buyers' seminar we discussed," Will said softly. "Is the offer still open?"

"It certainly is. As a matter of fact, I have already counseled three of the borrowers who attended our meeting."

"Yes, I know. I understand Sealand gave them preferred rates, and that you wrangled several builder upgrades for Mrs. Parker. She thinks you're a saint." He focused on her as if no one else existed. "I appreciate your working with them. Thank you."

"I want to thank you, too," Mrs. Whitehead added. "I don't know you very well, but I have a lot of respect for the way you handle yourself. You're a very special young lady."

"Thank you, Mrs. Whitehead."

They said their good-byes and she guided Marc around the crowd who had gathered to purchase CDs. Stealing a backward glance and finding Will's dejected look hard to take, she gripped Marc's arm, knowing she had to get past her feelings.

Over coffee at her place, Marc invited Susan to a special showing of Renaissance art.

"I don't know a lot of people who share my interest in art, and certainly not many who are familiar with paintings from that period."

"I'm sure I'm not as enlightened as you are, but I do enjoy art. The first painting that caught my eye from that movement was a Giotto. I don't remember the exact date of the painting, but I spent a lot of time studying the peak of the Renaissance."

"Maybe you're better acquainted with art than I am. Are you interested in other periods, or just the Renaissance?"

"Once I became interested I followed the artistic movements through history, but I'm not very knowledgeable about modern painters."

With Will's face popping up before her, Susan managed to stay focused until Marc mentioned something he observed earlier in the evening.

"Maybe I'm out of line here, but I detected a great deal of tension between you and Willie Cartwright. Was this all about the Cedargrove mess?"

Susan thought of what Will meant to her, even now. He was not just on her mind, but in her heart. His touch, his smell. The wonderful joy he brought to her life.

"Will and I could have had a relationship, but the Cedargrove thing destroyed that possibility."

"I don't mean to doubt you, but neither of you seemed to have moved past that relationship. I'm not trying to nose into your private life. I'm just thinking of what I would like to see happen between us, and that's not possible if you're still hung up on him."

She repressed her pain. "Will and I were just getting acquainted, but the feelings were intense. The fallout from the Cedargrove incident made me realize having such a high-profile person in my life would threaten the things I value."

"Such as?"

"I value my privacy, and I'm a creature of habit. I need to have a certain measure of control over my daily life, and not live waiting to run to someone's aid when the phone rings. There may be feelings left on both sides, but it could never work."

"I'm sorry if you were hurt," he said, tracing her cheekbone with his fingertip. "After meeting you, my family keeps quizzing me about our relationship. I hope to tell them, very soon, that you and I are a couple."

She smiled wistfully. "I hope so, too."

The music was soft and relaxing. Susan rested her head on Marc's arm and felt her fatigue turn to pleasure. Will was gone and Marc was there beside her. Even with Will in her heart, her body responded to the man whose arm encircled her waist and drew her close. *To hell with it! I don't have time for backwards thinking. This man is gorgeous.*

Marc lowered his face to hers and she leaned back expectantly. But instead of feeling his mouth on hers, she heard a shrill scream.

"You have a cat!"

He pushed her away, jumped up and backed against the wall. A terrified Dino scampered under the coffee table.

"That's Dino. He's perfectly harmless."

"Can you get him out of here until I leave?" His voice trembled. "I hate cats."

Susan took Dino into her arms and carried him to the bedroom. She tried not to laugh at the terror on Marc's face.

"They are the kindest and cleanest creatures in the world," she said, no longer able to repress her laughter. "I'm sorry. It's just that you look so . . . so ridiculous. He's just a cat. Domestic, not a wildcat."

"I was unaware that you had a cat. He caught me off guard."

The mood had soured. Marc left and Susan lay down on the sofa next to Dino until the phone rang. It was Angie.

"I hate to keep bringing this up, but unless you have a strong attraction to Marc, which I doubt, I suggest you call Willie Cartwright now. That man is head over heels in love with you."

"Why are you bringing this up now? I thought you wanted me to hit it off with the handsome Mr. Paxton, who, by the way, is ridiculously afraid of cats. "

"The obvious feelings between you and Will are hard to ignore. Besides, you and Marc have been going out together long enough for you to know if he's the one, and he's obviously not. If you felt the same attraction for him that you felt for Will, you wouldn't be alone right now. I know you're still hung up on Rev. Cartwright, and from what I saw tonight, he's still hung up on you."

"Okay, Angie, what did you see tonight?" She was assuming Angie had read the same pain on Will's face she had seen, and hoped neither of them could read her thoughts of falling into his arms.

"That man had tears in his eyes when you walked away with Marc. Carl saw it, too. His face was lined with love when he looked at you. I know how you value your pride and being in control, but those things don't keep you warm at night. If you don't want to call him, just go over and visit his church. I'll even go with you. That's how strongly I feel about the two of you."

"Okay, I'll go to his church the first Sunday after I get back, so plan to go with me. I don't know how he feels about me, but you're right about my feelings. Seeing Will made me realize just how much I love him. It's all still there, Angie, even stronger than before. It took all the strength I had to let him walk out of my life, even when I wanted to wring his neck. Later, I realized how difficult a life with him could be, and decided it would never work. Now, I think I'll spend eternity wondering if I was wrong. Maybe I should run to him. That is, if he'll let me."

"Take it from me, he'll let you."

The holiday slowdown at Sealand began the week before Thanksgiving. Travis was spearheading the company's Adopt a Family for the Holidays drive, and Susan assisted in organizing the donations. They worked side-by-side, sorting and bagging clothing and labeling each bag according to age and gender. The hostility between them had vanished, and Susan was glad.

She was doing a slow countdown to three o'clock, Friday, the time of her flight to Canton, when she received an interesting Friday morning phone call.

"Miss Cross, this is Lillie Mae Whitehead."

"Hello, Mrs. Whitehead. It's good to hear your voice." She quickly brainstormed and decided Mrs. Whitehead was calling about the seminar she had promised to hold. "What can I do for you today?"

"I remembered that you're from Ohio, and I know how lonesome holidays away from home sometimes are. We have special Thanksgiving services at our church, and I thought you might like to come, maybe to the Wednesday night service."

"Oh, Mrs. Whitehead, you're so kind to think of me. I'd love to come, but I'm going home today. My youngest brother is getting married next Saturday."

"That's wonderful. I'm glad you'll be with family for the holiday. I hope you have a safe trip."

"Thank you, and thank you again for remembering me. I plan to start visiting churches when I get back in town, and my friend Angie and I decided to attend your first Sunday in December service." She paused and added sweetly, "Rev. Cartwright is well, I trust."

"He's just fine. I'll let him know you asked. I'm sure he'll be very happy to have you at our service. Very happy."

Angie came bursting through the door just as she hung up.

"Girl, my kids are going ape over that cat of yours. You would think Dino was the prince of Egypt. Carl is going to kill all of us if they get so attached they start asking for one." She noticed Susan's pensive look. "Oh, no! I know that look. What is it?"

Angie's face broke into a grin as she listened to Susan's story.

"Told you. I don't care about that mess with Cedargrove. That man is in love with you. He probably put her up to call. I'm sure he also has that foolish pride."

"No, I don't think he was in on this. The evening he stopped by my apartment was when Mom informed me of Charles' wedding. Will knew I would be out of town for Thanksgiving. He didn't ask her to call."

"Well, she must have felt sorry for him and did it on her own. I sure felt sorry for him the other night. We talked about it all the way home and Carl, who opposes matchmaking of any kind, encouraged me to try and get the two of you together."

Susan left work feeling great. On her drive to the airport, she thought of nothing but Will and of visiting his church and looking into his face as he delivered the sermon for the first Sunday in December. She purchased an issue of *Cosmo*, boarded the plane, and relaxed. The phone call from Mrs. Whitehead had greatly increased her joy, making it possible for her to freely allow Will back into her thoughts. He had never been out of her heart.

She tore their relationship apart and examined each layer. It was the first case of instant attraction she had experienced. She admitted to loving him harder than she intended and to feeling a great deal of disappointment when he gave up without much of a fight. It was irrelevant now, she thought. If he wanted to continue his pursuit, she planned to allow herself to be captured.

She spotted her parents at the bottom of the escalator to baggage claims. "Mom! Daddy! I never thought I could miss anyone as much as I've missed you."

She clung to her father the way she had as a child. He was always there, so she had not experienced the separation anxieties of leaving home. She went to college in state and saw them frequently. When she and Stan married, they moved just four miles away from the home where she had grown up.

"I love you, both of you." She pulled them together in a group hug, thinking how simple life had been before she became an adult.

# CHAPTER 9

"Tell me about this new man in your life. Your mother says he's an attorney," Ralph inquired as they headed home from the airport.

"His name is Marc Paxton. He practices family law in a firm founded by his father. He represented Will and the others during our little confrontation, but his firm sometimes does work for Sealand. That's how Angie met him. She thinks he's great."

"What do you think?" Ralph asked.

"He's wonderful. Intelligent and intellectual. He likes art and classical music. We're going to an art show when I return. He's also handsome to a fault, and he hates cats. I don't think I could keep Dino if the two of us got together."

Tammy snorted. "Sounds boring. Have you spoken with Will's son?"

"Why should she concern herself with a man who caused her so much anguish, Tammy?" Ralph objected. "Some Bible thumper who is probably not going to be a good husband and who can't give her the standard of living she should have. Leave her alone. She's dating a refined young man now, a professional with a lot of promise."

"Your father doesn't understand, but I do. Regardless of how perfect a man may be, there has to be chemistry. You'll find the right man, honey. I know you will."

Tammy looked at her daughter over the front seat of the car. "Speaking of Will Cartwright—"

"Tammy, what's the matter with you?" Ralph interrupted. "We're not speaking of that preacher. Just because his father is one of your heroes from the olden days doesn't mean our daughter should go around letting him treat her the way he did. I don't care if he is a preacher. If I ever see him, I'm liable to break his face."

"Just hush, Ralph. I know the kind of man my daughter should marry, and I think Willard Cartwright Jr. is perfect for her. I'll bet he didn't have anything to do with that church mess, and I'll bet he's in love with Susan."

Susan smiled broadly. "When I was growing up, I would always warn my friends about the two of you bickering before they came to visit. Bobby had assured me that you would walk over hot coals for each other, and your little digs were just part of your love. I've missed it."

She felt their love and knew she was included. "Will did not have anything to do with the newspaper article. I know that now, and I'll tell you something, but only if Mom promises not to take flight again."

"Pay no attention to your mother, honey. You know how she is. What do you want to tell us?"

She relayed the story of Mrs. Whitehead's call and of Angie's blind-faith assurance that Will loves her.

"We're going to his church when I get back. The first Sunday in December. I think Angie is right about the reason she called. Now, don't carry on, Mom, but I have never found a man I wanted to be with as much I want to be with Will. Marc is interesting and incredibly handsome—pretty handsome—not the strong masculinity of someone like Will. I want to fall in love with him, but I'm still hung up on Will. I think the only way to handle my feelings is to give our relationship another chance."

"The heart wants what it wants," Tammy said. "Don't apologize for your feelings. Explore them. If you're in love with Will and he with you, don't let anything or anyone come between you. Men like Will don't grow on trees."

"Good," Ralph said. "If they did, you'd be out in the woods trying to find one for her to marry. Honey, you need to take your time. Weigh this thing out before making a decision."

"Thanks, Dad, but I've waited long enough. I want Will back in my life as soon as possible."

Susan felt totally relaxed back in her old room and enjoyed having her parents to herself for now, knowing their attention would be divided when Bobby arrived with the baby and Charles with his bride-to-be. She frowned at the bridesmaid's dress that was waiting for her, and thought the suggested hairstyle was a cross between Doris Day and Grace Jones, but kept it to herself.

After breakfast the following morning, she went to McMyrtis Department Store to select a wedding gift from the bride's registry. She reviewed the remaining pieces of china and settled on eight plates to round out a dozen place settings. She waited patiently behind the two customers, but froze when the tall man behind the counter turned her way.

"Susan!" Stan rushed around the counter and held out his arms. "My last customer purchased a gift from your brother's bridal registration, and I was wondering if you were in town."

A closed chapter of her life stood before her.

"Hello, Stan. I didn't know you worked here."

He looked at her quizzically. "Your parents didn't tell you? I see your mother in here all the time."

"My parents never talk about you." The pain of their failed attempt at togetherness was gone. Looking into his eyes, she only felt grains of sympathy. She accepted his brief hug.

"Did you just get in?"

"I arrived last night. How are you doing?" she asked, managing a small smile.

"I'm fine," he said too quickly. "My wife is expecting twins, so I work here on weekends to build a little nest egg for the babies."

"Congratulations. I didn't know you were married." His intense gaze was unnerving. "I just came in to get a gift for Charles."

"The list is right here. I just printed it for the other customer." He nervously placed the four sheets of paper in front of her.

"I already looked at the computer registry," she said, placing her credit card on the counter. "Just let me have eight plates."

"Yes, we've been married about seven months. We started a family right away. Do you plan to have kids?"

"Certainly not without a husband. Do I know your wife?" She had wondered where Stan turned after they divorced. She never inquired about him, and quickly changed the subject when her friends offered updates.

"I don't think so. She's younger . . . she's just twenty-two."

"What does she do?"

"Do? Oh, you mean a job. My wife doesn't work; she's never worked. I'm the breadwinner in our family. I'm doing quite well on the job." He turned and spoke to a gray-haired woman. "Millie, can you handle things for about ten minutes? I need to take a short break. I need to get eights plates for this customer." Turning back to Susan, he said, "This is my ex-wife, Susan Cross."

Susan wondered why he felt the need to explain their connection.

"I took this little side job just in case there are complications with the twins, but I'm doing great financially. We just purchased a house down on Saint Peter Street. A two-story with large windows. I'm doing great."

She knew the house very well. They had talked of replicating it.

Resisting the urge to smile, she said, "Yes, I can see." He continued talking, and she pretended to look at a grouping of crystal and he went in the back room for the plates.

"I just mentioned you to my wife. She was watching something on television that was taking place in Houston. How is it down there?"

"Hot as hell." She signed the credit slip and took the plates. "I need to have these wrapped, and I have a few more things to buy, but it was nice talking to you, Stan. Good luck on your marriage, and I hope you like fatherhood."

Without emotions clouding her vision, she was able to see the complex texture of his character. She now saw the insecurity she had previously missed. The thought of a working wife diminished his role as a husband and was, in his eyes, emasculating and demeaning. *God, I hope I had no part in creating that pathetic image.*

She walked through the children's department and her heart lurched. As soon as Will had mentioned children, she had started imagining a little boy who looked like his father.

"My mind began moving in strange directions," she confided to Barbara over lunch.

"Seeing Stan just made me realize how much I want to reconnect with Will, but it also made me wonder about our marriage. I loved Stan when we married. You've known me for most of my life. Do you think I'm too overpowering? Too controlling?"

"I know you, and I know Stan. His problems aren't your fault. Stan could never be the strong man you need, and you would have wasted away trying to be the passive woman he needs. He has the right woman now—at least for the time being. She's young, uneducated, and needy.

I'm sure he didn't tell you that she already has two children with different fathers. She is Sandra Becket's younger sister."

Susan was shocked. "That's probably why my parents never mentioned it. You're right. He has someone who needs his care."

"And you need to get back with your minister friend and make a life for the two of you." Barbara patted Susan's hand. "I was there when you fell in love with Stan. You were happy back then, but your face beams when you mention Rev. Cartwright. It has to be right."

Susan was grateful for the reassurance. She had missed Barbara and enjoyed spending time with her as the week wound down and all thoughts turned to Thanksgiving and to the wedding. Susan had lunch with Barbara on Wednesday, and then had her hair cut short before visiting her favorite aunt.

"Why did you get all of your hair cut off?" Aunt Virginia asked. "A woman needs that crowning glory, and you need to think about getting married, honey. Women were meant to have families. God made them that way," Aunt Virginia declared. "I think you should fine-tune your domestic skills and find a man to give you a good home and a few babies. I got an education, married, and had four kids. I still worked. Teaching school is a great profession for women. You'll have more time to spend with your family. That's important."

"Not all women want children, Aunt Vee. I do, but I love my career." Not wanting to ruffle the feathers of a mentor who had taught her to sew and cook, she listened to the anti-feminist views and realized how closely they mirrored Stan's.

"I really love Aunt Vee," she told Tammy at the wedding rehearsal. "I just don't remember her being so anti-feminist. Did she and Uncle Harry have a nice marriage?"

"They had a great marriage as far as I could tell, but that's because they were both dinosaurs," Tammy whispered. "Virginia ran around like Edith Bunker; 'yes, Harry, anything else you need, Harry? Can I lick your feet, Harry?' She was a great mother; that's why you liked her. She's the most domesticated woman I know."

"That does explain it," Susan answered, trying to smooth the puffy sleeves of her bridesmaid's dress.

"You can't do anything with those sleeves." Tammy folded the dress across a chair. "I do love Trish a lot, but that girl has the worst taste in clothes I've ever seen. Those bridesmaid dresses are *Gone With the Wind* revisited. Photographs of this wedding will get laughs for generations to come."

"I was thinking the same thing," Susan replied. "She is a nice person. So meek. I thought my brother would have chosen someone more dynamic, but if he's happy, then I'm very happy for him."

"I don't know exactly how to break this to you, but I think Bobby is also a dinosaur," Tammy said, laughing softly. "He chose a woman who will pamper him the way his big sister did."

Susan made a mental note to keep the pampering to a minimum in all future relationships with men. She helped with the holiday meal and enjoyed her parents' bickering. She saw that her father was more excited about spending time with his first grandchild than he was about the wedding. During dinner, Susan noticed that everyone at the table was paired except her and the baby. She smiled at her parents' renewed little tiff over the canceled wedding of Ralph's niece.

"They need more time. My sister spent a fortune, and they need more time. I don't know what's wrong with young people today," Ralph groused as he carved the turkey. "You have to wait to get married, and then plan your children. Everything has to be planned. Your mother and I didn't wait and we didn't plan. We loved each other and wanted to be together so we got married, just like Charles and Trish."

"Our kids are sure of what they want," Tammy interjected. "Not everyone is. Choosing the person with whom you'll spend the rest of your life is not an easy thing and should never be rushed into without thinking of every possibility."

"So what does that mean, Tammy? If you're thinking you should have dated more and you want to get back out there, you can just forget it. Nobody is going to put up with your mess the way I do."

"You put up with my mess? I'll have you know that I'm the one who makes the concessions in this marriage. You haven't changed one iota since you said I do. I've bent in a thousand directions just to keep peace in this family."

"Pay them no attention," Susan told a clearly perplexed Trish. "We've been hearing this all our lives. They love each other madly. This is just the show they put on for the rest of us." She shook her finger at her father. "I don't want to hear any of this when I bring a man home to meet my folks. You'd surely scare him away."

"If you bring Will's little boy home with you, I'll sit on Ralph if he starts to run his mouth. I want so much to meet him."

"Who is Will's little boy?" Charles asked.

Ralph took a sip of wine. "He's that preacher's son who made your sister's life miserable a couple of weeks ago. His father was one of those nose-into-everything slamming, sweating, and screaming preachers from back in your mother's day. I think she had a crush on him. She has never met his son, and even after he upset your sister the way he did, she still thinks he's the greatest man on earth. I think your sister would be better off with this nice attorney she's dating. Now he sounds like a real catch."

Susan was silent. Running into Stan had removed any doubt she had of a relationship with Will. Seeing him had made her realize the full dimensions of her need. She admired powerful men with strength, courage, and humility. She had been madly in love with Stan, and at the time, he seemed to have the qualities she needed to be happy, but there was much she had not realized.

She spent a restless night comparing the men she knew. Remembering that the "perfect husband is one with the perfect wife," she thought of her needs and theirs. Travis was adorable, kind, and intelligent, but limited by his own insecurities. Marc was everything rolled into one handsome package, but witnessing his flight of terror from a cat had altered her perception of him. She needed a confident man who would allow her to love him completely without demanding constant attention. She needed Willard Joseph Cartwright Jr. She knew her mother was only half joking about making concessions in their marriage. Her father was the steadfast and mighty oak tree. Her mother had relaxed her views on small issues over the years, while her father still held his original beliefs. She remembered the clamor when Ralph brought home a puppy for her and her brothers. Tammy had refused to entertain the notion of having an indoor dog, but relented when Ralph insisted it was best for the children. It had been a huge indulgence on her mother's part, but small in comparison to the enormous love her parents shared.

Susan considered the framework necessary for a successful marriage. Her parents, as well as Angie and Carl, were supportive and respectful of each other. Her aunt and uncle had shared the same antiquated views on the role each spouse should play. Love had many helpers.

Pink roses, streamers, and happiness filled the aisles of the church where Susan and Stan had married. She saw her brother, all grown up and handsome, waiting for his bride. Trish wore a traditional white lace gown with a multi-tiered skirt. *Who cares if I'm wearing a sickly pink dress with ruffles and puff sleeves? Their happiness is all that matters.*

Charles took Susan aside before leaving the reception. "Mom told me you were having a rough time in Houston, but you didn't mention anything when we talked. Is everything really okay?"

"Everything is fine," she answered, touched by his concern. "Work is going quite well, I have a few friends, and I told you about Dino. You would love him."

She stood with the rest of the family and yelled their congratulations as Charles and Trish left for Honolulu. Bobby and his family left for the short drive to their home in a neighboring town, and Susan went in to pack.

"Can we come in, honey?" Ralph asked, poking his head in the door.

"Sure, Dad, I was just packing."

She stopped and sat on the edge of the bed. Tammy took Susan's right hand and held it out. Ralph placed a small velvet bag in her palm.

"That was my mother's. She wanted you to have it. Tammy wanted to give it to you when you and Stan got married, but I told her to wait for another special occasion."

"Thank you, Daddy." She removed a gold chain with a small, heart-shaped locket. Inside was a tiny photograph of her grandparents on their wedding day.

"This is beautiful." She batted away the tears. "I love it, but why are you giving it to me now?"

"Because we're so proud of you," Tammy answered, placing her arm around Susan's shoulder. "You walked down the aisle when Bobby was getting married with your head held high even though your marriage to Stan was ending. Now you're here for Charles instead of whining about your own problems. Your father and I are so proud of you. No parents could be luckier than we are."

"Your mother's right, honey," Ralph added. "I'm proud that you make that great big salary, that Charles is going to be a doctor, and that Bobby has his own business. I'm proud of what you've accomplished, but you've all made me happy by being good people. Your mother and I can sit back and thank God that you are all exceptional adults."

"The three of us are very lucky, too. We have wonderful parents." She hugged them and said a silent prayer that, given the opportunity to become a parent, she would copy their style.

"You might think I'm brave, but I do get frightened sometimes. Mostly of myself. I saw Stan the other day."

"Yeah, we've seen the little flea standing behind that counter and looking pathetic. You're well rid of that weakling," Tammy declared.

"Is it possible that I *turned* Stan into a weakling? He wasn't that way when we married. Am I too domineering for most men?"

"I'll answer that. No," Ralph said, taking her hand. "Hell, no. Stanford was always insecure and fragile. With you, he felt bested, so he retaliated the way most cowards do, by exerting brute force. Unfortunately for him, he got the worse end of that, as well."

She dropped her head on her father's chest. "I feel sorry for him."

"Now you listen to me, honey. You are never to stifle yourself to boost anyone's ego. When the right man comes along, he'll be happy that you are the way you are, just as I'm happy to be married and madly in love with this overbearing woman standing here." He reached for Tammy.

"Your father's right, Susan. Just hang in there, and please don't try to change. Your prince will come. If not Will Cartwright, or this attorney you're dating, it will be someone equally dynamic."

"Thank you. I feel so much better after talking to you and to Barbara. I'm ready to go back to my new home."

When Ralph left to put her bags in the car, Tammy took her to the living room.

"I have something to give you." She took an envelope from a book, opened it, and placed a yellowing photograph in Susan's hand.

"What . . ." Her eyes widened. Her heart sang. "Is this . . ."

"Willard Cartwright Sr. when he was maybe twenty-one, twenty-two. That's Dr. Martin Luther King Jr. in the background." Tammy sighed.

"How did you get this?"

"My cousin Freddy took it at a rally in Washington. When he bragged that he had attended the rally and showed me the photograph, my eyes fell on Will Cartwright. One of the doctors offered me a thousand dollars for it years ago. I had almost forgotten about it. I want you to give it Rev. Cartwright. I'm sure it would mean more to him than it could to anyone else."

She stared at the likeness of the man she adored. "I can't believe the resemblance. I also can't believe the feelings I have for this man, and I don't really know him."

She didn't sleep at all on the plane ride to Houston. Remembering Will's arms around her made her dizzy. She heard his voice, saw his face, and felt the wonderful closeness they had shared, if only briefly.

She deplaned, retrieved her car from the roof level of the airport parking garage, and began shedding garments and fussing about the heat. "Did a calendar get stuck on sweltering?" She kicked off her shoes, sang with the Christmas songs already playing on the radio, and rehearsed her lines for the conversation she planned to have with Will.

As soon as she entered the apartment, Susan felt the absence of her companion. After dropping her bags on the bedroom floor, she decided to call Angie and see if it was too late to come for Dino. But first she checked her phone messages and heard a distressing call from Angie.

"Susan, call me immediately. Immediately, before you do anything else."

"Oh, God! Something's happened to Dino." Her imagination gone wild, she frantically dialed Angie's number. "I should have taken him with me. Daddy would just have to tolerate having a cat in the house. If Mom can get used to a dog, he can . . . Angie, it's me. What's wrong? Did something happen to Dino?"

"Susan, calm down. You have to calm down before I can tell you."

Angie's words usually sprang from her lips at break-neck speed, but now they were slow and deliberate. Her patronizing tone frightened Susan even more.

"It's not Dino. Other than being spoiled rotten by my girls and lying around on his big, fat butt, Dino is fine. What I have to tell you is very bad news."

"It's not the girls. Carl? Please don't—"

"Honey, we are all fine. Just calm down."

Her mind was spinning. It wasn't Angie, the kids, or Carl, and Dino was okay. There was no one at work she cared about to the point of hysteria, so it had to be Will.

"It's Will, isn't it? He's gone and got himself engaged?"

Angie didn't answer.

"Married? Angie, you're scaring the daylights out of me. Is it Will?"

"Yes, it's Will. There was an accident—"

"Will's dead!" The scream came from a body quaking with pain and fear.

"No, he's not dead. His car was struck by an eighteen-wheeler. The driver ran a stop sign going over sixty miles an hour in a residential neighborhood. Will was pinned inside his car."

Numbness had taken over. She gripped the phone with both hands. Her body was rigid. Her eyes were fixed on the wall. She couldn't speak or move.

"Susan? Susan, you have to be strong. Susan, answer me."

Trembling, she found her voice. "I'm okay. Is he . . ."

"The doctors are saying it doesn't look good at all. His brain is swollen, and there are possibly serious internal injuries. They think that even if he lives, he . . ."

"What?"

"They think there could be . . . God . . . they think his motor skills may be severely limited and that he may even be . . . brain dead. He has shown no sign of awareness. News reports said he was in a coma, and then changed it to unconscious, then back to comatose. I called the hospital and, after getting some serious runaround, I called his father's house. I told Rev. Cartwright I was your friend and that I needed to know what to tell you when you returned."

"W-w-what did his father say?"

"He said to tell you to get to the hospital as soon as possible. That's why I wanted you to remain calm. If you plan to drive—"

"Why him, Angie? Why Will? Aren't there enough lowlifes out there who could have been in the way of that truck? Why did this happen to Will?"

"I don't know, honey, but I want you to promise me that you'll sit there and calm down before attempting to drive to the hospital. The only thing worse than this would be to have something happen to you. It's still early. Why don't you call his parents' house first? Get a pen and take the number down."

"Why? Are you thinking that maybe he's already . . . dead?"

"I'm not sure, Susan. The news reporters kept using phrases like 'the doctors are doing all they can as he hangs on.' Just call his folks."

"Okay, I'm sitting. I'm breathing slowly. Will was in an accident, and I have to get to him. He's going to be all right. He has to be."

When Angie felt comfortable enough to let her off the phone, she alternated sipping water and taking deep breaths. Surely, God would not take him now, she thought, dialing the number Angie had given her.

"Rev. Cartwright, I'm so sorry to bother you now. This is Susan Cross. Do you remember me, sir?"

"Yes, and I'm glad you called. They said you were out of town. He's in bad shape, Susan. Bad shape. My wife just called. The doctors say he's just holding on."

Tears streamed down her face and her legs turned to rubber. "Do you think I should go—"

"The rest of the family is down there now. Go to him."

She hung up before realizing that she didn't know what hospital he was in or how to get there. Dialing the number again, she sobbed uncontrollably.

"Rev. Cartwright, I don't know where he is. Please tell me how to get to Will."

Susan broke a few traffic laws during her rush through the Sunday evening serenity. She had passed the medical center area only once and was not sure which hospital was which, but knew it was a sprawling community in itself.

"First I have to find the South Freeway, 288." She repeated the directions Rev. Cartwright had given her.

"McGregor exit coming up." She squinted at the signs until she found Ben Taub Hospital. Thankful for the ease with which she maneuvered her Jeep into a cramped parking space, she ran through the door marked "Emergency Entrance."

"Excuse me, can you please help me? I'm here to see Willard Cartwright."

A white-clad staffer asked if she was family.

"I'm his fiancée." The words came without thought.

Susan was directed to a glass-walled area in intensive care. The nurse took her to the middle section and cautioned her, holding her hand up until she finished speaking.

"He's unconscious. His family was in there a minute ago but they're gone, so I guess it's okay for you to go in."

She tiptoed into the sterile room. Her heart was thumping audibly, and her hands were cold as ice. Pausing just inside the door, she listened to the monitor's rhythmic bleeps, took a deep breath, and forced her feet to move. Will's head was bandaged, and his face swollen and distorted. His right hand was taped to a board, and his vein was puffed up around the needle in his skin.

Shock and disbelief mingled with foreboding. Inching closer to the bed, she touched the fingers of his right hand, instinctively fell to her knees, and prayed out loud.

"God, please give me the chance to let him know how much I love him. Please don't take him away."

Her mind began to rummage through the pages of her life, in search of something positive to hold on to.

The prayers were not just for his life, but hers as well. A weekend in his arms, a day on the beach, holding hands and laughing. No matter what fate awaited him and their relationship, she knew her views of love would be forever defined by their precious moments together.

Guilt was also a factor in her jumbled thoughts. Foolish pride and vanity had prevented her from responding when he had reached out to her. "I love you, Will. Please hear me. I love you so much."

Hearing voices in the hallway, she looked back through the glass and saw Mrs. Whitehead. Her aching head was spinning. She went into the hallway, feeling that her heart would explode.

"She's shaking like a loose hubcap." Mrs. Whitehead grabbed Susan's shoulders. "Get a nurse."

"I think she's about to faint," Mrs. Cartwright said, hailing a nurse. "Can you get some smelling salts or something?"

She guided Susan backwards as Mrs. Whitehead and Terri held a chair. Terri fanned her with a magazine while the nurse broke an inhaler under her nose. She coughed and sat upright.

"Drink this water, sweetheart, and breathe slowly." Mrs. Whitehead continued holding her hand.

Amy Cartwright took Susan's other hand. "You really do love him, don't you?"

Susan nodded and said, "With all my heart."

She regained her composure and looked at the tall, statuesque woman standing before her. Though they had not met, Susan knew she was Will's sister.

"Has anyone informed you about Willie's condition?"

"I-I was told that his condition is grave," Susan stammered.

Mrs. Cartwright introduced them. "This is my daughter Eugenia, Miss Cross. Jean is the skeptic in the family, but we're sure Willie can beat this."

"I was just wondering why you're here, Miss Cross. Unless I've been misled, you and Willie broke up because you accused him of engineering that Cedargrove mess. Right now my brother needs to be surrounded by people who love him, not the ones who caused him pain."

Stunned by the harshness of Jean's words, Susan did not respond.

"I believe my son will get well and walk out of this hospital, hopefully on your arm. Willie had nothing to do with that story in the paper," Mrs. Cartwright assured her. "He would never do anything to hurt you. He's in love with you."

"I'm in love with him, too," Susan said. "After all that happened, I thought it best that we not see each other, for his sake as well as my own, but I was wrong. Before you called me, I had already planned to visit your church to find out if there was a chance for Will and me. I can't stand to lose him twice."

A gray-haired man with a friendly smile touched her arm.

"My name's Clarence Bradford. I'm Amy's brother. Just call me Uncle Chitty. My nephew has great taste. You're just about the prettiest thing I've ever seen."

Susan tried to smile at the impish brown face, but felt the heat of Jean's scowl.

"This is my sister Dalia and my brother Chitty." Mrs. Cartwright took Susan's arm and steered her away from their stares. "I'm glad you're here, Miss Cross. Willie loves you. I know that, and I think your presence might help him recover. Jean means well, but as I said, she's the family pessimist. Don't take her too seriously."

"I feel the same way, Miss Cross," Mrs. Whitehead said. "When we saw you at that concert, I knew you and Willie had to get back together. I knew he loved you, but I saw that same look on your face, too. We talked about it later. Willie said your good-bye had been final and that you would not reconsider. I told him he was wrong. That's why I called. Willie's face lit up when I told him you were coming to church. He smiled the rest of the week until . . ." She cried softly.

Susan waited with the family, in spite of Jean's baleful stares. Since only two people were allowed in the room, she took her turn going to his bed, each time reminding him that she loved him. After dozing briefly in a waiting room chair, she awakened at 5:16 and prepared to leave.

"Mrs. Cartwright, I've got to put in an appearance at work. I've been gone for a week, but I'll be back as soon as I can. Please call me if there is any change."

"Before you go, would you please join me in a prayer for Willie's recovery?"

With tears in her eyes, Mrs. Cartwright took Susan's hand and led her to the bed. They kneeled together, and Susan said a desperate prayer of her own. She kissed

Will's cheek and left her cell and home phone number with Mrs. Cartwright and Mrs. Whitehead.

"I'll return as soon as I can. In the meantime, please call me if there's any change."

She drove home in blind numbness. She was determined for Will to live because that was the only scenario that made sense. If he needed and still loved her when he awakened, she would become his wife, his nurse, anything to keep him in her life.

The warm water of the shower washed away some of the knotted tension in her body. She relaxed just enough to feel the need for sleep. After starting the coffeemaker, she noticed the red blinking light on the phone and remembered she had not spoken with her parents. They would be up now, she thought.

"Mom, it's me. I'm sorry I didn't call you last night. The most terrible thing has happened. Will has been hurt." She told her mother the details and added her fears, "Mom, they don't think he's going to make it. They have really good doctors here, but each of the ones I overheard said brain injuries are unpredictable. Even when the swelling subsides, they're unsure of his level of recovery. His mother believes he'll get better, but his sister thinks there will be complications even if he does live. I'm so frightened. I don't know what I'll do if he dies."

Tammy offered to come to Houston. "You've been through a lot in the past few months. I don't want you to go through this alone."

"Let's wait, Mom. It's possible that he . . ." She couldn't say the words.

Stumbling into her office after retrieving a basket of mail from the secretary's desk, she sat wearily down, her head falling forward in exhaustion.

"Susan?" Travis walked in. "You're here early. How was your vacation?"

"It was fine." She lifted her head but avoided eye contact.

"Did you hear what happened to Rev. Cartwright? Talk about paying for one's sins. I heard he's barely alive . . ." He stopped and came closer. "I'm an insensitive oaf. You've been at the hospital . . . you're in love with him, aren't you?"

She nodded but couldn't speak.

"It's okay. I understand. I'm sorry, Susan. I felt angry that he was able to hold your interest and I wasn't. I was also angry that he hurt you, but I never thought anything like this would happen." He cautiously placed his arm around her.

"It's been awhile since I had an intense conversation with God, but I still have his number, and I'll use it for you and Will. Please try not to worry."

"Susan." Angie was at the door. "How's he doing?"

"There's been no change. He's shown no signs of awareness. I was there all night. His mother is trying to be optimistic, but the doctors aren't very reassuring."

Travis headed for the door and turned back, his eyes filled with compassion. "Susan, I'm so sorry for everything you've been through, and I meant what I said. I'm here if you need me."

"I'm praying for him too, Susan, and I'm optimistic, just like his mother." Angie sniffled. "He's going to be all right. You've got to believe that."

Trying to believe what Angie said, Susan filled her coffee mug and headed for the Monday meeting. Perry lingered after the meeting adjourned. Taking her arm, he escorted her back to her office.

"I can tell something is wrong. Do you want to talk about it?"

"Perry, it's Willard Cartwright. He's . . ."

"An accident, yes, I heard it on the news. Is he going to be okay?"

"The doctors are not at all positive. He's still unconscious. They've even mentioned brain dead. I've been such a fool, Perry. Will came to my apartment the evening after our meeting with the people from Cedargrove. He assured me he had nothing to do with the story in the papers, and I believed him. What I didn't believe was that I could be happy in a relationship where so many people depended on him, leaned on him, *and* tried to stab him in the back. I let him walk out of my life, and now . . ." She shook her head.

"I'm so sorry," Perry said, embracing her. "Don't give up. The one thing Houston has is an abundance of medical technology. I'm sure he's getting the best care available. He's a strong man. He can fight this, and you'll have to remain positive."

"I'm trying. I was there all night last night." She felt the need to unburden her heart. "I never should have allowed this Cedargrove mess to come between us and now, if he doesn't make it, if I'll never have a chance to tell him how I feel, I don't think I will be able to forgive myself."

He took her hand. "I thought you were in love with him. I saw it on your face . . . and his. Why don't you go back to the hospital and check on him and then go home and rest? Deeds won't be back until the week of Christmas, and there are no emergencies. We'll hold down the fort another day."

"I'll leave a little later. I need to focus on something else right now, and I'm sure there are a few things that need my attention."

She sorted her incoming mail, made phone calls, and then took Perry's advice. When she arrived in the intensive care ward, she found the Cartwright family huddled around the doctor. Unnoticed, she stood on the perimeter of the circle and listened.

"Swelling is our main concern right now. There's no fluid build-up . . . that's a good sign. It's just too early to tell. The ribs on his left side are cracked, as is a bone is his left arm, and he's badly bruised, but those things will heal. He could open his eyes any minute . . . or this could continue indefinitely."

"Doctor, is it okay for us to be with him?" Mrs. Cartwright asked.

"I think that's the best medicine right now. Don't crowd the room, but stay with him as much as possible. Talk to him, sing, pray, any stimulant you can think to use."

Jean moved forward. "Doctor, what about his emotional condition? Am I correct that any kind of stress can harm Willie right now?"

Susan's heart stood still as she watched the doctor rub his chin.

"Stress is harmful, regardless of the situation, but the love of his family is vital. Some would say that being subjected to anxiety could be harmful, and some will say anything that stirs emotion, either good or bad, can help him regain consciousness. Love is a strong emotion. Unfortunately, so is hatred."

A sharp pain cut into Susan's heart. Terri spotted her and nudged her mother, and they all turned. Susan bravely stepped forward.

"I couldn't help overhearing, and I want you to know that I would never do anything to harm Will. I love him, but I'm not family. If you think it best that I leave, I'll do so."

"Miss Cross, you must understand that my daughter is just trying to protect Will. I want you to stay here. I think your presence will make a positive difference. Will loves you. There's no way that could be bad for him." Mrs. Cartwright moved to her side.

"Thank you." She looked at Jean and Terri. "This is a trying time for all of us. I want to do what's best for Will, and I would never want my presence to make any of you feel uncomfortable."

"I'm just trying to look out for my brother, Miss Cross," Jean retorted. "You see, I never saw him in the elated state that my mother and Auntie are speaking of. I saw only sadness and desperation emerge from your relationship. When that whole mess was over, the meeting at your office, we sat at home and waited for Will's return. He was a broken man. That's the face I remember. You say you love him, so why didn't you believe him?"

"It wasn't simply a matter of believing him. In time I came to believe him, but there were other factors to consider in our relationship. I made a decision based on what I thought was best for both of us."

"Please understand where I'm coming from, Miss Cross. I'm afraid you'll stay here now because you feel sorry for him, maybe even guilty, but later, if God chooses not to give him back all of his physical or mental abilities, you'll leave him again. Losing his baby and having Tracey turn away from him, even blaming him for the loss of their child, was almost too much, even for a strong man like Willie. He's suffering now. Let him get through this before you come back into his life."

"I don't agree, but I do understand. Do you mind if I visit him one last time?"

"You go right ahead, honey. Talk to him. I pray that he will hear your words." Mrs. Cartwright's steadying faith seemed to have been shaken by her daughter's doubts and fears.

Susan approached the bed with trepidation. Fearing she would break down, she placed her hand over his, bowed her head, and spoke as if he was awake and listening.

"Hello, darling. I couldn't work this morning for thinking of you. I love you so much. You must hear me. I know you do. Please try and come back to us. So many people are praying for your recovery but I, most of all, need you back. There's so much I want to tell you, and if you'll let me, I want to love you for the rest of my life." She touched her lips to his stiff, bloated fingers.

Mrs. Whitehead was waiting outside the door. "Miss Cross, please keep coming to see him. Will loves you more than any of them know. I saw it in his eyes. I heard it when he spoke of you. Please visit him and talk to him. Amy and I are sure he'll hear you."

"Mrs. Whitehead, you don't have to beg me to see him. I want to be with him more than anything in the world, every minute for the rest of my life, but I can't take the risk that Jean might be right. What if hearing my voice upsets him further?"

Mrs. Whitehead took her arm and guided her to the far end of the room. "I don't want you to abandon him now. I don't know what tomorrow holds. None of us do, but if you love him, and I can assure you that he loves you, the two of you will be very happy together. Jean is very protective of Will, always has been. I'm sure she thinks you not being here is best, but I know better. You put the first real smile on Will's face since his baby died. I saw his joy."

Susan smiled and took Mrs. Whitehead's hand. "Please let me know how he's doing."

"I'll call you every day."

Jean stepped in front of them. "I'm sorry, but I can't help the way I feel. My brother is very important to me. He's a kind, generous man who has been taken advantage of more times than I can count. I don't know you, but I know you hurt him, and that alone makes me feel that it's best for you to stay away."

"No need for further explanations. You're certainly entitled to your feelings." Susan was hurt and angry and this time, unable to control her emotions. She responded in kind: "Just as I would have to live with knowing I caused him harm, you'll have to live with knowing that I might have helped him recover. Love is a wonderful thing, and I couldn't love your brother more than I do."

Not waiting for a response, she brushed past Jean and the rest of the family and hurried to the elevator.

Unable to sleep, Susan called her mother. As expected, Tammy was livid.

"Who does this woman think she is? Don't listen to her. If Will's mother and father want you to visit him, you go ahead and do it. Tell his sister to go to hell. If you're not up to the task, I'll gladly come to Houston and do it for you."

"I can't do that, Mother. She's only doing what she thinks is best. I'll just wait and see how things go. I pray that he'll wake up and be able to make decisions for himself. Will is not like any other man I've known. If I never have a chance to tell him how I feel, I'll have regrets for the rest of my life."

Angie called later, also outraged at Susan's story.

"I can't believe this. How could it possibly harm him for you to be there? Is she so blind she can't see how much that man loves you? So the Cedargrove thing wasn't his fault. It wasn't your fault either, but you were hurt personally and professionally. If you hadn't been strong enough to go in there and defend your position, this mess could have ruined your career."

"She doesn't know that, and she doesn't know me. Honestly, I would probably feel the same way if Bobby or Charles was lying in that bed." Susan chose a softer subject and relived her brother's wedding in hilarious detail. Before the call ended, Angie laughed and so did she.

Lying back on the bed, she pressed her hands to her throbbing temples. "I let him go because I feared the uncertainty of a minister's life. Now he's dying and I can't even be with him. I cheated him and myself. Right now, being in control doesn't mean a thing. Pain comes when you least expect it, and you fall in love when you'd rather not. Maybe the only certainty is uncertainty."

The hospital smell lingered in her nostrils, and the ghosts of what could have been danced teasingly around her. She tried to brush away the pain only to find herself encountering memories of Stan, the love she had felt for him when they married and the disappointment she had felt when his weakness smothered their future. Seeking comfort, her thoughts returned to Atlanta and the feel of Will's arms around her—his magnificent presence, the touch of his hand. She closed her eyes.

"Dear God, please let him live."

Susan's Tuesday was no better than her Monday. She plowed through mounds of papers, keeping as busy as possible, but her thoughts did not stray far from that hospital bed. As promised, Mrs. Whitehead called, reported no change, and added a personal note.

"Jean and Terri have to work. They're here only in the evenings. As far as immediate family is concerned, there's just Amy and myself here during the day. Will is here sometimes, but he wants you to see Willie as much as I do."

Susan thanked her but did not change her mind. "Will is on my mind every second that I'm awake, but I can't chance causing problems for his family and maybe for him. I greatly appreciate the updates. Just please keep me informed."

Having accepted Marc Paxton's invitation to the art exhibit, she felt compelled to attend. She kept a forced smile and tried to remain alert to his conversation, but it was no use. She could not focus on the paintings or on Marc.

"Want to tell me what's troubling you? You're not here at all."

"A friend is in the hospital. He had a bad auto accident and he's in a coma. I'm very concerned." Her smile was small and weak.

"Would that be Rev. Cartwright?"

She nodded.

He cupped her elbow and guided her to a quiet corner of the museum. "Are you in love with him, Susan?"

"Yes. Our relationship is over, but I never stopped loving him."

"I see. Let's get out of here," he said, walking toward the exit. "I won't pretend not to be upset. We've not known each other very long, but I had hoped that—"

"So had I. I'm learning that things seldom go as we plan or hope. I'm sorry about tonight. I've tried to focus on other things, but I can't. I don't know . . . if I had met you before I fell in love with him, I know things would be different, but I can't change the past. Right now, I'm not doing a very good job of dealing with it. I'm very sorry."

"Don't be. Willie Cartwright is a good man, Susan. If the two of you are in love, as much as I want you, there'll be no hard feelings. If things don't work out for whatever reason, I hope I can make you love me with as much passion as I heard when you spoke of him."

He took her home and she tossed and turned until sleep finally came.

# CHAPTER 10

Susan made it through the week with the help of daily updates from Mrs. Whitehead. There was no change in Will's condition. The only positive note was that his vital signs had slightly improved. Swelling around the brain was still the main concern, and time was not on his side. For every second he remained comatose, the likelihood of his recovery grew more distant.

On Saturday Susan slept late, made an appointment with a massage therapist, and spent the evening on the balcony with Dino. Feeling hungry, she made a sandwich and ate it in front of the television. Just as she was about to head for the shower, the phone rang.

"Susan, Travis. I just called to see if you're okay. I know you've been spending time at the hospital and haven't been getting proper rest, and I'm concerned." His voice was sweet and tender.

"Thanks, Travis, thanks a lot. I'm okay. I was able to get some rest last night and today, so I'm feeling and, I hope, looking much better."

"Well, I won't keep you. I just wanted to remind you that I'm here if you need me—for anything."

"I appreciate your concern. I really do. You were my first friend in this city, and that friendship still means a lot."

In the uncomfortable silence that followed, Susan wanted to reach out. Travis had been a bright spot in her life until his feelings progressed to ones she could not match.

"I won't lie and say I don't still have strong feelings for you, but I would never impose. As I said, I'm here if you need me."

She wanted to need him. She wanted to need Marc, to want him because he was wonderful and he was available, but she loved Will and knew that was not going to change. She thanked Travis and promised to call if she needed him.

"I had lunch with Travis yesterday," Angie said when Susan told her about the call. "We were in the deli at the same time and he asked if he could sit at my table. It was the first time I've actually had a conversation with him that didn't concern work. He's very sorry for helping Price."

"I know he is, and I'm trying to get past that."

"He started the conversation by saying how much he liked working with Tom Baden, and how the entire atmosphere in lending has changed since you brought Tom in to take Price's place. Then he mentioned the loan commitment, and finally said he was so glad to have you here. I let him talk until he said how sorry he was that you had such a hard time getting settled. I told him you didn't have a hard time getting settled; you had a hard time fighting off evil bastards."

Susan shook her head. "I'm sure he doesn't consider himself in that group."

"He's not stupid. He said he knows we're friends and was sure you had told me about him ratting to Price. Then he went on about how he had befriended you when you first arrived and that you two had spent a lot of time together. I know he saw the look on my face when he said you two weren't intimate, but he assumed your relationship was going somewhere."

Angie flexed her eyebrows, as was her habit when reaching the highlight of her message. "I told him you spent time with him because you liked him as a friend, and that the first three letters of assumed spelled the kind of friend he turned out to be. I also told him you had men swarming around to spend time with you when you first arrived. I made that part up, but I do remember being in the deli when Chance Howard said you were the first women he would gladly give up his black book to be with. Travis also heard; he was sitting at the next table."

"Chance said that?" Susan was mildly surprised that the head of accounting would say that, especially in public.

"Chance isn't the only one, but he's the cream of the crop. Women make all kinds of excuses to go to accounting so they can gawk at Chance, just as men come to the twenty-sixth floor to gawk at you. And why not? You're not just beautiful, you're stylish, intelligent, and, as my mama use to say, 'you got class,' and that's something money can't buy. Men and women both notice this, just as they notice the breathtaking and pleasant Mr. Chance Howard." She dropped her head. "I can't say I'm proud of myself, but I've done a little gawking at him, too, and I'm not into blondes."

Susan laughed. "You know you always make me feel better. Thanks for being here for me."

◈

On the first Sunday in December, Rev. Willard Cartwright Sr. delivered the morning sermon at Cedargrove Baptist Church. From his wheelchair, the message rang clear. "When I was in the hospital, I heard the prayers you said for me. More importantly, God heard those prayers. He heard and he answered. Please join hands and pray with me for my son's recovery. Ask God to awaken him and bring him back to us, to direct his feet back into this pulpit."

Sniffles were heard throughout as the congregants joined hands in prayer. The most heartfelt appeal came from the first pew, center. Susan sat with one hand clinched in Angie's and the other entwined in Mrs. Whitehead's.

Before leaving, she hugged Rev. Cartwright and told him how much she enjoyed his sermon. "I mentioned that my mother remembered you from your civil rights crusades, especially the summer you worked with Dr. King." She placed the photograph in his hand. "She wanted you to have this."

"My goodness." His eyes became misty. "Where on earth did she get this?"

"My mother's cousin was in college there and attended the rally. His camera caught only a bit of Dr. King's profile, but my mother recognized your face and kept the photograph. She received a hefty offer for it from a collector, but she felt it was a poignant moment that belonged to you and the dedicated members of that gathering."

His eyes blazed and then dimmed. "I don't know what to say. Give your mother my thanks. I'd love to meet her."

"And I thank you for your inspiring message. I can now say that I've heard a sermon from a man my mother greatly admires and whom I also admire. God bless you, Rev. Cartwright."

"Thank you, and thanks for caring about Willie. My wife told me about my daughter's reaction, and I want to apologize. We're going over to see Willie now. I want you to come by and say hello. I'll be there for as long as I can stand to sit in this old chair. I really want you to come."

Jean and Terri joined them, flanked by Mrs. Cartwright and Mrs. Whitehead.

"Hello, Miss Cross. I'm surprised to see you here today," Terri said, giving her a brief hug and standing back. "I think you should stop by and see my brother before you go home. I know you want to, and I think he'd want you there."

Susan tried to smile. "This is my friend Angie. She and I had planned this visit before I left town for Thanksgiving. Mrs. Whitehead invited me." She didn't feel any explanation was necessary, but wanted to counter his sister's doubts.

"Yes, I did. I told Will she was coming and he sat there grinning from ear to ear. That smile had been absent from his face for too long, and when his eyes can focus, I want him to see Susan and know that she loves him. I want to see that smile again." She began to cry.

"Miss Cross, please don't misunderstand my concern. I know my brother loves you, but I also know that he's been hurt—"

"Jean, we'll have no further discussions of this," Rev. Cartwright said sternly. "I just invited Miss Cross to join us at the hospital. I want her to feel welcome here in this church, and I want her to feel free to visit Willie. Sometimes our love is so strong that it smothers those it intends to protect. We love Willie and want him to be happy. Life will never be one long day of sunshine, but it's the raindrops that make things grow. Please don't make an issue of this again." He lowered his head as his wife assisted him in maneuvering his chair to the door.

Susan and Angie walked to Angie's car in silence. Angie started the engine and looked around.

"Well, where to?"

"Angie, I want to see him, but I can't deal with this. I don't want his sisters to feel that I'm intruding, and no matter what his father says, I don't feel welcome at the hospital as long as Jean feels the way she does. Did you see the look she gave me? I don't need that. Maybe they don't know it, but I'm hurting, too."

"Well, if you want my opinion, I think you should go. If you don't and something happens to Will, you'll always wonder if your presence would have made a difference. I'll go in with you if you want to see him. I think you'll feel better. We won't stay long."

The waiting room was packed with church members and family. Susan walked around the crowd and made her way to the door with Angie at her side. His father was in with him, and Mrs. Cartwright was standing guard.

"Go on in, Miss Cross. Will wants you to see him, and so do I." She smiled and held the door.

"Come on over here by the bed," Rev. Cartwright said, smiling up at her. "He was restless at first, but he's peaceful now. Maybe that means he is no longer in pain. I'll leave you two alone. Tell my son how you feel, and we'll all pray he can hear you."

Taking small steps, she walked past him and looked down on Will. She tried to speak, but the words never came. His eyes were closed and sunken, the stubble on his face had a sprinkling of gray, and his strong hands lay limp on the bed. It was more than Susan could take. She rushed from the room, determined not to cry, and praying not to faint.

"Susan. Honey, hold on." Angie was beside her. "I know it's hard, but you've got to be strong for Willie."

"I can't handle this, Angie."

"You can and you will, because when you go in there, you won't see him in that bed. When you look at Willie, you'll see the strong, handsome face you fell in love with. Stay with me now, Susan."

Susan felt darkness closing in and focused on Angie's face.

"Susan, listen to me. I don't think I told you this, but I've never had a wedding. I wanted one, so I'll just plan one for you and Willie. I have this cousin, Vernon Bailey.

He's a designer. We grew up together before he moved to New York. He's gender-confused, but that boy is good at what he does, and he's relocating to Houston. I'm going to call him and have him design a gown for you."

She squeezed Susan's hand. "Think about this. You'll have the most glamorous wedding Houston has ever seen. You'll walk down the aisle in this stunning gown, train and all. You'll walk down the aisle to Willie. Can't you see him, Susan? Standing there waiting for you? Standing, waiting for the woman he loves."

The Cartwright family, and a curious few from the waiting room, crowded around. Mrs. Whitehead brought a wet towel for Susan's face.

"Now you pull yourself together and go back in there and tell him how much you love him. Tell him about the wedding. He'll hear you. I know he will. And you just keep thinking about that smiling face waiting at the altar, and the story doesn't end there. We'll all come back to this hospital, upstairs, to the maternity ward. You'll have a beautiful, healthy baby boy who looks just like his father. You know how you love Willie's deep voice? Well, your baby will have that same voice. Can't you just hear him? Crying in baritone?"

Susan was alert, her mind straining to hold the image Angie had painted. She walked back into the room and over to the bed.

"Hi, honey. That's my friend Angie. She's a little over-wrought right now, but she's a very nice person. Do you know what she's doing? She's planning a wedding for us, and she says we'll come back to this hospital to have our first baby. According to her, we'll have a son. I love you so much, Will. Please don't leave me. I want that wedding. I want to have your children, and spend the rest of my life loving you. You can't leave me."

She stroked his face until a nurse came in to check his vitals. Susan walked out and found Angie crumpled in an embarrassed heap in the corner of the room.

"I'm sure you think I'm nuts. I could tell you were about to faint, and I didn't know what to do. I don't even know where those words came from."

"The words came from God." Mrs. Cartwright put her arm around Angie's shoulders. "I believe everything you said will happen. My son will walk out of here and he will stand waiting to take Susan's hand in marriage, just as you said."

Mrs. Cartwright's brother came over, his arms outstretched. "Miss Cross, I'm glad you came back. Willie is gonna wake up and talk to his Uncle Chitty again, and he'll marry you just like that lady said." He leaned close to her ear. "And if he don't, I will."

"It's nice to see you again, Uncle Chitty. I hope and pray you're right, and that it happens very soon." She smiled and then caught a glimpse of Terri and Jean sipping coffee by the window on the other side of the waiting room. Terri smiled when their eyes met, but Jean glowered with anger. Susan left Mrs. Cartwright and Angie deep in wedding-plan conversation and headed back to say good-bye to Will, but Jean cut her off in the hallway.

"Well, Miss Cross, I see you made the best of your visit. Such dramatics," she said scornfully.

"I've had enough now," Susan said, turning sharply. "I understand your feelings for Will, but is there more to this? You don't know me. I've never done anything to you, but I detect pure hatred in your voice. We were both hurting when we said good-bye, but there was no animosity between us, so why do I feel so much from you?"

"I'm not concerned about Will's future if he regains his health, but what happens if that handsome face you fell in love with turns out to be the slack-jawed drooling one in there now? Don't tell me you'll love and want to marry him then. You'll destroy him, Miss Cross. I can see—"

"Eugenia!" Mrs. Cartwright yelled. "What is wrong with you?"

"Now you hold on a minute." Angie pushed past Mrs. Cartwright and stood between Jean and Susan. "You have no right talking to Susan that way. She almost lost her job over that Cedargrove mess and, whether your brother was involved or not, she had every right to be upset. She paid a hefty price. Your brother wasn't the only one hurt, and Susan wasn't just thinking of herself when she broke up with him. Susan is the least selfish person I know, and you're way out of line here, sister. She's too polite to strike back, but I'm not. If you love your brother the way you say, you'd know that she loves him, too."

Jean moved away, but Angie continued.

"Susan is a woman—make that a black woman—in a white man's world. She's more intelligent and qualified than most of them, but she's the one always having to prove herself. I know. I was on that same stage, but Susan made my life better. She even went to bat for the people in Cedargrove against staggering odds. She got Sealand to waive fees that have already mounted to over well over sixty thousand dollars. She's unselfish, caring, and the best friend I've ever had."

"Jean, please don't let me hear you refer to your brother that way again." Mrs. Cartwright's eyes were filled with tears. "Will is going to recover."

Susan placed her hand on Mrs. Cartwright's arm.

"I shouldn't have come here today. None of us need this extra stress right now." She grabbed Angie's arm and fled.

"I can't believe her. She must be a lot older than she looks to be so hateful. I guess that was her broom I stumbled over in the hallway." Angie's voice carried across the corridor. "His parents want you to stay, and that should be enough."

"It's okay, Angie. As much as I love Will, it doesn't seem that our relationship is meant to be. I pray to God he awakens, but I don't think the wedding you described will ever take place. Not if I have to deal with this."

Susan kept busy preparing operation manuals for the new production manager. She and Angie incorporated all available lending regulations into very detailed guidelines for each area of production, including Angie's new position as quality control manager.

Susan accepted dinner invitations from both Deeds and Perry. She was comfortable with her stand-alone position. No man was required.

Marc called several times to see if she was okay and to check on Will's condition. She mentioned the holiday functions she was expected to attend and the fact that she dreaded going alone, mostly because she did not know a lot of people on the Houston social scene. He offered to accompany her as a friend, and she accepted.

A Board of Directors' formal dinner party was the first event. Thanks to Angie, Susan had found a wonderful salon that tended to all her grooming needs. She spent the afternoon at Fountain of Youth getting a facial, massage, manicure, and pedicure, as well as a shampoo and style for her short, easy-to-manage hair. Her holiday outfits were not exactly suited for Houston's weather, and she was relieved when the sixty-seven degree daytime high dropped to tolerable mid-forties before the event. She wore a red suit with rhinestone trim on the plunging neckline and cap sleeves. The skirt stopped just above her sparkly designer shoes and had deep slits on both sides.

Marc's eyes widened when she opened the door.

"You look wonderful in red. Of course, I've never seen you wear anything that didn't look wonderful on you."

"Thank you." Thinking of the Travis debacle, she cautioned; "You're a good friend and you volunteered for this, but I would never want to hurt you and right now, I'm still too wound up in the past to look ahead."

"I understand. I offered to escort you as a friend. I expect nothing in return but friendship," he said, his lips parting in a wide smile. "Of course, when two people are thrown together, things sometimes happen, so if you find yourself needing more than a friend, hey, I'm your man."

She felt comfortable, and Marc knew many of the other guests. They mingled during the reception and Marc engaged another attorney in deep conversation during dinner, but he remained attentive to Susan. When they returned to her apartment, he kissed her cheek and prepared to leave.

"The holidays are here, Susan. I know you're concerned about Will, but you can't go on this way. I am your friend and I wish you'd allow me to try and put a smile back on that beautiful face."

She thanked him and sincerely considered his offer. Will was out of her life. She would never forget him and what they had shared, but knew she had to try to love again.

"You're great company and I did enjoy myself. I'm getting better, but I don't want my dark mood to spoil your holidays."

"My holidays have been brightened by your company, and I'll gladly be your escort should the need arise again."

Perry gave a party at his home and Susan attended alone, as Marc was out of town. By simple elimination, she was paired with Travis. The two of them talked as they had when she first arrived in Houston, but her protective wall kept the conversation neutral. Her mind was now clear. If Will was permanently removed from her life, she would have to open the channels of her heart to other possibilities. She still prayed faithfully and refused to stop hoping for his survival.

Mrs. Whitehead still called with updates and Mrs. Cartwright called several times, the last to issue an invitation to visit Will, which Susan quickly declined.

"Mrs. Cartwright, as painful as it is to see Will in that condition, I would be there every second of the day if I wasn't aware of the discord my presence brings to your family. I'm trying to understand your daughter's anger, but I can't tolerate it. If Will . . . when Will awakens, if he wants to see me, I'll be there. If Jean is right and he doesn't, my heart will break again."

"Honey, Will loves you. There's no question in my mind about that. I can't control my daughter. Jean has a mind of her own, and right now she's going through some personal pain that makes her even more mistrustful. I know you love Willie and I know he loves you. I wish you would come to visit him, but I understand your feelings."

Susan wanted to disagree. They did not understand her feelings, and for the most part, neither did she. In a short time, Willard Cartwright had taken over her heart.

She tried to get into the holiday spirit, but nothing could penetrate her agony.

She accepted a lunch invitation from Perry and unintentionally blurted out her feelings. "I'm sorry, Perry. I didn't plan to drop this on you. I guess you're now the big brother I've always relied on. I hope you don't mind."

"I don't mind at all. I'm flattered that you feel close enough to trust me with your feelings. Unfortunately, ugliness tends to erupt during illness or death. Cheer up. I have to side with Angie. I do believe Rev. Cartwright will recover, and I believe the two of you will be together. On a brighter note, Angie is a very capable employee and very witty. I enjoy our conversations."

She loved him for being there and felt thankful for the others who offered comfort.

Her heart lurched when Laura interrupted the Monday staff meeting with an urgent call from Mrs. Whitehead.

"Miss Cross, his eyes are open, but he's not focusing. I think the doctors are giving up. Please come with me to see him. I think it would make a difference. You can't let Jean's doubts interfere. Willie loves you, Miss Cross. I know he does."

"I believe he loves me, and I know I love him. Please tell Mrs. Cartwright that I've not stopped praying or believing, but I think it's best that I stay away."

During a conversation with her mother, Susan opened her soul. "I don't know what to do. Every time I close my eyes, I see his face before me, laughing and happy. Then the scene shifts to that hospital bed."

"I know how independent you are, but you should not have to go through this alone, especially when you have family who loves you and wants to be with you. Let me come and stay with you until this crisis passes."

"Thanks, but no one knows how long that could take. With the holidays approaching, I know you're busy. Besides, there's nothing you can do but grieve just as I'm doing."

On Wednesday she was immersed in final drafts of her manuals when Ann came to the door. "Excuse me, Miss Cross. There's a Mrs. Oliver here to see you."

"My next appointment isn't until two. What is this regarding?"

"She only said it was personal."

Susan closed the binder and placed the papers on the end of her desk. "Okay, show her in, please."

Not knowing what to expect, she walked over to the credenza for the coffee carafe; when she turned, Jean was standing inside the door. She hadn't known Jean's last name, and was disconcerted by her sudden appearance.

"Good morning, Miss Cross. Thank you for seeing me. I didn't call first because I didn't want to give you the opportunity to say no."

"I wouldn't have said no. Please come in and have a seat. I take it Will's condition has . . ." Her legs weakened and she grabbed the edge of the desk for support.

"He's basically still the same. The doctors called us in this morning and asked about our long-term plans for Willie's care. We agreed to look into nursing homes in the area, but my mother acted in accordance with Willie's wishes and asked that they not resuscitate if his heart . . ." Tears fell onto her blouse. "A nurse came in and placed a red DNR on his chart. Nothing has ever hurt me this way."

"I'm so sorry." Remembering from her night at the hospital that Jean took black coffee, she poured a cup and placed it next to the trembling hand resting on her desk.

"It was easy to pretend he was sleeping when his eyes were closed, but now . . ." She stifled a sob. "He stares like a blind person, looking right through you. I believe this will kill my father. He's taking it harder than anyone."

Susan had listened to her talk, waiting for the part explaining why she was there. Finally, she asked, "Is there anything I can do?"

"My mother and father feel that you can get through to him, and everyone is angry with me for keeping you away." She spread her hands and bowed her head. "I don't know anymore. I'm so worried about my brother that I'll do anything to help him. I'll understand if you don't want to do me any favors, but if you love him, please go to the hospital for him. Willie doesn't deserve this. He's not a minister simply because of our father. His Christianity comes from the heart. He lives what he preaches."

Susan felt torn in many directions. "I stopped coming to the hospital because I love him too much to take a chance on your being right." She fought back a rage of tears. "I think your feelings are irrational, but I understand you were only doing what you felt was best. I have two brothers. The younger is the baby of the family and, I, along with my parents, spoiled him rotten. I would try in every way imaginable to protect him."

"It's not always easy being a preacher's kid, living by the turn-the-other-cheek rule. I watched both of my parents endure untold heartache, and they never stopped dishing love on the ones who wronged them. I've seen the same thing with my brother. That was certainly the case when Rev. Otis called the newspapers behind Willie's back. Right now I'm living in a marriage with a man who cheated on me with my best friend—in my bed with our children asleep upstairs. I can't stand the sight of him, and I want a divorce. He has begged for forgiveness, and my father has asked that I try and mend our marriage. I can't. The harder I try, the more contempt I feel."

Susan straightened in her chair. "I'm very sorry for your troubles. I'm sure you respect your father's teachings, but it seems unusually cruel to have to live that way."

"It's degrading. I respect my father's advice, so I'm being the dutiful daughter, wife, and mother. I guess you could say I'm a little bitter right now, Miss Cross. When I learned what happened with Cedargrove and how Willie was hurt, I saw this as just another example of what happens to those trying to do the right thing. Will would do anything to help the people in that neighborhood, and not because he's a minister—because he's a good man."

Susan stood and paced, searching for the right words.

"I love your brother, Jean. In the short time we were together I was happier and more fulfilled than I thought possible, but I've always tried to maintain control of my life. I set boundaries, I take precautions, and I avoid leaving controllable things to chance. With Willie, I saw that control slipping away, and I was frightened. I wasn't sure I was cut out to be a preacher's wife, and I didn't want to suffer or cause him to suffer while we were finding out."

She poured a glass of water, returned to her chair, and passed a box of tissues to Jean. "My doubts made me believe it best for all concerned to abandon a relationship that had come to mean everything to me. I know that if Willie doesn't recover, I'll always wonder."

"I was the last one to know about your relationship with Willie. I didn't see the happiness that everyone else witnessed. I also didn't realize that you could have lost your job over what Clyde Otis did. Willie praised you for being a strong woman. I suppose being strong doesn't mean indifferent or uncaring. You just handle your pain differently."

"We all have a story, a reason for being the way we are. I try hard to get beyond the pain of my past, including a marriage that I expected to last forever. When it didn't, I was devastated, but I knew my life had to continue, and I certainly didn't want to burden my family."

"Do you mind my asking what happened to end your marriage?"

"No, I don't mind. We were both young, but I felt all of the love and respect that one can feel at that age. I made a lot of career advances, my husband's confidence began to sink, and he blamed me."

Jean dried her eyes and sat attentively.

"The tension escalated and became physical. Needless to say, our marriage ended after that. I've run those things through my mind a million times, wondering what I could have done differently. I knew that any man who entered my life had to be strong and self-assured."

She smiled. "I transferred here from Ohio, and on my first day here at Sealand, I looked up and saw a man who literally took my breath away. Willard Cartwright Jr. swaggered through that door and my heart stood still. He was insulting enough to make me want to slap him and fascinating enough to shake my calm. I was only half angry with him. The other half was my realization that I had allowed a man to get under my skin and into my heart enough to shake my resolve. I was almost afraid to love him, but I couldn't deny the attraction."

Jean smiled. "From what I've heard, I don't see you being afraid of anything."

"I was afraid, and plenty confused. By the time we finished our insults and met on neutral territory, I knew the feelings I had were real and that my life would never be the same. I had several reservations about his profession, starting with having to carefully choose the things we talked about. I didn't know his position on . . . having a glass of wine, or sex. Woman to woman, I've never wanted a man one-tenth as much as I wanted him, but when we first spent time together socially, I found that just holding his hand, sitting next to him, watching him take the podium at that convention brought something magical into my life."

She paused to refill Jean's cup and then continued. "I returned from Atlanta and found that story, and in its aftermath, I exposed a few people at work who wanted to make me the scapegoat for something I knew nothing about. In the end it was not just a matter of believing Willie. What I saw in the future was frightening. Willie is a minister with a large congregation. He's a man of the people, because—as you said—he cares. There are a lot of people depending on him, and I can handle that. I don't need constant attention. I understand his commitment and the duties of his profession. What I can't handle is having those people rumble through our lives."

"So you didn't break up with him because you thought he deceived you?"

"At first, but I soon came to understand the role Rev. Otis played in the whole media thing. The ordeal was upsetting for me, and I saw what it did to Will. He was trying to balance his responsibility to Cedargrove, his beliefs, and our relationship. I didn't want to think of another failed marriage."

"Do you still feel that way?"

"I had made up my mind before leaving for Thanksgiving in Canton that I would allow our feelings to chart the course. The impact he has had on my life is overwhelming. I couldn't imagine happiness with anyone else. I still can't."

"What about Marc Paxton? Terri said you two were at the concert together. Marc is one of those men every woman wants."

"Marc is a wonderful, sweet, and loving man. I only found two things wrong with him. He's terrified of cats." She smiled at the image of Marc cowering against her living room wall. "The other thing is . . . he's not Willie."

Jean dried her eyes. "Thank you for understanding. I'll tell my parents and Auntie that you're coming to see him. If his love for you is as strong as what you described, he'll come back to you."

Watching her walk to the elevator, Susan hoped and prayed that Jean was right.

# CHAPTER 11

Susan punched three numbers on the telephone and spoke softly into the mouthpiece. "Angie, please come to my office. You'll never believe what just happened." While waiting for Angie, she thought of Jean's words and felt her heart sink. *The doctors have given up.*

"What's going on?" Angie ran in, breathless.

Susan told her about Jean's visit and the doctors' prognosis.

"So what are you still doing here? Go to him."

"I've got a meeting with Chance at one, and another appointment an hour later. I can't leave now." Her head and heart were both pounding. "We spent one weekend together, but I feel as if I'm losing someone who has been a part of my life forever. I don't know if I can go there and not fall apart."

"I'll go with you if you like, but you have to go."

"Excuse me, Miss Cross. I'm sorry to interrupt, but there's someone here to see you," Ann said, standing in the doorway. "Mrs. Cross."

Susan leaped up. "Mom! Oh, Mom, I'm so happy to see you. Why didn't you tell me you were coming?"

"Because you would have talked me out of it, and I knew you needed someone here with you."

"Mrs. Cross, my name is Angie, and if you hadn't come, I was going to start calling every Cross in Ohio until I found you. Your daughter is as stubborn as a mule, but I'm sure you know that."

Susan introduced her mother to her new best friend, and then recounted the latest news about Will's condition.

"Susan has an appointment she can't cancel," Angie said. "I'm starving, so please join me for lunch while she finishes her work."

"Thanks, Angie. I am a little hungry."

"Try to stay calm while we're gone," Angie told Susan. "We'll bring you something back. You have to eat." She looked at Tammy. "I want to get your phone number before you leave—all of your numbers."

Susan settled back in her chair thinking of the 'do not resuscitate' sticker on Will's chart. By the time Angie and Tammy returned, she had concluded her last appointment, cleared her desk, and was ready to leave for the hospital. She took a few bites of the sandwich they brought her, locked her door, and helped Tammy with her bags.

"I've heard things are bigger in Texas, but I didn't know that also meant the heat. It feels like I landed south of the equator." Tammy removed her jacket and threw it on top of her overcoat in the back seat. "Angie said you were just invited back to the hospital, so I guess I sharpened my claws for nothing. I know the Cartwright family is suffering, but that's no reason for that woman to treat you the way she did."

"It's okay, Mom. We had a long talk, and I think we understand each other better now. I'd be a raving maniac if something like this happened to Charles or Bobby. You know that."

Tammy brought her up-to-date on things back home. "Your baby brother is so happy with his new wife. He thinks they'll end up in Houston at some point. I want that same happiness for you, and I know you'll have it, with or without Will."

When they arrived in the hospital's intensive care wing, Susan found Rev. Cartwright standing next to his wheelchair. Seeing him on his feet for the first time, she felt hopeful and proud.

"There's Rev. Cartwright. Come on, Mom." She rushed to his side. "Rev. Cartwright, it's great to see you standing, sir. How are you feeling?"

"I'm feeling fine physically. I'm just so worried about my boy." He took her hand. "I'm glad you came."

"I want you to meet my mother." She looked around for Tammy. "She was right behind me. She probably had to go to the restroom."

"Mom?" Susan turned around and looked down the hallway. "She didn't go that way. I would have seen her."

"Some people are frightened of hospitals. I'll certainly understand if she is."

Susan spotted the formidable Tammy Cross huddled against a wall. "There's no chance of that. She's a scrub nurse. Mom, come meet Rev. Cartwright."

Tammy shook her head and Susan walked over and tugged at her sleeve. "What's the matter with you? Why are you acting this way?"

Tammy followed, but kept her eyes down.

"Mom, this is Will's father, Rev. Cartwright Sr. Sir, this is my mother, Tammy Cross."

Standing in her daughter's shadow, Tammy took his hand. "Hello, Will. I'm sure you don't remember me, but we met a very long time ago."

He looked up, squinting and frowning. "How do you do? Your name is Tam . . . wait a minute . . . not Tammy Spears? It can't be."

Susan watched, bewildered, as Rev. Cartwright stood tall and took her mother's hand.

"Baby, you go on in and see Willie," he suggested. "The rest of the family went down to the cafeteria. I just couldn't stand to smell that hospital food. It was bad enough when I was in here. Go on in. Stay as long as you want."

Susan turned and walked away, but glanced back in amazement and wondered how they could possibly know each other. Hesitating at first, she pushed the door open and prayed. Will seemed agitated. He rustled against the sheets and his eyes blinked with great rapidity, but failed to focus. Trying to remember what Angie had said, she strained to bring his smile to mind, to think of happy times to come.

"Hello, Will, it's Susan. I know you can hear me, so I want you to try very hard to focus on my face." She leaned down to him. "I'm here with you. I love you, Will. I'll always love you. Please wake up. We've got a lot of life ahead of us. A lot of happiness. Please wake up, Willie Joe. I love you so much."

She thought she saw a glimmer of consciousness in his eyes, but knew it was only wishful thinking. "My mother is here. I'll bring her in later. She and your father know each other. I'm not sure how that happened, but I'll find out. Jean came to see me today. I think she understands how much I love you, how much I need you in my life. I'll never find another man to make me feel the way you do. I don't want anyone but you. You've got to come back to me, sweetheart. You've got to let me show you how much I love you."

The swelling had gone down and, except for the beard and a couple of scratches on his face, he looked much as he had before. One side of his mouth drooped slightly, but the big difference was his blank stare. She leaned down and kissed his forehead and remembered Angie's advice.

"I hope you wake up soon, because Angie has already spoken to a cousin of hers that makes the most beautiful wedding gowns in the world. I trust her taste, but I don't really care about the wedding. I just want you in my arms."

She passed her hand over his face, hoping his gaze would sharpen, but it did not.

"Look at me, Will, please look at me."

She leaned over for a final kiss and felt him move under her.

"Will? Did you try to move your arm? I know you can hear me. Your parents are outside. Your father is doing much better. I left him standing next to his wheelchair and talking with my mother. It would mean so much to be able to go out there and tell him you're responding. Please try, baby. Please."

She stared at his blank eyes.

"You have to come back to us. If you don't, Angie is going to be really disappointed. She never had a wedding, so the one she's planning for us is very special to her. She also knows how much I love you."

She touched his chapped lips with her fingers. "I want to kiss you so badly right now. I want to feel your arms around me again. It was the greatest feeling I've ever had. It can't end this way, Will. Please hear me."

His eyes held hers for only a brief second, but she thought there was recognition.

"In the short time we were together, you loved me better than I could hope to be loved. I'll wait for you, Will. I love you so much."

She kissed his forehead over and over, hating to leave but wondering what was going on out in the hallway. The fact that Rev. Cartwright and her mother had a history was shocking; Tammy had never mentioned it.

The two of them were standing close together behind Rev. Cartwright's wheelchair and speaking softly. The conversation appeared private and intense. Susan was fascinated. Her mother was smiling coyly, the way she did when Ralph whispered in her ear.

Susan turned in the opposite direction and took the elevator down to the gift shop. There was nothing she wanted, but a couple of gift items with the Rockets logo and one from NASA caught her eye. Her father had a garage wall covered with mementoes from around the globe, so she purchased one of everything they had. She also knew that present circumstances notwithstanding, Tammy Cross would never visit a city with great shopping facilities without buying as much as she could get away with.

The Cartwright family, including Uncle Chitty, had returned to the waiting room when Susan went back upstairs, and Rev. Cartwright was making the introductions.

"It's good to meet you, Mrs. Cross," Mrs. Cartwright said, hugging Tammy. "I know my boy will get better and we'll all be family, so it's best that we meet now rather than during the wedding. Those events are so hectic."

"I don't want a big wedding. Will and I were both married before. As I told him, I've had a fancy wedding. Now I want a wonderful marriage." Susan looked back at Rev. Cartwright. "I know he's going to be well and when he is, I don't see how I'll ever be able to leave his side."

"Did you get any response?" Mrs. Whitehead asked.

Susan wanted to say she thought he had moved and that he may have tried to speak, but dared not raise their hopes in vain. "Not really. He was fidgeting quite a bit.

His expression changed several times. I thought I saw deliberate movement, but I'm not sure."

"Amy thought he moved his fingers earlier, but the doctor said it was just a nervous twitch," Rev. Cartwright said.

"Yeah, I experienced that as well." Susan added. "I just know he hears me. His eyes seemed to focus for a second. He heard me. I just know."

Mrs. Cartwright and Tammy chatted about Will and Susan's romance, and Uncle Chitty had found a new attraction in Tammy. Unfortunately for him, she did not accept his flirtation as well as Susan had.

"Oh, I know you didn't pinch me." Tammy spun around with her open hand poised for a slap. "I'm sorry, but I can't seem to remember your name."

"Just call me Chitty. I'll never forget your name, Tammy, baby."

Susan watched a smile stretch across her mother's face when she lowered her voice and spoke close to Chitty's ear. Susan and Mrs. Whitehead could hear her words, which belied the sweetness of her smile.

"It's good that we're in a hospital because if you pinch me again, old man, I'm going to break every bone in your arm. If you like your fingers, you'd better keep them in your pocket. Where is your wife? I know you have one. I'm sure she would want me to slap the salt out of you."

Susan did not react until she saw Mrs. Whitehead's grin.

"It doesn't surprise me that your mother would be the one to set Chitty straight. He's always been that way. He doesn't mean anything." She frowned. "At least I don't think he does."

When Tammy began yawning, Susan stood to leave, but went into Will's room to make a final, desperate plea.

"My mom is here, sweetheart." She sat on the edge of the bed and stroked his hand. "She and your family are getting along just fine. Except for Uncle Chitty. He really is a lecherous old dude, but Mom can handle him. She'll probably slap the stew out of him before she leaves."

His head moved slightly toward her, but his eyes remained walled and unfocused.

"I have to go now. Mom has had a long day, and she's getting sleepy. I'll be back as soon as I can. Look at me, Will. Let me know you can hear me. Please come back to me while my mother is here, so she can meet the man who stole her daughter's heart."

Feeling the weight of her concern, she kissed his cheek and left.

"They all seem nice," Tammy commented when they were in the car. "That one sister is a little bossy, but Willie's mother is—"

"Cut the crap, Mom. Why didn't you tell me you knew Rev. Cartwright? How do you know him, and please don't say what I think you're going to say."

"It was a long time ago," Tammy shrugged. "I didn't think he would remember me."

"Well, he did, Tammy Spears. Even if he hadn't, that's no reason for you not to tell me. How did the two of you meet?"

"When I tell you, you'll understand why I never admitted knowing him." She wiped her hand across her furrowed brow. "Don't ever repeat a word of this to your father or anyone in the Cartwright family—not even Willie. I was sixteen at the time, and we were on spring break. Mama tried to get me interested in college by sending me to spend a weekend on campus with your Aunt Estelle. I went to a protest rally with her, her roommate, and these two young men from Howard. One of them was a young and incredibly handsome Willard Cartwright."

Susan gasped.

"Before the evening was over, Estelle's friend, Frieda, left the four of us and never came back. Since Estelle and this other boy were paired off, that left Will and me. I was completely awed by him, and he thought I was another college student. Imagine how I felt. Sixteen years old, in D.C., and hanging out with the college crowd. We spent the entire weekend together. All of it. I never told Will my age, but I was stupid enough to give him my phone number. I never thought he would call, but he did."

"Wait a minute. Back up. You spent the weekend with Rev. Cartwright doing what?"

"Let's just say Will Cartwright put the divine in divinity, okay? I was so young and stupid. I couldn't get over the fact that a handsome college man could mistake me for nineteen. He was so sweet. He even said he loved me, and I damn near fainted."

"This is incredible. How am I supposed to act when we're all together? I'm surprised someone didn't suspect something in there tonight. They would have if they had seen the look on your face, and his."

"Susan, listen to yourself. That was . . . let's see, I was sixteen, I'm now . . ."

She mumbled, and Susan remembered that Tammy would never tell her age.

"Let's just say it was long before you or Will were born. When we're all together, just act like nothing ever happened. That's what I intend to do."

"Okay, so what happened next?"

"He called and your grandmother hit the ceiling. She told him I was sixteen and not yet allowed to date, especially a twenty-two-year-old divinity student."

"Wow."

"What my mother didn't know was that I had fallen madly in love. I pitched a fit when she wouldn't let him call me. I threatened to run away from home, the whole nine yards. We wrote to each other for a while, but his letters stopped and I never heard from him again. I followed his career for a long time, just wondering if he had really loved me. The memory was strong. Still is. Of course, I met your father, fell in love, and that was the end of my first romance."

Susan shook her head. "This ranks among the most amazing stories of all time. Why didn't you tell me? I would have understood. I do understand."

"I was sixteen years old and posing as a college student. I spent a weekend in the arms of the most adoring man in the world, next to your father, that is. That is not something you want to tell your daughter. I've never told anyone. Mama didn't know the whole story, just Estelle, and since she would have been blamed, she sure wasn't telling."

"And he remembers, too. That's amazing."

"I'm surprised at that myself. My life has been rather ordinary next to his. Don't get me wrong, I wouldn't trade my life with your father for anything in the world, but there was no one between Will and your father. I dated and dated, looking for someone who measured up, but none did until I met Ralph. Will might have been a divinity student, but he was hot to trot, so I'm sure he dated a whole troop of women before and after me. I've never regretted marrying your father and I couldn't love him more than I do, but I'll always remember that weekend."

She looked at Susan and dropped her head. "I remember what you told your father and me about marrying Stan. I didn't want to admit that I hadn't waited."

Susan recovered from deep reflection. "I waited, but if Willie had been the man in my life, I don't know if I could have. I'm not upset about you and Rev. Cartwright. It's quite possible that it was the most unforgettable weekend of his life as well."

"I almost passed out when you said the name Willard Cartwright. He said his heart was broken when he learned I was only sixteen. I've often wondered what would have happened . . . well, no use wondering. I'm happy, he's happy, and I know you and Willie will be happy. That's why I kept insisting that you try and make the relationship work. I could well imagine how enticing that man was."

Susan said nothing, but to her, it was a sign. She and Will were meant to be together. She was more confident than ever that he would awaken.

Susan and Tammy went to the hospital every evening, stayed late on Friday, and returned early Saturday morning. They stayed until noon, went to lunch, and then to the Galleria to shop. The telephone was ringing as they walked in the door of Susan's apartment.

"Miss Cross! Oh, Miss Cross! He heard you!" Amy Cartwright screamed into the phone. "I knew he would. I knew you could reach him. He heard you. He looked at me and spoke. He said, 'Mama, I thought I heard Susan.' You brought him back to us, Miss Cross. You brought my boy back."

Grabbing her purse and Tammy's hand, Susan ran back to her Jeep. "I knew he would come back. I prayed harder than I've ever prayed for anything. I knew God would hear my prayer, and I knew Will heard my voice."

She drove quickly but carefully, threw her keys to a parking attendant and ran into the hospital corridor. "Come on, Mom. Get ready to meet your son-in-law."

She found Mrs. Cartwright in the hallway and ran into her arms.

"Is he awake?"

"He's asleep now, but I want you to stay with him until he opens his eyes." She hugged Susan hard. "He looked at me." She wept. "He knew you were there. Thank you." Taking Susan's hand, she pulled her past the others and into the room.

Will's face was turned to the wall. His eyes were closed.

"The doctor came in and checked him. He's breathing well, and his temp and blood pressure are okay. It's still too early to tell if he sustained any permanent injuries, but he's awake, and that's the best we could hope for.

"Will, darling, it's Susan. I'm here, Will. I'm here, and I'll never leave you." She rested her head on the pillow close to his, stroking his fingers gently. "I love you, Will. I'll never leave you."

As she caressed his face, a faint sound traveled to her heart. It was the sweetest sound she had ever heard.

"Promise?"

Mrs. Cartwright, who had been praying at the foot of the bed, jerked upright. "He spoke. Willie? Can you hear me, son? I'm here next to you, and so is Susan. We're both here, Willie. Please try and open your eyes."

He moved about but his eyes remained closed.

"What did he say, Susan? Did you understand what he said?"

Susan answered through joyful tears. "I told him I would never leave him again. He heard me. He asked me to promise."

Mrs. Cartwright ran out to tell the others, while Susan kept stroking his face and speaking softly in his ear. Mrs. Cartwright summoned the doctor.

"He was awake. He spoke."

After a brief examination, the doctor smiled at the two of them. "Try and be patient, Mrs. Cartwright. Your son spent a long time in darkness. His awakening will be gradual, so don't get upset when he drifts off, and don't expect too much when he's awake."

Susan and Tammy stayed with the family until Tammy fell asleep in a chair next to Mrs. Whitehead. The next morning they prepared to visit Cedargrove Baptist Church.

"I can't tell you how often I've thought of Willard Cartwright over the years. I wondered if he was happily married, if he ever thought of me. Of course, when he learned my age, he probably thought I was a shameless liar."

"I still can't believe all of this."

"Just don't tell your father. I only told him that I had met Will, and this is not the time for him to learn otherwise. You and Willie are going to marry. We'll be family, and I don't want anyone to be uncomfortable with that."

"This will be our little secret, but honestly, I don't think I can sit there in church and listen to him preach without thinking of the two of you together."

"Why did you have to say that? Now I'll think that way, too." Tammy frowned.

"Don't kid me, Mom. You would have thought it anyway. If he was anything like his son, I'm sure it was quite unforgettable."

Her heart was light as they prepared to leave. She had slept the night before. It was her first restful night of sleep since the accident. She felt happy and refreshed.

Tammy was impressed with Cedargrove Baptist, and they both looked on with adoration as the elder Rev. Cartwright spoke from the festive pulpit.

"My heart is filled with gratitude this morning. My son is awake. I just spoke to the nurse, and they're taking him to a private room." He waited for the cheering to cease.

"I'm not going to make a speech this morning, but I want each of you to know that your prayers are deeply appreciated. Giving honor and thanks to God for His mercies, I thank you for your concern, and I especially want to thank a special young woman, who I hope will soon become an official part of our family. This is Miss

Susan Cross and her mother, Mrs. Tammy Cross. Please stand, ladies. Some of you have met Susan before at Sealand, and I'm here to tell you that these are two very special ladies. Very special, indeed."

After the sermon, Susan hurried to her Jeep and Tammy lagged behind.

"Hurry, Mom. I want him to be awake. I have to tell him how I feel, and I want to do it before the others arrive. What were your thoughts in there?"

"Honey, right now my feelings are indescribable. I'm elated that Willie has pulled through, and I hope and pray the two of you will marry. Angie bent my ear with her plans. Do you know she's already ordered the material for your gown? Her cousin is having it shipped from New York."

Tammy shook her head. "This situation really is inexplicable. I'm a very lucky woman to have known such a wonderful man and to have married one even more wonderful. I know your experience with Stan was disturbing, but I'm glad you've gotten past that, and I hope you and Willie have many happy years together."

Susan walked into the hospital laden with flowers and a scrapbook she had made of each day's news headlines. Will's eyes were open and, though his voice was gravely, his words were sweeter than honey.

"Susan." He reached for her hand. "You cut your hair."

"You noticed," she said, laughing. She carefully leaned and kissed his forehead. "I've been so worried. Thank God, you're okay."

"You made me a promise. I heard you say you'd never leave me again. Did you mean that?"

"From the bottom of my heart."

She hugged him gently. "I love you so much. I'll never leave you. Ever."

⁂

Susan didn't want to leave him that evening, but the doctors insisted. Each family member, and some of the church's congregation, had visited to praise his recovery. His speech became slurred and Susan helped Mrs. Cartwright clear the room. Tammy went outside with Mrs. Cartwright, and Susan kissed Will again and again.

"I know you have to work tomorrow, and you'll be tired afterwards, but—"

She placed her fingers over his lips. "I'll be here tomorrow, the day after, and the day after that. Plan to live forever, because that's how long it will take for me to tell you how much you mean to me."

Tammy went home Sunday night, making Susan and Angie promise to keep her informed. Susan rushed through her Monday morning workload, smiled throughout her meeting, and left at lunchtime to visit Will. This time he was wide awake.

"I've been waiting for you," he said when she walked into the room. "Someone was stupid enough to give me a mirror. I was shocked, especially before they shaved my face. If you can come in here for weeks and look at this wreck, you really must care."

"I care. I almost made the biggest mistake of my life, and now God has sent you back to me. I've read about things like this, but I never thought it would happen to me. We were meant to be together, Will. I know that now."

"When Auntie told me you were coming to visit our church on the first Sunday in December, I couldn't stop smiling. I was thinking of you when I saw that truck and when I lay there, going in and out of consciousness. I thought it was such a shame that I had found you, lost you, and found you again, only to have—"

"Don't. It was a terrible experience. You can talk about it if you need to, but let's try and look ahead."

"There is so much I want to remember and many things I hope to forget, but I need to talk about my feelings. I was semi-conscious for some of the time. I didn't realize how badly I was injured, but I couldn't feel my legs."

She placed her fingers over his mouth. "Maybe you shouldn't talk about it. I know it was horrible, but you're here with me now. We'll have plenty of time to talk about it later."

"I fell in love with you the first time I saw you. I wanted to marry you right then and there, but things kept getting in our way. I don't ever want to lose you. If I did . . ."

"I'm not leaving your side. You couldn't push me away if you tried."

❧

Will became an outpatient the week of Christmas, and Susan became a regular at the Cartwright home.

"They're all so nice," she told Tammy on Christmas Eve. "Even Uncle Chitty. The only time I sensed tension was when Jean's husband was there."

"He didn't hit on you, did he?" Tammy asked.

"No, but let's just say I wouldn't want to be left alone with him. Will doesn't like him, and neither does Rev. Cartwright. I could see it in their eyes, especially Will's. I can see a lot more than he thinks, and I'm worried. He's in pain and he still isn't moving his legs. I was there for most of the day helping Mrs. Cartwright in the kitchen and watching Will and his father enjoy football on television."

"That's great, and you're right to help in the kitchen. If you want to become a part of the family, don't act like a guest. Most women will decline if you offer to help, but don't offer. Just go in there and pitch in. That's the first thing I noticed about the women your brothers brought home."

"I did just that. Mrs. Cartwright kept saying I should sit down and relax. When I didn't, she finally said it was nice to have someone in the kitchen with her. She seemed surprised that I knew my way around a kitchen." Her heart sank. "I watched Will when he didn't know I was looking. I saw him flinching and squirming. The doctors aren't saying anything about his future, which probably means they don't know."

"Just remember what he's already overcome. I'm sure he has both physical and emotional hurdles ahead. By the way, I told your father about me and Will's father, and I'm so sorry I did."

"You mean Daddy is jealous of something that happened when you were sixteen?"

"No," Tammy grumbled. "He's not jealous at all. He could pretend to be a little jealous. I had told him about my brief encounter with another man when we first met, and he has been teasing me ever since I told him that man is Rev. Cartwright. He thinks it's hilarious. I might just find me someone else and leave him here to laugh at the walls."

Susan chuckled. "Now that's the reaction I would expect from Daddy. I want a man with the same strength and confidence."

"You have one, honey. I know things will work out. Just stay close and let him know how much you love him."

That was not difficult for Susan to do. She had declined Mrs. Cartwright's invitation to spend the night with the family, but returned early Christmas morning. She felt relieved to hear bits of Will's familiar laughter as she entered. The family room was packed, but when their eyes met, there was no one else in the world.

"You look great today." She kissed his forehead.

"And you look great every day." He smiled broadly. "Sit down. We can watch something else on television if you'd prefer."

"And spoil your holiday sports fest?" She hugged Rev. Cartwright. "No, thank you. I'll see if I can help in the kitchen."

The day reminded her of a holiday TV special. The door remained unlocked, and guests came and went. Susan had met most of them, but when a tall, striking woman dressed in red came in with a young boy, only the sound of the sports announcer could be heard.

She swished a mane of chestnut, and obviously fake, hair over her shoulder and sauntered across the floor. "Hello, everyone. Merry Christmas." She let go of the child's hand and hugged Will's neck. "Oh, Will, I just heard about your accident. I don't know why someone didn't call me, but I'm here now."

She kissed his lips, and a surge of anger washed over Susan. She looked at the perplexed faces in the room and back at the stranger, who was wearing the same red knit suit she had started to purchase until she decided it was too dowdy. Now the material clung to a voluptuous figure and the jacket was unzipped down to cleavage that was tightly clinched. Susan felt a thud in her chest when she heard Will's greeting.

"Hello, Tracey."

"I came to town yesterday and heard what happened. My mother thought you were still in the hospital. She hadn't called me because she thought someone in the family would have let me know. I called there and one of the doctors told me you'd been released." She caressed his face. "I'm so sorry for your pain. I would have been there for you had I known."

"How were you able to speak with a doctor?" Jean asked.

"I'm his wife." Tracey fussed with Will's robe and continued stroking his cheek. "I would have appreciated being told, but I'm here now."

Jean slammed the newspaper she was reading down on the coffee table. "You mean you didn't know about Willie's accident until yesterday?"

"You forget, Jean. I don't live in Houston anymore."

"You live in Baytown, not Beijing. The story was in the paper and on every news channel. How could you not have known?"

"I don't really have time to watch television anymore. I'm just getting my real estate business off the ground. I'm constantly on the go, and I have Danny to care for." She pulled the child into her lap. "This is my son, Daniel. Stepson, actually, but I don't like that term."

The easy laughter in the room had been replaced with blank stares.

"It's good to see all of you." She hugged Rev. Cartwright. "Hi, Poppa. How's my second favorite minister?"

Rev. Cartwright alertly bent his head into his hands to avoid her kiss. "I'm still here," he mumbled.

Tracey smiled around the room but stopped when she spotted Susan. "Hi, I don't believe we're met."

"This is Susan Cross, Will's fiancée." Jean's loathing was as obvious as Will's discomfort. "It's time to check that last batch of rolls. Wanna help me, Susan?"

Jean began ranting before the kitchen door was closed. "I can't believe that woman. Waltzing in here and calling herself Willie's wife. She's lying like a dog, too. She's not married. I know the sleaze she's with. And why would she bring a child here who is about the age Trey would have been? She's not worried about Willie. She's up to no good."

"Mom should ask her to leave," Terri said as she joined them. "If she stays for dinner, I'm leaving. I can't stand the sight of her, and I can see what her little charade is doing to Willie. You should go back in there, Susan. Don't let her do this."

Before Susan could think of a suitable answer, Mrs. Cartwright called her name.

"Will is a little tired, dear. He's going in to take a nap. I thought you might like to sit with him until he falls asleep."

"Of course." She watched Will brave the pain of movement when he maneuvered the wheelchair around the furniture.

"I'm back home for awhile, and considering where I've been, taking orders from Mom doesn't seem so bad. It was good to see everyone today. In case you're gone when I finish my nap, enjoy this special day." He grinned courageously. "Thanks for stopping by, Tracey."

Susan hurried to push the chair. "Your mom is right. Enjoy naptime while you can." She returned Tracey's stare with a phony smile and a nod.

Terri's husband, Jerome, helped Will from the chair and into bed.

Susan wrapped her arm around his neck. "We're finally alone. Do you know how much I love you, Rev. Willard Joseph Cartwright Jr.?"

"After all I've put you through, I don't see how you can. I'm sure the little scene in there was awkward. Tracey and I don't talk. Haven't since the divorce. I have no idea why she did this. I'm so sorry."

"Don't apologize. You didn't do anything wrong. I'm here with you, and that's all that matters." She leaned her head on his chest. "I made a promise. Remember?"

*❦*

"Everyone was at a total loss for words," Susan later told her mother. "Mrs. Cartwright's solution was to suggest a nap for Will and ask me to sit with him."

"She's a gracious lady," Tammy answered. "I would have just slapped the shit out of that woman. Do you think she knew about you and Willie before she came there?"

"Both Jean and Terri think she had been told he was serious about someone, but not that he was engaged. And since we're not exactly engaged, Jean's answer shocked me a little, too. Angie stopped by with a gift for the two of us that really made him smile. You should see it, Mom. She said she felt comfortable choosing the material for my wedding dress, but she wanted me to choose the design. She had her cousin compile a book of dresses and tuxedos, complete with fabric swatches. It's amazing. The last few months of my life have been amazing. I can't tell you how much I love that man, but I'm so worried about him."

"I know. Has his movement improved?"

"He can swing his body from the sofa to the wheel-chair with assistance. He's very strong. He'll wheel himself into the bathroom and back. It hurts so much to see him that way."

She spent the next week compiling year-end reports, which proved to be a difficult task. There were miscalculations and missing documentation that she knew could be attributed to Price's inefficiency, but she chose not to take that route. Even with the workload, her concern for Willie was foremost in her mind. When she arrived at the Cartwright home on New Year's Eve, Mrs. Cartwright met her at the door.

"Go on in, dear. He's waiting for you. He refused to take a pain pill so he could be alert when you arrived, so would you please see that he takes one? Jerome is napping upstairs. The rest of the family already went to the church for watch night. We'll be back a little after midnight." She took Susan into her embrace. "I hope you're still here when we get back."

"Enjoy watch night. I'll be here." She smiled and hurried to Will's bedroom. He was lying against a stack of pillows, watching television. Clean-shaven and alert, he looked as he did before the accident.

"Hi, handsome. You look terrific."

"No, I don't. I'm just a great big blob sitting around waiting for the woman he loves." He opened his arms. "You look marvelous, but you always do."

They kissed and she settled into his arms.

"I see that little smile or smirk, I'm not sure which, on your face, Rev. Cartwright. Something is up, isn't it?"

"And you have a suspicious nature, Miss Cross." His smile grew wider.

She sat next to him and ran her hand down his chest and up his ribs. "I noticed something when we were dancing in Atlanta. You're very ticklish." She pressed her fingers against his side. "Now, either you tell me what's going on, or I'll tickle you silly."

She poked him lightly and received a hearty laugh.

"You wouldn't do that to a sick man, would you?"

"If the sick man is holding out on me, you bet I would. Tell, or I'll tickle." She poised her fingers near his side.

"Okay, but I have to be sitting up for this, so move your beautiful body."

She held his hand and helped him push against the pillows. "Talk."

"The accident was terrifying, but there's something I need to tell you." His smile disappeared. "I heard you, Susan."

"W-what?"

"During the time I was out, there were things . . . sounds, voices mostly, and flickers of light. I heard your voice. I knew I wasn't physically moving, but in my mind I was running, following your voice, trying to find you. I heard the sound of movement around me almost constantly, waves of sound. I heard doors open and close, saw the light brighten and dim, but your voice was the only thing I recognized."

"You actually heard me?"

"My mother says it was your voice that brought me back. I can't substantiate that, but I can tell you that as I lay there in the darkness, I heard you speaking to me and I tried to answer. I heard you say you loved me."

She looked at him through misty eyes. "I love you with all my heart."

"Susan, I don't know how complete my recovery will be. I do have feeling in my limbs. The doctor spent a long time examining me this morning. He seemed satisfied with my progress, but I still don't know the outcome. What I'm trying to say is that through some higher power, I've found the one woman I want to spend the rest of my life with. I don't ever want to lose you again. Will you marry me, Susan? Can you take this broken and battered shell of a man into your heart?"

She looked into the eyes that had evoked fiery anger and blinding desire. Touching her lips to his face, she whispered, "You're already in my heart, and you always will be. Yes, I'll marry you. Today, if you want."

"I'm all for that, but we don't want to break Angie's heart." He took her left hand. "If you don't like this, you can choose another one."

"My God. I don't like it; I love it. It's breathtaking . . . and huge. There's no need to spend a lot of money on a ring. Simple bands are just fine."

He kissed the tips of her fingers. "I asked my friend Saul to bring over everything he had befitting a princess, because that's what you are. Auntie is the only one who saw it. She helped me pick it out."

He coughed and winced in pain.

"I'm getting your pain pill. Your mom said you didn't take one."

She brought the pill and a glass of water. "Take the pill and lie back a little. I know coughing must hurt, but it will help if you take this pillow and press it against your ribs."

"You're a good nurse." He stared at her and shook his head. "I love you more than I can say. My whole family loves you. Mama says she has another daughter, whether we get married or not. Dad said I'd better not do anything to drive you away, and Uncle Chitty said if I didn't marry you, he would."

"I love you. I love the ring. I just want you to get better. And by the way, we'll have to have a long talk about Uncle Chitty one of these days." She kissed her forehead. "Lie back and relax. Don't tire yourself."

"Whatever you say. You're in control."

"Hey, you two," Jerome called from the doorway, "are you engaged yet?"

"Yes, we are." Susan held out her hand. "I'm the luckiest woman in the world."

"And I know the two of you will be happy together." He hugged Susan and took Will's hand. "Congratulations, man. I need to run to the house for a few minutes. Can I do anything before I leave?"

Jerome helped Will to the bathroom. Susan fluffed the pillows and straightened the bedcovers.

"Think you can keep him in line until I get back?" Jerome asked as he helped Will back into bed.

"I think I can." Susan arranged the pillows around him. "Take your time."

She closed the bedroom door. "I think he's giving us a little privacy." She grinned, seductively, and sat next to him. "I know we'll have a lifetime to be together, but I don't want to waste one second."

She kissed him softly, enjoying his closeness and the taste of his mouth. He deepened the kiss.

"Keep that up and you'll get in trouble."

"I think a few of my parts still work, Miss Cross. I'm just not sure how rewarding it would be for you."

"I want you more than I can say. I just didn't want to cause you more pain."

"I'm hurting pretty bad right now, and you're the only one who can make it stop."

The lust she heard in his voice stoked the already raging fire inside her. "I'll be gentle."

Fighting to keep her urges under control, she unbuttoned his pajamas, stopping to taste and tease. He groaned her name, and she kissed him before removing her blouse and pants and hovered over him. "I hope no one comes home because I couldn't stop now if I wanted to. I love you so much. I'm so thankful you came back to me."

She knew he was everything she wanted in a man, a husband, and a lover. Control took on a new meaning. Her movements became more intense, but she stopped abruptly when he groaned.

"Am I hurting you?"

"No, no, baby. You're making me feel better than I have since the last time we were together. Please don't stop."

They rang in the New Year with a toast of ginger ale and a promise to never allow anything or anyone to separate them. The family returned and they celebrated. Susan thanked Mrs. Whitehead for helping pick out the ring and accepted the family's open arms. Her love for Will had brought another family into her life. Susan felt doubly blessed.

# CHAPTER 12

Susan received a convincingly sincere congratulation from Travis when he saw the ring on her finger. Angie coordinated the wedding details with Tammy and Barbara through phone calls and e-mails, but Will didn't want to set a date until he received a firm prognosis on his recovery. He did show Susan photographs of his house in the hill country, and they decided to honeymoon there.

His pain worsened and he was readmitted to the hospital on the twelfth of January, with Susan at his side. She sat with the family and prayed until a team of doctors joined them in the waiting room. Susan read the grim prediction on their faces.

When surgery was announced to relieve pressure on Will's spine, she felt a fist squeezing her heart. The surgeon explained the involved process while advising that the procedure was not very invasive, but required expert precision. Everyone held hands, and Rev. Cartwright led them in prayer. Susan prayed hard. *There are few more deserving men than Will Cartwright in this world. God, please let him walk.*

Susan's heart cried out when she saw him on the gurney, dazed but trying to smile. She kissed his cheek. "I love you, baby. I love you so much. Now, hurry up and get this over with. We've got a wedding to plan."

Susan sat with Mrs. Cartwright and the rest of the family, barely speaking during the three-hour wait. The procedure went well according to Will's physician, but a wait-and-see was the only prognosis they were given. Mrs. Cartwright was steadfast at her husband's side. Terri and Jean consoled each other, and Mrs. Whitehead stayed close to Susan.

When one visitor was allowed in recovery, Mrs. Cartwright insisted on brief visits from everyone except Susan. "Stay with him as long as you can. You brought him back once," she said. "He still needs you."

Susan sat next to the bed and held his hand. She spoke lovingly when he was awake and prayed each time he closed his eyes. "I'll be with you forever, no matter what. I love you."

Mrs. Whitehead came in just before midnight and laid a reassuring hand on Susan's shoulder. "Jean and I will stay until tomorrow. Go home, dear. You need to rest and stay strong."

Sleep was a few restless dozes for Susan, and ended with an early-morning phone call from Jean.

"He's awake, but still groggy, so don't rush to get here," she told Susan. "The doctors seem hopeful, so just pray they're right."

Susan didn't wait for lunchtime to visit, but took off after the staff meeting. She had called ahead for a very capable florist at The Empty Vase to prepare an arrangement of white calla lilies. With an armload of flowers and a fearful heart, she hurried to the hospital. There was no one in the waiting area so she pushed against the door and knocked, but there was no answer.

"Will?"

He was lying on one arm, facing the wall. His other arm was draped across his face. She could tell by his breathing that he was not asleep. After placing the vase on the nightstand, she went to the bed and poked her finger under his arm.

"Wake up, sleepyhead."

His arm came down and pushed her hand away.

"Will?" A wave of fright washed over her. "Will, is something wrong?"

She waited for what seemed like an eternity before he turned over, and when he did, his stare was much like it had been when he was comatose, except she knew he was fully conscious.

"What's wrong? Are you in pain? Can I get a nurse? Doctor?"

"The doctor just left," he muttered.

She asked, but was afraid to hear the answer. "What did he say?"

"He said I'll be released soon." His face was ashen, his expression angry. "Any day now, you can just come in and wheel me out."

"Will, you're scaring me. Tell me what the doctor said."

"Just that. I can go home very soon and spend the rest of my life in a wheelchair."

Susan's heart dropped. "I'm sure the doctor will prescribe physical therapy. You'll be walking in no time."

She bent to kiss his forehead. He pushed her away.

"Sweetheart, I know that's not what you want to hear, but you're not in pain, and that's a great start. We knew there could be complications."

When he didn't speak, she tried to sound cheery. "I love you so much. I'll be with you every second. I'll take a leave of absence from Sealand. I think they can survive without me for awhile."

She tried to lay her head on his chest, and again, he pushed her away.

"I'm so sorry, Will, but you can't let this get you down. We sat here for weeks, wondering if you would live. You're very much alive. We'll get through this together. Please don't push me away."

"I'm doing you a favor. You're a young, vital woman. Why would you want to be tied down to a cripple? Go on." He motioned with his hand. "Run for your life."

"Okay, now you're talking nonsense. We'll leave this hospital together and we'll be married as soon as possible. I prayed hard for God to bring you back to me, and He did. I prayed for you to recover from surgery, and you have. The fact that your legs don't work doesn't make me love you any less."

"Maybe you should have amended that prayer and asked God to bring me back whole. I can't drag you into this, Susan. I won't. What kind of life would we have? I'll join Dad in front of the television and you can watch with the rest of the family. Two cripples, just—"

"Stop it! I can't believe you're reacting this way. Where is your faith in God and in me? I love you."

"Sure, now you do, but what happens when your friends are out dancing and you're babysitting your husband? How will you see me then? You'll hate me, Susan. You'll hate me, and I'll hate myself. You and I just weren't meant to be."

Shocked, she stood and walked to the window. "I swore I would never leave you, and I meant it. I can also see into the future, and I see the two of us married and very happy together."

"Then you must be still playing that game Angie made up, because it would never be that way. I can't marry you, Susan, and I think it's best if you leave and don't come back."

"You don't mean that." She watched his disgust through the water welling in her eyes. "I won't stop loving you because you can't walk. I won't stop loving you—ever."

"Quit trying to be noble. It doesn't become you." His voice was hard, cold, frightening. "I'll say it again. Please leave."

Frozen in disbelief, she finally stood and stared.

"See, it's started already. Let's feel sorry for the poor cripple. Well, I don't need your pity, so leave. Please."

Susan saw traces of tears in his eyes just before he turned his back. She clutched her purse and stumbled from the room. Jean, Terri, and Mrs. Whitehead got off the elevator, chatting gaily—until they say her face.

"Susan?" Terri reached her first. "What's wrong? What . . . something happened to Willie."

Terri and Jean ran into the room and hurried back to where Susan and Mrs. Whitehead stood, clinging to each other.

"Willie wouldn't talk to us," Jean said. "Tell us what's going on, Susan."

"He can't walk," she answered. "He thinks he never will, so he asked me to leave."

"Oh, God." Mrs. Whitehead gasped. "Come on over here." She guided Susan to a chair.

Jean went into Will's room, returned shortly, and placed her hand on Susan's shoulder. "He says he can't marry you as long as he's in this condition, but he doesn't mean it. Just give him time."

"And what am I supposed to do? He doesn't want me here."

She hurried into the elevator, dazed and heartbroken. Mrs. Whitehead and Mrs. Cartwright called her later, but Will had not rescinded his rejection. Susan went back early the following morning. Mrs. Cartwright met her in the hallway.

"I'm so sorry, Susan. He asked me not to let you come in the room. I know he doesn't mean it, but he's a proud man. This whole thing is too much for him right now. Just have patience. The doctor will be in shortly. Let's pray there's a positive change."

Susan started to leave but stopped when she saw Tracey coming out of Will's room. "Okay, it's my turn to ask questions. What's going on here? He doesn't want to see me, but she's welcome?"

"I'm sorry, honey." Mrs. Cartwright shook her head. "She was here when I arrived, sitting there talking to him about some stupid deal she's working on."

"Okay, I guess that says it all." Susan went back to the office and into Angie's arms.

"I can't take it anymore. This yo-yo relationship, worrying myself sick over his condition. It's making me crazy, Angie."

She called Mrs. Cartwright's cellphone at lunchtime, but Will had not changed his mind. Feeling worse than she had when he was comatose, Susan went to the hospital after work. Rev. Cartwright was with Will.

"Can I come in?"

Will turned away. "No. I've asked you not to come here. Just let it go, Susan. I'm not the man for you. I'm a cripple with little hope of change. Go back to Marc. The two of you looked quite handsome together."

"That's not fair, Will. I love you. I want to be with you."

"I don't want you here. You're just making this worse for yourself and for me. Go on with your life. Pretend we never met."

Susan went home but could not sleep. Staring at the mirror, she saw the toll pain and anxiety had taken on her face. Her eyes sagged, and the corners of her mouth seemed permanently downcast. Nothing appeared real. The weeks leading up to now seemed like a dream, or a very sad movie.

She avoided talking about her feelings, even with her mother. There was nothing left to say. Hours ticked by the next day. Realizing everyone had gone but the cleaning crew, Susan rested her head on the desk and tried to block away the love, the disappointment, and the pain. The message light on her phone was blinking when she got home, and the clock read 8:35.

She sprawled across the bed, wounded and drained. No longer able to ignore the ringing telephone, she picked up the cordless and mumbled hello.

"Susan? I know you're not asleep this early," Tammy said. "Did you just leave the hospital?"

"No, I'm just very tired, Mom. This running back and forth is catching up with me. Can I call you tomorrow?"

She had barely hung up when the calls began. Mrs. Whitehead and Mrs. Cartwright, both saying Willie was in shock and not himself. Angie called, and then Terri with the same message. Their words did little to soothe

the pain. She had endured too much heartache during her relationship with Will. She was through.

Angie was waiting at her office door the next morning. "I couldn't sleep last night, and I know you didn't. I hate to say this, but this little merry-go-round has to stop. You look drained."

"I am drained." She removed the ring from her finger. "Can I ask you to take this to Mrs. Cartwright, Mrs. Whitehead, anyone in the family?"

"No, you can't return this ring. He'll snap out of it. I know he will."

"I called on my way to work. He told me good-bye, asked me to please leave him alone, and hung up. I want him to have his ring back, and I'll get on with my life. That's not the way I want it; that's the way it is."

*❦*

Susan worked on the files and stack of papers on her desk until Angie's assistant rapped on her door just after eleven o'clock.

"Sorry to bother you, Miss Cross, but I need a signature on this report and Angie isn't back yet."

"That's okay, Shauna." She took the papers and realized what Shauna had said. "Did Angie go to lunch already?"

"I don't think so. She said she had an emergency and left about two hours ago."

Concerned, Susan signed the report, waited for Shauna to leave, and then dialed Angie's cell number. "Are you okay?"

"I'm turning into the parking lot. Hold on and I'll tell you when I get upstairs."

When she learned Angie had gone to see Will, Susan shook her head. "Don't you get it? I was wrong. We're not meant to be together. Didn't he tell you that?"

"No." Angie shook her head and held out her hand. "Put this back on your finger and get over to that hospital. He wants to see you." She smiled. "Now."

"I don't think so, Angie. I can't keep going through this, not even for Will. Do you realize how my life has seesawed since I've been in Houston?"

Angie started to speak and Susan talked louder. "I get a promotion that's too good to be true, so I wonder if it is. A stranger walks in my first day on the job and gives me another reason to wonder. He pisses me off and takes my breath away at the same time, and I give it right back to him. We get together, we part, I suffer. I guess he suffered, too. I come back home after convincing myself to find out if we can make it work, and he's comatose. I damn near lose my mind with worry, he comes back, we get engaged, and now we're apart again. On top of that, the ex-wife he claims to have no contact with waltzes in and takes my place at his side. I can't deal with this anymore. I don't want to. I know you're trying to help, Angie, but it won't work. There are too many women in Will's life, so I'll gracefully, and at his request, step aside."

"I know you're upset, and with good reason. That's why I went down there. I told Jean that I was concerned about you just like she was concerned about her brother, and though I realize he's going through a tough time, I needed answers."

She took a deep breath and continued. "Just as I finished giving her my version of what happened, his ex-wife came back. I thought Jean was going to faint. She went into the room and we listened outside the door. She was talking to Will about some real estate deal she's trying to close. Jean called her out of Will's room, grabbed a handful of that fake hair and pulled her to the elevator."

Susan gasped. "She did that?"

"She did, and I was right there to back her up. She told Tracey to never set foot near her brother again or she would kick her ass. Jean accused her of trying to get back in Will's life because she needs money for this deal she keeps talking about. I think she's right."

"You really think this woman would pull some crap like that when Will is lying there suffering? That's pretty low."

"She's a bitch, plain and simple. I don't know if she was that way when she married him or not, but she is definitely a bitch now." Angie hugged Susan's shoulders. "Now, you have to go to the hospital. I wouldn't tell you to go without good reason. You were right all along. You two do belong together. The wait will only make it that much sweeter. Go, now. That good-looking man needs you, and believe me, he won't ask you to leave."

Taking her purse from the credenza, Susan spoke over her shoulder. "Okay, I'll go, but if I'm invited out of there one more time, I'm never going back."

Glancing apprehensively at Angie's smiling face, she left and hurried to her car. The drive was short, and not knowing what to expect, she stood by the elevator and tried to prepare for another disappointment. Mrs. Cartwright was waiting in the hallway.

"Miss Cross. Wait here for just a minute."

She hurried away and Susan inched closer to Will's door. Mrs. Cartwright came out smiling.

"Go on in. He's waiting for you."

Susan got the same sly look she had received from Angie. She pushed the door open just enough to peep inside.

"Come on in." Will was standing. Flanked by Mrs. Whitehead and a nurse, he leaned on a walker and took shaky steps before sitting on the bed and holding out his arms. "First, tell me what a fool I am, and then please say you'll forgive me."

"You're walking."

She stood inside the door, waiting for her heart to react. Mrs. Whitehead and the nurse hurried from the room.

"Not very well, but this will do for now. It seems I have to keep saying this, but once again, I'm sorry. When Dr. Hines told me—"

"I understand your apprehensions, but you didn't trust me. You didn't believe I could still love you, and that was so unfair. You pushed me away. It hurt, Will."

"I know. We both keep trying to make it easier for the other, and in the process we cause a lot of pain. I'm so sorry, but you're wrong; I did believe you. I knew you would be there with me even if I never walked. That's why I had to let you go. I couldn't allow you to spend your life loving a man who wasn't all you should have. I know I hurt you. I just thought it would be best to do it now rather than over the course of our life together. Please forgive me."

She stood in place next to the door. "When did this happen? When did you first walk?"

"I moved my right foot yesterday, but there wasn't much after that. I was afraid to hope. The therapist came in this morning and started flexing my feet. I felt a slight rush and realized I could move my toes. Dr. Hines came in and jabbed me with a pin, and it hurt like hell. They helped me stand." He closed his eyes.

"I prayed and tried with every bit of strength and faith in me. I felt my foot move. Just as Dr. Hines told me things looked great, my mother stormed into the room with Angie on her heels. Between the two of them, I feared I'd better be able to run in case they started flogging me. Mama had already fussed at me, but Angie gave me the full dose, including telling me what a rough time Jean gave you when I was unconscious. They both said she had been vicious, but you kept coming back. On top of that, my ex-wife barged in and caused a scene. Jean thinks she wanted money, and as much as it disturbs me, I agree. Jean threw her out today, saving me the trouble."

"I was a little uncomfortable when she came to your parents' house on Christmas, but when I saw her in here after you asked me to leave, I was furious. I still am."

He wiped his hand across his face and looked into her eyes. "Please don't be. She's out of my life, and certainly out of yours. My sister acted the way she did because she's always tried to protect me, and I guess I was trying to protect you. I apologize for my stupidity and for Jean's harshness, as well as Tracey's intrusion. I couldn't marry you without knowing the state of my health." He stopped speaking and looked into her eyes.

"Your eyes look so hard and cold. Maybe I hurt you more than I thought, or maybe this whole thing has been too much for you. Do you still love me?"

"I just don't think I can do this," she answered.

"But you do love me. Being a minister's wife isn't the greatest, but I'm making you a solemn promise. If my profession interferes with our happiness, I'll give it up."

Susan shook her head. "You can't do that."

"I can and I will. The only thing I can't do is let go of what I feel for you. I'm positive I'll never love anyone the way I love you. Please don't walk away now."

She worked her way through layers of anger, pain, frustration, worry, and rejection.

"You can't leave me now, Susan. I love you; I need you."

She heard confidence and charisma in his voice and she saw the future. Hands and hearts entwined.

"I just don't believe I . . ." She let the words trail off and sat next to him. "I don't think I can live another second of my life without having your arms around me."

A full-page ad in the *Houston Chronicle* announced the engagement of Rev. Willard Joseph Cartwright Jr. and Susan Michelle Cross. David Chestnut, who had met the couple in the middle of a feud, wrote an article of love surviving the obstacles of life.

Angie, Tammy, and Barbara trumped Susan and Will's wishes for a simple ceremony. Engagement parties with mass choirs, rehearsal dinners, and bridal showers filled Angie's home and the Bayou City Club with an outpouring of love and support from family and friends. Will's best man, Robert Wise, assembled a group of former classmates from college and rented a private room at Constantine's Restaurant for the bachelor party. Will called Susan at eleven o'clock.

"Would you do me a favor and pick me up? The guys are having fun and I don't want to ask them to leave their cigars and tall tales, but I want to be with you. I need to be with you."

"Good excuse, Rev. Cartwright," she answered, laughing. "I'll be there in ten minutes."

As they lay in each other's arms, Will confessed his relief that his bachelorhood was over.

"I'm glad you said that because I decided to discontinue my birth control products in a couple of months. I'm ready for that little boy with his father's baritone voice."

On the first Sunday in April, Rev. Cartwright Sr. stood, unaided, on the dais at Cedargrove Baptist Church. His son stood at his side. Clutching her father's arm, Susan glowed in a Vernon Bailey original, her mother's pearl earrings as something borrowed, and a bouquet wrapped with a sky blue ribbon with Angie's lucky horseshoe attached.

She walked confidently down the aisle. Trust, faith, and a very large helping of love had diluted her need for control.

## THE END

# ABOUT THE AUTHOR

Joan Early lives in Kingwood, Texas, with her husband where, together, they own an automobile dealership. *Look Both Ways* is her first novel for Genesis Press. Her second book, *Fireflies*, will be published by Genesis in October 2009.

## 2009 Reprint Mass Market Titles

### January

I'm Gonna Make You Love Me
Gwyneth Bolton
ISBN-13: 978-1-58571-294-6
$6.99

Shades of Desire
Monica White
ISBN-13: 978-1-58571-292-2
$6.99

### February

A Love of Her Own
Cheris Hodges
ISBN-13: 978-1-58571-293-9
$6.99

Color of Trouble
Dyanne Davis
ISBN-13: 978-1-58571-294-6
$6.99

### March

Twist of Fate
Beverly Clark
ISBN-13: 978-1-58571-295-3
$6.99

Chances
Pamela Leigh Starr
ISBN-13: 978-1-58571-296-0
$6.99

### April

Sinful Intentions
Crystal Rhodes
ISBN-13: 978-1-585712-297-7
$6.99

Rock Star
Roslyn Hardy Holcomb
ISBN-13: 978-1-58571-298-4
$6.99

### May

Paths of Fire
T.T. Henderson
ISBN-13: 978-1-58571-343-1
$6.99

Caught Up in the Rapture
Lisa Riley
ISBN-13: 978-1-58571-344-8
$6.99

### June

Reckless Surrender
Rochelle Alers
ISBN-13: 978-1-58571-345-5
$6.99

No Ordinary Love
Angela Weaver
ISBN-13: 978-1-58571-346-2
$6.99

## 2009 Reprint Mass Market Titles (continued)

### July

Intentional Mistakes
Michele Sudler
ISBN-13: 978-1-58571-347-9
$6.99

It's In His Kiss
Reon Carter
ISBN-13: 978-1-58571-348-6
$6.99

### August

Unfinished Love Affair
Barbara Keaton
ISBN-13: 978-1-58571-349-3
$6.99

A Perfect Place to Pray
I.L Goodwin
ISBN-13: 978-1-58571-299-1
$6.99

### September

Love in High Gear
Charlotte Roy
ISBN-13: 978-1-58571-355-4
$6.99

Ebony Eyes
Kei Swanson
ISBN-13: 978-1-58571-356-1
$6.99

### October

Midnight Clear, Part I
Leslie Esdale/Carmen Green
ISBN-13: 978-1-58571-357-8
$6.99

Midnight Clear, Part II
Gwynne Forster/Monica
   Jackson
ISBN-13: 978-1-58571-358-5
$6.99

### November

Midnight Peril
Vicki Andrews
ISBN-13: 978-1-58571-359-2
$6.99

One Day At A Time
Bella McFarland
ISBN-13: 978-1-58571-360-8
$6.99

### December

Just An Affair
Eugenia O'Neal
ISBN-13: 978-1-58571-361-5
$6.99

Shades of Brown
Denise Becker
ISBN-13: 978-1-58571-362-2
$6.99

## 2009 New Mass Market Titles

### January

Singing A Song…
Crystal Rhodes
ISBN-13: 978-1-58571-283-0
$6.99

Look Both Ways
Joan Early
ISBN-13: 978-1-58571-284-7
$6.99

### February

Six O'Clock
Katrina Spencer
ISBN-13: 978-1-58571-285-4
$6.99

Red Sky
Renee Alexis
ISBN-13: 978-1-58571-286-1
$6.99

### March

Anything But Love
Celya Bowers
ISBN-13: 978-1-58571-287-8
$6.99

Tempting Faith
Crystal Hubbard
ISBN-13: 978-1-58571-288-5
$6.99

### April

If I Were Your Woman
La Connie Taylor-Jones
ISBN-13: 978-1-58571-289-2
$6.99

Best Of Luck Elsewhere
Trisha Haddad
ISBN-13: 978-1-58571-290-8
$6.99

### May

All I'll Ever Need
Mildred Riley
ISBN-13: 978-1-58571-335-6
$6.99

A Place Like Home
Alicia Wiggins
ISBN-13: 978-1-58571-336-3
$6.99

### June

Best Foot Forward
Michele Sudler
ISBN-13: 978-1-58571-337-0
$6.99

It's In the Rhythm
Sammie Ward
ISBN-13: 978-1-58571-338-7
$6.99

## 2009 New Mass Market Titles (continued)

### July

Checks and Balances
Elaine Sims
ISBN-13: 978-1-58571-339-4
$6.99

Save Me
Africa Fine
ISBN-13: 978-1-58571-340-0
$6.99

### August

When Lightening Strikes
Michele Cameron
ISBN-13: 978-1-58571-369-1
$6.99

Blindsided
Tammy Williams
ISBN-13: 978-1-58571-342-4
$6.99

### September

2 Good
Celya Bowers
ISBN-13: 978-1-58571-350-9
$6.99

Waiting for Mr. Darcy
Chamein Canton
ISBN-13: 978-1-58571-351-6
$6.99

### October

Fireflies
Joan Early
ISBN-13: 978-1-58571-352-3
$6.99

Frost On My Window
Angela Weaver
ISBN-13: 978-1-58571-353-0
$6.99

### November

Waiting in the Shadows
Michele Sudler
ISBN-13: 978-1-58571-364-6
$6.99

Fixin' Tyrone
Keith Walker
ISBN-13: 978-1-58571-365-3
$6.99

### December

Dream Keeper
Gail McFarland
ISBN-13: 978-1-58571-366-0
$6.99

Another Memory
Pamela Ridley
ISBN-13: 978-1-58571-367-7
$6.99

## Other Genesis Press, Inc. Titles

## Other Genesis Press, Inc. Titles (continued)

## Other Genesis Press, Inc. Titles (continued)

## Other Genesis Press, Inc. Titles (continued)

## Other Genesis Press, Inc. Titles (continued)

## Other Genesis Press, Inc. Titles (continued)

## Other Genesis Press, Inc. Titles (continued)

| | | |
|---|---|---|
| Still Waters Run Deep | Leslie Esdaile | $8.95 |
| Stolen Kisses | Dominiqua Douglas | $9.95 |
| Stolen Memories | Michele Sudler | $6.99 |
| Stories to Excite You | Anna Forrest/Divine | $14.95 |
| Storm | Pamela Leigh Starr | $6.99 |
| Subtle Secrets | Wanda Y. Thomas | $8.95 |
| Suddenly You | Crystal Hubbard | $9.95 |
| Sweet Repercussions | Kimberley White | $9.95 |
| Sweet Sensations | Gwyneth Bolton | $9.95 |
| Sweet Tomorrows | Kimberly White | $8.95 |
| Taken by You | Dorothy Elizabeth Love | $9.95 |
| Tattooed Tears | T. T. Henderson | $8.95 |
| The Color Line | Lizzette Grayson Carter | $9.95 |
| The Color of Trouble | Dyanne Davis | $8.95 |
| The Disappearance of Allison Jones | Kayla Perrin | $5.95 |
| The Fires Within | Beverly Clark | $9.95 |
| The Foursome | Celya Bowers | $6.99 |
| The Honey Dipper's Legacy | Pannell-Allen | $14.95 |
| The Joker's Love Tune | Sidney Rickman | $15.95 |
| The Little Pretender | Barbara Cartland | $10.95 |
| The Love We Had | Natalie Dunbar | $8.95 |
| The Man Who Could Fly | Bob & Milana Beamon | $18.95 |
| The Missing Link | Charlyne Dickerson | $8.95 |
| The Mission | Pamela Leigh Starr | $6.99 |
| The More Things Change | Chamein Canton | $6.99 |
| The Perfect Frame | Beverly Clark | $9.95 |
| The Price of Love | Sinclair LeBeau | $8.95 |
| The Smoking Life | Ilene Barth | $29.95 |
| The Words of the Pitcher | Kei Swanson | $8.95 |
| Things Forbidden | Maryam Diaab | $6.99 |
| This Life Isn't Perfect Holla | Sandra Foy | $6.99 |
| Three Doors Down | Michele Sudler | $6.99 |
| Three Wishes | Seressia Glass | $8.95 |
| Ties That Bind | Kathleen Suzanne | $8.95 |

## Other Genesis Press, Inc. Titles (continued)

| | | |
|---|---|---|
| Tiger Woods | Libby Hughes | $5.95 |
| Time is of the Essence | Angie Daniels | $9.95 |
| Timeless Devotion | Bella McFarland | $9.95 |
| Tomorrow's Promise | Leslie Esdaile | $8.95 |
| Truly Inseparable | Wanda Y. Thomas | $8.95 |
| Two Sides to Every Story | Dyanne Davis | $9.95 |
| Unbreak My Heart | Dar Tomlinson | $8.95 |
| Uncommon Prayer | Kenneth Swanson | $9.95 |
| Unconditional Love | Alicia Wiggins | $8.95 |
| Unconditional | A.C. Arthur | $9.95 |
| Undying Love | Renee Alexis | $6.99 |
| Until Death Do Us Part | Susan Paul | $8.95 |
| Vows of Passion | Bella McFarland | $9.95 |
| Wedding Gown | Dyanne Davis | $8.95 |
| What's Under Benjamin's Bed | Sandra Schaffer | $8.95 |
| When A Man Loves A Woman | La Connie Taylor-Jones | $6.99 |
| When Dreams Float | Dorothy Elizabeth Love | $8.95 |
| When I'm With You | LaConnie Taylor-Jones | $6.99 |
| Where I Want To Be | Maryam Diaab | $6.99 |
| Whispers in the Night | Dorothy Elizabeth Love | $8.95 |
| Whispers in the Sand | LaFlorya Gauthier | $10.95 |
| Who's That Lady? | Andrea Jackson | $9.95 |
| Wild Ravens | Altonya Washington | $9.95 |
| Yesterday Is Gone | Beverly Clark | $10.95 |
| Yesterday's Dreams, Tomorrow's Promises | Reon Laudat | $8.95 |
| Your Precious Love | Sinclair LeBeau | $8.95 |

# ESCAPE WITH INDIGO !!!!

Join Indigo Book Club©
It's simple, easy and secure.

Sign up and receive the new
releases
every month + Free shipping
and
20% off the cover price.

Go online to www.genesis-
press.com and click on Bookclub
or
call 1-888-INDIGO-1

# Order Form

**Mail to: Genesis Press, Inc.**
**P.O. Box 101**
**Columbus, MS 39703**

Name _____
Address _____
City/State _____ Zip _____
Telephone _____

*Ship to (if different from above)*
Name _____
Address _____
City/State _____ Zip _____
Telephone _____

*Credit Card Information*
Credit Card # _____ ☐ Visa ☐ Mastercard
Expiration Date (mm/yy) _____ ☐ AmEx ☐ Discover

| Qty. | Author | Title | Price | Total |
|------|--------|-------|-------|-------|
|      |        |       |       |       |
|      |        |       |       |       |
|      |        |       |       |       |
|      |        |       |       |       |
|      |        |       |       |       |
|      |        |       |       |       |
|      |        |       |       |       |
|      |        |       |       |       |
|      |        |       |       |       |
|      |        |       |       |       |
|      |        |       |       |       |

Use this order

form, or call

1-888-INDIGO-1

Total for books _____
Shipping and handling:
  $5 first two books,
  $1 each additional book _____
Total S & H _____
Total amount enclosed _____
*Mississippi residents add 7% sales tax*